SOUL OATH

THE EVERLAST SERIES BOOK 2

JULIANA HAYGERT

COPYRIGHT

This book is a work of fiction. Names, characters, places, and incidents either are products of the author's imagination or are used fictitiously. Any resemblance to actual persons, living or dead, events, or locales is entirely coincidental.

Copyright © 2017 by Juliana Haygert.

All rights reserved. This book or any portion thereof may not be reproduced or used in any manner whatsoever without the express written permission of the publisher, except for the use of brief quotations in a book review.

Manufactured in the United States of America.

First Edition November 2013

Second Edition June 2016

Third Edition November 2017

www.JulianaHaygert.com

Edited by H. Danielle Crabtree

Proofreading by Running Ink Edits

Cover design by Moonchildljilja at Fantasy Book Design

Any trademark, service marks, product names, or names featured are the property of their respective owners, and are used only for reference. There is no implied endorsement if one of these terms is used.

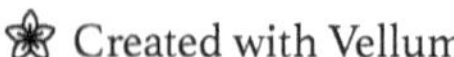 Created with Vellum

1

A NEW DAY, THE SAME DARK WORLD.

The blue bus stopped at its usual spot inside NYU's north gate.

I stared at it and wished, for once, I could have a normal day. I wished I could arrive at the hospital without any hassle, I could contain the urge to look out the windows and see the destroyed world, I didn't hear anything about bats, my day at the hospital was easy and fast, and more than anything, I wished I could forget the last year of my life.

The doors opened, and I stepped into the blue bus, looking around. Only seven people, plus the other three that came in with me. Total of eleven. Less than yesterday, and much less than last week. Each day there were fewer people around, as if they had given up living in this world. Or they had been taken from it.

I chose a seat in the front of the bus, far from the others, and avoided looking out. However, once we were outside the campus, the pull was much stronger than my will, and I gave in. My eyes scanned the streets as the bus drove north.

Dark. Everything was dark. A few lamps illuminated the sidewalks here and there, but I would rather they didn't, so I couldn't see anything. Trash everywhere, broken doors and windows, dead bushes, people with crazed looks or holding guns assaulting others, people on the ground—if they were sleeping or dead, I would never know.

"Hold on, everyone," the driver announced.

Holding my breath, I braced myself for it.

Screams and shouts surrounded the bus, followed by bangs on the metal, shaking the entire bus.

"Let us in!"

"I need to eat!"

"My kids are dying!"

"Please, help us!"

Tears stung my eyes. I wanted to clamp my ears, close my eyes, and sing so it would drown out the melancholic sounds from the streets. It was the same almost every day, but it never ceased to shock me.

The driver maintained his speed, ignoring the protests until a gunshot rang through the darkness. My heart stilled for a moment and I gasped. Cracks spiderwebbed over a glass window in the front.

I silently thanked God that the university had bought armored buses and vans a few weeks ago.

The driver cursed. "All right. Hold on." He sped up. Many of the assailants stayed behind, but a couple ran with the bus. "I hate doing this," the driver said, his fingers reaching for the red button under an acrylic cap on the dashboard. He pushed the button, and the cries of the people outside made goose bumps prickle my skin.

This time, I did clamp my ears and hum a song.

The button activated electric cables located under the

bus's bodywork. Anyone who touched the bus would receive a powerful electric charge. It wasn't fatal, but it was enough to make them collapse on their knees.

I felt bad about it, but I couldn't do much; I couldn't change the world by myself.

Change the world.

I hadn't heard from any of them—Victor, Micah, Ceris, Morgan, or the Fates—in three months. Which was good and should bring me relief, but it didn't. It actually worried me. What if they had—?

The bus stopped in front of Langone's courtyard, and I jumped from my seat. The others stood too.

"Thanks," I said to the driver as we waited for him to open the doors. The drivers could only open the doors if the surrounding area looked safe—one of the many new rules.

I scanned around with him. The streets were deserted and almost clean here, save for a few ambulances coming in and out of the emergency entrance to the right and a couple of cars entering the garage—after being checked by the security personnel—to the left. The two guards walking around the hospital's courtyard seemed relaxed, even though their hands rested over the guns at their waist, and the other two guards stationed at the main entrance past the courtyard were conversing as if they were old friends in a coffee shop.

Besides the darkness and the permanent feeling that the world was ending, nothing seemed out of the ordinary.

The doors opened, and I stepped out of the bus clutching my tote close to me.

Two other buses stopped behind the one I had just disembarked. Red buses. I watched as the doors opened and armed police officers helped sick people out. They dragged themselves to the emergency entrance.

The red buses were a new thing, substituting most ambulances. They drove around New York City, including dangerous neighborhoods—thus the police protection. They stopped at specific, government-appointed places, where medics and nurses triaged to see who needed to go to the hospital and who didn't, and then they brought them here.

At least four dozen sick people scrambled out of those two buses, some with only a heavy cough, others with open wounds and profuse bleeding.

A heavy sigh escaped my mouth. With the influx, I was going to have a busy day. Better get on with it then. Get in, check in, work, and help.

I was crossing the courtyard when the first shriek reached my ears.

My blood turned cold, and I almost tripped. "Oh no," I muttered looking up.

A black cloud moved across the others, descending from the sky and coming toward the ground at incredible speed.

Another shriek echoed through the courtyard, waking me up from my stupor. Waking everyone. People screamed and ran. I raced toward the main entrance as the guards turned their guns to the sky.

"Hurry, hurry!" one of guards shouted.

They shot. More screeches and screams filled the air. The hospital alarm blared, and metal sheets slid closed over the windows and doors.

"Oh, God." Cursing, I pushed my muscles as hard as I could and ran.

In front of me, a boy tripped and fell on his hands and knees. His mother yelled, but a guard pulled her forward. Without thinking, I skidded to a stop and hauled the boy up.

"Come on," I said, putting one of his arms around my waist. He clutched at me and we ran.

Inside the glass doors, his mother wailed, pushing the arm of a guard, frantically trying to get to her child.

A man rushed past us, bumping his shoulder against mine and almost making me fall.

Jerk!

Then the first bat fell on top of a woman beside us.

The boy yelled. Heart pounding, I held my breath sure I was as white as the Fates' hair.

I covered the boy's eyes with my hand so he would not see as the bat clawed the woman's chest, then bit into her face splashing blood everywhere. One big splat fell on the tip of my boot. Nausea revolved in my stomach and my knees felt weak, but I couldn't give in now.

"Hurry," a guard said. He stood in front of the glass doors, pulling people in before the metal sheet closed all the way down. "Hurry!"

I grabbed the boy's shoulders and pushed him forward, hoping the guard would catch him first and help him. Ten feet from the main door, the guard stepped out and grabbed the boy's hand. Then his eyes went wide and the air swished behind me.

Oh, God.

Blood throbbing in my ears, I glanced over my shoulder. A claw hovered a couple of feet from my face.

My body slowed down in shock. The claw came at me.

A bird flew directly into it, stabbing his beak into the creature's skin, hard enough to make it recoil.

Rok, the raven.

What the—?

A hand closed around my upper arm and pulled me

forward. The guard practically threw me past the glass doors. He came in right behind me. Then the metal sheet touched the ground and something large bumped into it.

My heart stopped, and I jumped back touching my back on the front desk.

"Damn bats," said the guard, who had thrown me inside. His hands trembled.

Mine did too.

I turned around and stepped into chaos. The alarm still blasted, and the red lights flashed along the walls casting eerie shadows to the place. People cried and screamed. Some held bloody hands or arms or legs, while others lay on the ground barely breathing.

I pushed my feelings and shock aside and forced myself into action.

After throwing my tote under the front desk, I rushed around the place evaluating who was in a grave state and needed immediate attention, and who could wait until the mess around us subsided.

Three hours later, I leaned against a wall and took a deep breath.

"Jeez, that was close," said Jill, a young nurse. Shoulders sagged and expression weary, she sat on a chair behind the desk at the nurses' station and fidgeted with the computer. "Nadine, are you all right?"

I nodded. "I guess so."

"You look pale." She gestured for me to come around the desk. "You should sit down."

"No, I'm fine." What a lie. My heart still pumped in my chest, and my hands still shook.

"Those vicious bats. This is the third time this month," she complained in a low voice.

Yes, the third time this month a group of *bats* had attacked people on the streets, close to the hospital. This was the first time I had seen it, been in it, and it was surreal. It was one thing to watch it on TV—a news channel had been able to record last week's attack for two minutes—but another thing to live through it. The creatures simply flew over Manhattan in a solid black cloud and descended on the streets, slashing people with their claws and biting them with their teeth. It was a slaughter.

Of course, everyone still called these creatures giant bats, but I knew the truth. They were demons.

Nausea surged up again. God, I couldn't think about it, or I would curl up and cry. "Yeah. Their attacks are becoming more frequent."

"More frequent and just ... more. It's like they reproduce by the thousands. Soon, we won't be able to leave our houses because not even armored cars will be able to protect us."

Oh, if only she knew how true her statement was.

A loud bang came from the metal cover on the window across the hall. I jumped and Jill screamed. Whatever bat had bumped into the metal had actually left a dent on it.

"They can't break through the metal, can they?" she asked.

I swallowed. "I don't know."

The alarm fell silent. My ears thanked whoever had a hand in it. However, the red lights continued flashing, indicating the doors and windows were locked. No one could get out or come in.

I tried not to think about the sick people who needed to get into the hospital *now*, or the people on the outside that weren't able to escape and yet managed to crawl to the hospital, only to find its doors weren't open. No. They would bleed to death outside, or they would end up eaten.

Jill touched my shoulder, bringing me back to the present. "Are you sure you're all right?"

I blinked back tears. "Yeah, I am." I went to the computer on the side desk and signed in. I should have done that the moment I arrived, but with all the craziness around us, it didn't even cross my mind until now. "I think I'll wash my face, then find something to eat before helping some more."

"See you later," she said as I walked away.

Besides these terrible moments, this job had been godsend. Almost literally. If it weren't for Cheryl—or Ceris— I would still be making coffee and cleaning tables at the cafe. Here, as a patient care technician, I worked normal hours around my class schedule and was in the environment I wanted, where I planned to work in the future. I also made more money, which meant I could send more to my parents.

Since Victor and Micah found out who they were, things had gotten worse. Small businesses closed, the majority of the population was unemployed and some turned to robbery to survive, and agriculture was dead. Without the farm, my father didn't have a job anymore. Now, he worked here and there, wherever he could find an odd job to do. Some days he helped in reconstructing the town's church, others he was a chauffeur, while other days he cleaned the town's streets. My mother tried to help by taking care of people's children while they were at work—the ones who still had jobs. My parents' place had become a daycare.

I halted when a woman stepped in front of me. I recognized her. The mother of the boy I had ran inside with. She had him tucked under her arm now. My heart squeezed. He was probably twelve years old, the same age Troy, my late brother, would be if he were alive.

"I wanted to thank you for what you did," she said, her voice breaking.

I swallowed the tears. "It was nothing."

"To me, it was everything." Tears sprouted from her eyes, and she smiled. "Thank you."

Holding an awkward, forced smile I hoped looked strong and sure, I touched her arm. "You're welcome."

The boy looked up at me, his brown eyes shining with reminiscent shock. "Thanks."

I leaned forward and kissed his cheek. "My pleasure."

Before I broke down and cried too, I walked around them and through an authorized personnel door in the corridor, intent on washing my face and sitting down for a minute on a couch inside the locker room. However, as soon as I crossed the doorway, a hand closed around my wrist and pulled me into the dark room. Fear shot through me. I was about to scream, but another hand closed over my mouth.

I jerked, but then his scent hit me and I froze, gasping. He let me go, and I quickly reached for the light switch turning it on.

My breath caught.

Victor squinted against the bright light. "Hi."

2

—————

Victor stood before me in a five-by-five dressing room. His honey-colored hair fell over his sea-green eyes in a sexy, messy way, and his tall, strong figure seemed to be shrunk inside his thick, dark gray coat.

I couldn't speak. I could only stare. I hadn't seen him in three months, not since he disappeared from the top of Cathedral Rock with Ceris—his mate—and left me alone with Micah and hundreds of demons.

Somewhere amid my shock, my brain processed he didn't look right. He was too pale, and he was trembling.

"Victor, what is it?"

He groaned and fell to his knees. "Need ... healing."

I stepped into his personal space and cupped my hands around his face. The effect was immediate. The energy flowed from me to him as a warm, pleasant sensation. I didn't know how it worked exactly, or if he could take too much of my energy and kill me, but I knew it made him better.

His trembling subsided with each second that passed. He finally stopped shaking and took a long, deep breath. A little apprehensive, I pulled my hands away and put some distance between us.

Victor stood. "Thanks." He looked better. He wasn't pale anymore, his chest and shoulders no longer sagged, and his eyes shone. He was gorgeous, as always.

"You're welcome." I curled my fingers around a strand of my hair. "If it was this bad, why didn't you come sooner?"

He looked away. "I wanted to avoid drawing attention. The demons are probably here because of me. They sensed my aura and came."

Could it be? I thought they were coming because of my aura. But if the demons were here because of Victor's aura this time, what could explain the other times?

His eyes returned to me, and I held my breath once more.

How could this man, who had been shaking like a scared child a few moments ago, be a freaking almighty god? I couldn't believe it. I had three months to absorb and believe, but I still couldn't wrap my mind around it. When I closed my eyes, it was easy to tell myself that what happened had been a dream.

A dream. Hallucinations. Maybe visions. Maybe Ceris hadn't taken the Destiny Gift away, and this time I was living within a vision, trapped forever.

"How have you been?" he asked.

I frowned. After all these months, that was what he asked me? "Good," I said, my voice more bitter than I intended.

His gaze ran the length of me before settling on my eyes again. "You look good."

What was that supposed to mean? I looked down. My hair was messy from running, my face was probably flushed, my clothes were battered and dirty after all I had been through this morning, and one of the heels of my boots had been glued on with crazy glue. Oh, and there was the brand new splat of blood on my boot. I felt anything but good.

"How's your family?" he asked, surprising me.

"Good," I lied.

"And Raisa and Olivia?"

What was with him and small talk? "They're good too."

He ran a hand through his hair. "Look, Nadine, we should probably ta—"

"If there isn't anything else I can help you with, I should probably get back to work," I said, putting as much confidence as I could in my tone. It wasn't easy.

The shine in his eyes changed. "No, no. I'm fine now. Thanks again."

"Sure."

Holding my head high, I strolled out of the room. Once in the corridor, I let out a huge breath and fought against the sudden tears. Why was I feeling disappointed and frustrated? He didn't owe me anything. He had left with his *mate*, and said mate had fabricated my feelings for him. Nothing that happened between us had been real, and I should be over it.

I shook my head. Apparently, I wasn't really over it.

I entered the restroom, washed my face, and then dropped down on the couch in the locker room.

Before my mind could drift and my muscles relax, my cell phone vibrated with a new text message. It was from my boss. *Where are you?* She sounded mad even if I couldn't hear her voice or see her face. I knew she was mad.

Cursing I pushed up from the couch and rushed out.

This day couldn't get any worse.

THE BUS RIDE BACK TO CAMPUS THAT EVENING HAD NO incidents, thank goodness. It dropped me inside the north gates, and I walked the couple of blocks to my dorm, located on the east side of campus.

Last semester, Raisa and I had shared an apartment outside the walls, but this semester, the university's policy had changed. All students were required to live in the dorms inside its walls for security reasons. Olivia, however, was long gone. When things started to get worse, her parents told her to come home. Raisa's parents were trying to convince her to do the same. My parents tried to convince me too, but I wouldn't budge. There weren't many jobs available where they lived, if there were any, and I would be one more mouth to feed. I couldn't give up yet.

I glanced up at the electrified cables they had put atop of the walls, creating a wrought dome that fried the demons wherever they touched it. It was like living in a prison, but if it meant the university could keep us safe so I could finish my degree and help my family, I was okay with it.

The dorm building wasn't too bad. Most students were scared shitless, and a few had left. There were parties, but not too many anymore, not since the world kept getting worse and worse.

I opened the door to my room and sighed. The room was tiny compared to our old apartment, but that was the only truly bad thing about living here. One room with dull white walls; a boring window that opened to the courtyard at the heart of the other dorm buildings; two squeaking twin beds; two desks that looked like they would break if we put one more book on them; two chairs; a decaying sofa; two tall shelves that passed as closets; a counter with our coffee machine and such; and a bathroom with plastic curtains and stained tiles and a sink, but at least we didn't have to share it with anyone else.

I closed the door, and threw my coat and my tote on my bed. I thought about taking my boots off and throwing myself on my bed too, but I would have to leave for class soon. If I got comfortable now, I knew I wouldn't go.

I turned on the coffee machine, and Raisa stepped out of the bathroom.

"Hey, you," she said, her hazel eyes inquisitive. She had a towel draped around her, and her short brown hair was wet, dripping all over the linoleum floor. "I saw the bats' attack around the hospital. Was it too bad?"

"The usual. Lots of hurt people and lots of people we couldn't help."

"I'm sorry," she said.

I nodded, and she disappeared inside the bathroom again. She turned on the blow-dryer, and I leaned against the window while waiting for the coffee machine.

The raven was perched on the limb of a dying tree. Thank goodness, it was all right. I hadn't forgotten it had saved me from a demon, but with all the chaos inside the hospital, I couldn't really stop and wonder about it. Besides his presence wasn't news. Rok had been following me since I came back from that boring Croatian island. Each time my eyes landed on the bird, my thoughts turned to Micah and mixed feelings invaded me. I was angry with him for leaving me alone on that damned island. I thought of all he had done: sticking up for me, defending me from demons, killing Brock so my identity and family would be safe. I didn't understand.

I scoffed, trying to suppress such thoughts. However, the more I tried to put my mind on something else, the more it went back to him. I was angry with him, even though he didn't owe me anything. He was a god, an almighty god that would probably stomp on a human like me at the first opportunity. But if that were true, why would he send Rok to keep tabs on me? The only reason I could imagine he had was to know if I ran away right when he needed my healing.

My healing ... I had seen Victor today. Oh my God, I had seen Victor today.

My heart sped up.

Disappointment and frustration brewed in me. Three months. For three months, I had heard nothing from him. I thought I was free of this mess, save for the bird following me. I thought I could live my life, pretending I didn't know anything about why the world was the way it was, about how there were gods out there in the mortal world on what sounded like impossible quests that could bring light to our world of darkness, and about how I could help these gods.

I wished Ceris had taken away my healing ability too.

The coffee machine beeped. I dragged my feet to it and prepared my coffee. Black, no sugar. I hadn't drunk any mochaccino since the Fates brought me back. I was afraid I liked mochaccino only because Victor had told me he liked it during a vision, and I wanted to distance myself from coincidences like that as much as I could.

Raisa exited the bathroom dressed in tight jeans, a red blouse with a gray knit cardigan over it, and full makeup.

"Hmm, hot date?" I asked, not really interested, though I should be. She was a good friend and she deserved my attention.

She wiggled her eyebrows. "Something like that."

Raisa had been going out with the guy who lived across the hall. As the good friend she was—her words, not mine— she tried setting me up with her guy's roommate. There was nothing wrong with the roommate. He seemed okay, kind of cute even, but I wasn't into him.

"All right. Just please, if you come back after midnight, be quiet. I need to wake up early tomorrow."

She raised her eyebrows. "When don't you need to wake up early?"

"Good question."

She grabbed her purse from her closet and gave me a quick kiss on the cheek. "Don't wait up."

"Ha, as if." I reached for her hand and squeezed it. "Be careful."

"Don't worry. We won't leave campus."

"Good."

She waved goodbye and left the room with a wide smile.

Raisa went through life as if it was a party, even after demon attacks and other horrible stuff. She cared, of course, she was sad about those things, but she didn't let it bring her down. I guess she pretended it didn't happen and thought it could never touch her. I wished I could be that carefree.

Trying not to let my mind go back to the fact I had seen Victor this morning, I refilled my coffee mug.

"Hello, child."

I froze. My mug slipped from my fingers and crashed on the floor with a loud crack, splashing coffee everywhere.

No, no, no. Two unexpected visits in one day?

Slowly, I turned and faced the Fates.

Three identical women stood in front of my bed, wearing matching white gowns, and looking ageless and powerful. I shuddered.

I thought this day couldn't get any worse. Oh, God, how wrong I was.

The gray eyes of the one in the center met mine. "Good to see you, child."

I pressed my lips together before I said I didn't feel the same. "Why are you here?"

She stepped in my direction. "Because we need to give you your soul back."

Of all the things I expected to hear, this wasn't one of them. My mouth fell open, and I literally forced it closed. "What?"

"You'll need it."

"I'll need it? For what?"

She shook her head once. "We can't tell you that."

Typical. I crossed my arms. "And you'll just give it back to me? No favors? No deals?"

She smiled. "Child, we're not evil. We don't want you harmed. Actually, we want quite the opposite."

"But why?"

"Can't tell you."

I groaned. Talking to them was always confusing. Instead of answering my questions, they left me with more.

She extended her hand to me, and I squinted at it. What if they were messing with me? What if they were lying and whatever she did to me actually made everything worse? What if they brought me back to the center of the problem, even though all I wanted was to be left alone?

"I already told you, child. If we wanted to harm you, we wouldn't ask permission. We would have already done it a long time ago."

True, but that didn't make me less wary.

I couldn't deny, though, it would be nice to go to bed at night without worrying the Fates would show up and claim me.

I placed my hand in hers.

A rush of energy flowed into me, cold one second, warm the next. It was like when I was healing Victor or Micah, but receiving instead of giving. The energy cascaded into me and coursed up my arm, around my shoulder, and spread through my chest. I shivered. It coiled around my heart and into it. I gasped. My body became jelly, and I fell into a seated position on my bed.

The Fate let go of my hand. "Done. Your soul is yours now, and you may use it as you want."

"This damn cold," Raisa complained as we walked out of our dorm building. We had an early morning biology class together on the west side of campus.

There was snow everywhere, but I was happy about getting out. Since moving onto campus, weekends were terrible. Especially when snowing. We were stuck in our tiny dorms with nowhere to go. Well, almost nowhere. Raisa, for example, went to the room across the hall, and I didn't even want to know where the spare roommate went.

I tugged my beanie down over my ears and my scarf up over my nose and mouth. "The walking in the snow bothers me more," I said, kicking at the frozen fluff with the tip of my boots.

Raisa linked her arm through mine and pulled me with her. "I'm a walk-in-the-snow expert."

"Yeah, right." I remembered last year, when she had fallen on her butt in front of half the campus after slipping on an icy patch. I wouldn't let her drag me down with her this time.

"So," she said, "why don't you want to go out with Cale?"

Cale. That was the name of her guy's roommate. Just the fact that his name didn't stick to my brain told me volumes. "Again with that? I don't want to talk about it."

"You mean you don't want to talk about Victor?"

I glared at her. "Raisa."

"What? You never talk to me about him. I'm worried. The guy takes you on a trip, which I think is supposed to be romantic, and then you come back alone and never talk about the guy again. It's a little odd."

Oh, I thought so too. Especially because the romantic trip had no romance in it. Well, maybe one tiny moment, but even that had been misguided. I was sure it had been misguided.

"I don't want to talk about it," I whispered, glancing at the trees. Rok was there jumping from branch to branch, following me.

"But—"

"How's your guy?" I asked, interrupting her. I had to change the subject. I knew she couldn't help but talk about her love life. Unlike me, Raisa loved talking about everything.

She smiled. "He's okay, I think."

"Just okay?"

"Well, I'm kinda disappointed because he's considering going back to his parents."

"Because of how bad things are?"

"Yeah." She looked up, and I followed her gaze.

The wrought dome was there looking like a dark gray cage, swallowing our freedom. Most of the time I felt safe under it, but there were rare times when the air was gone and I suffocated. Like now. I took a long breath, willing the heavy arms of the dome to melt and let in the fresh air and the sunlight—as if both things were hiding behind it.

Breaking my daze, Raisa said, "I'm not sure I'll go home next week for Thanksgiving."

What? She had been talking about Thanksgiving break for weeks now, longing for a little vacation from our classes. She would go home, enjoy her family. I would stay here and work double shifts at Langone.

"Why not?"

"My father gave me an ultimatum last night. If I don't come home to stay when this semester is over, he'll cut me off."

"What?" My shock made me slip on the snow. Raisa held on to my arm, keeping me steady.

"He was serious. The thing is I'm afraid if I go home for Thanksgiving next week, he won't let me come back to finish this semester."

"He wouldn't do that." Maybe he would. I didn't know her father well enough to know what he would or wouldn't do.

"It sucks. My hometown sucks. Everything is closing or dying there, and the colleges nearby aren't as safe as this one. But he and my mom are worried. If I was a mother, I would be too."

I tilted my head, watching her. "Wow, that is so unlike you."

"I know." She smiled, but it was a sad one. "They got me thinking, you know. Even if I stay and graduate, what will I do later? Things are getting worse. It's not like I can walk out of these gates and have a normal life. Whatever normal might be. I'll have to go back to my parents or try my luck in a city like this." She gestured to the walls.

She was right. I had plans to work at Langone after I graduated from med school, but that wasn't a done deal because getting into med school wasn't a done deal. They could reject my application—fear gripped my chest each time I thought about it, making me sick—and housing did worry me. I was used to spending most of my time inside these walls. It would be hard and incredibly dangerous to live outside of them. I thought about bringing my family to live here with me, there was nothing left for them where they were, but I wasn't sure here would be much better.

"It's hard watching it get worse and worse, isn't it?"

"I wish there was something we could do about it," she muttered.

I glanced at her. "What did you say?"

"I know presidents and governors and all those big guys get together all the time to come up with solutions and ideas, but nothing they do is working." She paused. "I wish we could do something, but I don't know what. If the government can't do anything about it, we certainly can't, right?"

"Right," I said automatically.

I wish we could do something.

That thought stuck in my mind. I shook my head, but the thought stayed there in the back of my head, taunting me.

We reached the door of the science building, and a siren blasted through the entire campus.

My heart stopped for a second and fear locked my muscles.

"What the hell?" Raisa asked, squeezing my arms.

We whirled around. Red lights flashed from all corners of campus and above the walls. Guards appeared out of nowhere and ran to the gates. Students rushed out of the buildings, their faces lost and scared.

"What's happening?" they asked each other.

But nobody knew.

I looked up to the dark sky.

It seemed different. Darker. Heavier.

My knees shook, and I held on to Raisa. I saw them before anyone else. Just like that day at the hospital, but many, many more. A huge cloud of demons descended onto the city.

"This is Mr. Cornell, your dean," the voice boomed from the speakers strategically installed around the campus. "All students proceed to the basements in their residences at once. Please respect the guards and police officers doing their job and follow their orders." He sighed. "New York City is under attack."

He turned the microphone off and chaos erupted.

3

———

I DARED GLANCE UP AS THE DEMONS LANDED ON THE electrified cables.

The zapping sound was sick, but not as sick as their shrieks. Even with all the zapping going on, the demons didn't give up. They clawed through the cables.

Fear crawled up my spine.

Guards ran among the students and yelled at them to back away before turning their guns up. They shot the demons. More shrieks resonated through the frigid air.

The students and faculty members seemed frozen in place like me, entranced in the horrific sight above us. I tried counting, but I got lost before I reached twenty demons.

Holy shit.

A determined demon closed its claw around a cable, shrieked, and snapped it.

Everyone jerked into motion. High-pitched screams and shouts of terror echoed the crackling hiss of the cable, and students and faculty members ran looking like lost ants in a water-filling tank. Loud, ringing shots flew over our heads causing more frantic screams.

One of the guards, holding a fancy rifle, stopped before our group. "Everyone back to your dorms. Now!"

"Oh, God. Oh, God. Oh, God," Raisa muttered. She stood beside me, pale and trembling.

Pushing my fear aside, I took her hand in mine. "We'll be okay," I said, pulling her to walk with me.

A sea of desperate students engulfed us. Shoulders bumped, feet stepped on one another, and short people—like Raisa and me—suffocated. I didn't like it, but I pushed too, not wanting to see Raisa or me squashed. We went with the flow, a death grip locking our hands together.

Then the crowd dispersed a little. They were entering the buildings.

I looked up. "This isn't our building." We were on the south side of campus, near the gates.

Raisa's eyes bugged. "Oh no."

I squeezed her hand. "It's okay. We can still make it."

Wingless demons pushed against the gates. They were large, nasty creatures with pointed teeth and crippled bodies. Slobber dripped from their slanted mouths, and sharp claws protruded where fingers should be. The creatures looked like the ones I had seen at the pub in Wichita, and at the school where Brock locked me up a few months ago. Panic rushed into me at the memory of the pain their claws caused.

"Wh-what are those?" Raisa asked, her voice a thin whisper.

What I wouldn't give to have my visions back so I could see a way out of this mess.

"I don't know," I lied.

One of the wingless demons locked its yellow eyes on mine and snarled. Goose bumps covered my arms.

I tugged Raisa's hand and we turned, taking long steps away from the south gate. My mind raced, trying to think of a plan to escape this, any plan.

From above us, another snapping sound made us jump. Oh God, the winged demons were almost in. I glanced over my shoulder to the south gate. Wingless demons pushed against it, bending it bit by bit. Soon they would be in too.

The wingless demon from before stared at me. It bared and snapped its teeth. With its unnatural force, it let out a feral growl and pushed against the gate, breaking it down.

"Oh shit," I muttered, pulling Raisa to run with me.

A police officer appeared from a corner. He looked above our heads, and his eyes went wide. "Run!" he said as he pointed his gun past us.

He shot. I winced. Raisa whimpered.

He emptied the magazine of his gun, and then ran with us, changing the magazine on the move.

"Just keep going," he instructed. I intended to follow his order until I saw what was right above us. I pulled Raisa to a stop, and he bumped into us. "What the—?"

"There." I pointed up to where a winged demon was crawling through the snapped cables. We would never outrun it and, no matter which direction we went we would find more demons.

"Fuck." The cop scanned the area. "In there." He gestured to the Grey Art Gallery across the street. Three students opened the wooden doors and slipped in. "We can hide in there."

The winged demon was in, and it was looking at me. This was the second demon looking straight at me. Wait, this wasn't some random attack. If … if the demons were here for me, then it meant Imha and Omi knew about me.

Panic cinched my chest, and my body slacked with that overwhelming realization. The police officer tugged the sleeve of my coat, snapping me out of it. We rushed to the other side of the street, and I didn't look back while the cop unloaded his gun at whatever moved closer.

Raisa and I opened the door. The three of us entered the gallery and pulled the door closed. The cop locked it, and then fastened a pair of cuffs around the knobs.

"I doubt this will hold them for much longer," he said.

Raisa turned to me and grasped my arms, her nails digging into my jacket, her eyes wide. "Dear Lord, I can't believe this is happening. This isn't happening. Tell me it isn't happening."

I patted her hands. "Hey. Calm down. Breath in and out."

The cop shot us an evil eye. "We don't have time for this."

I glared at him before focusing on Raisa again. "I need you to calm down. Take deep breaths."

She reluctantly did it. "W-what was that?"

"I don't know," I lied, hoping she wouldn't notice it. Usually, she caught on to my lies easily, but with the panicky state she was in, I doubted she was paying attention to details. "But you need to calm down a little, okay?"

She nodded, and I passed my arm over her shoulders steering her to the main room of the gallery.

We crossed the room on high alert. Around us quivering students hid behind the exhibitions, some climbed up the stairs, and some entered the restricted area probably looking for secluded places to hide. Many pieces of art had fallen or been broke.

I glanced up to the cop. "I'm Nadine. This is Raisa."

"I'm Greg," he said as we stepped into a second room.

A large banner indicated an international medieval weapons exhibition had been on display. The weapons lined the glass cases along the walls and over the tables. There were swords, axes, spears, daggers, bows, and many others I didn't know by name.

"W-we should take one," Raisa said, her voice still quavering.

I stared at her. "What?"

"Well, better than running empty-handed." She shrugged, and I had the urge to hug her. I had never seen Raisa this unsure before. "In case they get to us, we can try something."

"That might not be a bad idea," Greg said. He walked up to a center table, where swords of many different lengths were laid. Behind the table a woman hid. "Hey."

The woman stood. She held her chin high, making me jealous of her flawless brown skin. Her chocolate eyes stared at us, not one bit afraid. "I should tell you not to rob the swords, but who am I kidding? The weapons are the last thing to worry about now."

She was dressed in a gray pencil skirt, a silk white shirt, and black pumps. She looked too elegant to be a student. She turned, showing a name tag pinned to her shirt. It read *Keisha Cross, Medieval Weapons Specialist.*

"Why didn't you run to the basement with the others?" I asked as Raisa approached Keisha. Beside the new girl, Raisa looked like a gnome. I probably did too.

"I-I don't know," Keisha said, pushing her long, black hair back.

"Okay," Greg started. "Let's grab some stuff and get away from here."

A huge cracking sound echoed through the walls, followed by loud growls.

My heart chilled, and I jumped back bumping into Keisha. Oh God, the demons were inside.

Greg pulled his fist back set to break the glass over the swords, but Keisha was faster. She gently pushed me aside, punched the glass, and grabbed two swords. Her expression was tight, and when she turned her head toward the doorway her eyes flashed—a spark of silver light shone from her irises.

I rubbed my eyes. What? I must have been more tired than I thought I was.

Greg handed a dagger to Raisa and me, and he picked an axe for him. The dagger felt heavy and cold in my hand, and I didn't like holding it.

With what sounded like sick battle cries, the demons charged into the room, and Keisha stepped toward them.

I reached for her. "What are you doing?"

Without answering me, she jerked away from my hand and lunged at the demons.

Keisha swung one of her swords at the demon in front of her. The hideous creature parried it with its arm as her second sword slashed across its stomach. Another demon turned to her. Teeth gritted, she whirled away from its claw and hacked its thighs with both her swords. A third and a fourth demon lunged at her. She parried the spear of one, dodged the swipe of another, gashed the throat of the one with the spear, and kicked the chest of the other. The demon she killed and the one she kicked fell to the floor as a third demon came at her. She spun out of its reach, then stepped back into it, and shoved her sword into its chest. By then the other demon was back on its feet. She swung her arm wide, slicing its face with the tip of her blade. The demon collapsed to the side, and she sunk her sword in its chest.

My mouth hung open.

"Dear Lord," Raisa whispered.

Greg's lips curled up. "That's hot."

Seriously? He was thinking about *that* while she was fighting for our lives?

She was fighting. A bunch of demons. By herself. Fighting. Like sword fighting. As if she was a knight in some Arthurian tale.

I couldn't believe my eyes.

Keisha stopped, took off her pumps, ripped the side of her pencil skirt up to her thigh, and wiped the hair from her face. She looked fierce and strong, like a warrior, and she probably wasn't much older than I was.

Then three more demons came at her, and she killed them with ease.

She looked through the doorway. "We're clear. For now." She rushed to a glass case, broke it with the hilt of one of her swords, and grabbed a bow and a quiver with arrows. "But there are more outside. Many more. It won't take them long to figure out there are people in here." She turned to us. "What?"

Raisa blinked. "Are you serious?"

"How did you do that?" I asked.

Keisha swung the quiver and the bow across her shoulders. "I don't know. I just took the swords and did it."

"Have you had any training before?" Greg asked.

Frowning, Keisha took a velvet cloth hidden under one of the tables and cleaned her swords. "No."

"That's odd," Greg whispered.

"It sure is, but we don't have time to wonder about it," I

said, knowing there were odder things in this world than a girl who suddenly could fight without any training. "We need to find a way out of here. Out of the city possibly."

"I know," Keisha said. "There's a room downstairs in the basement where precious items and artifacts are stored. The room has a corridor that leads to a door into an alley. They bring valuable stuff through there. We could get away that way."

"If the alley is clear," I added.

"If it's not, I'll make it clear," she said, not an ounce of doubt in her voice.

"Sounds like a plan to me," Raisa said, clutching her dagger as if she were a warrior too.

"Lead the way." Greg walked to the back door.

"Wait." Keisha went to another glass shelf. She broke it, picked a leather belt from a hook, fastened it around her waist, and then took a dagger from the wall and slid it into her new belt. Next, she caught a long sword from the wall, placed it inside a scabbard, and hung it on her belt too. "Now I'm ready."

I stared at her. She had three swords, a dagger, and a bow and arrows, while I held only one meager dagger in my hand.

Holy shit.

Keisha rushed to the back door and led us through a corridor. At the end, there was an employee's only door. She took her name tag from her shirt and turned it, revealing a card. She slid it in the card reader, and the door popped open.

Once we were all in, Greg closed the door, making sure it was locked. Keisha looked like she knew where she was going, so when she climbed down two sets of stairs and continued through a long corridor, I didn't question it.

However, I did look through a couple of doors with small glass windows. People cowered inside those rooms, hiding for dear life.

Keisha stopped in front of a white door with no glass windows. She used her card to open it and stepped aside, letting us enter before her.

Lights flickered on, probably due to a motion sensor, and I looked around my mouth open. The room was large—not as large as the one at the Metropolitan or the former MoMa, but still large—and filled with paintings, rugs, books, mirrors, statues, other artifacts and rarities, and many boxes.

"Through here," Keisha said, taking the lead again. We weaved around the items and boxes, careful not to touch anything.

We reached the back door, and Keisha turned to us. "This door leads to stairs up, then to another outside door. I'll go up and check if the alley is clear."

Without waiting for an answer, Keisha vanished behind the door.

Raisa sagged against the wall beside the door and looked at me, a shocked gleam still in her eyes. "Do you have any idea what's going on?"

Instinctively, I reached for a strand of my hair, but before I could start twirling it around my finger, I realized what I was doing and lowered my hand. "No," I said. I hoped she wouldn't notice the quiver in my voice. "I have no idea."

"How about you?" she asked Greg.

Beside us, Greg ran his eyes over the axe he had gotten from upstairs. It looked heavy and deadly and had a thick hilt and sharp blade.

"I have seen bats before, but not this many. However, I have never seen the other creatures. I wonder what they are."

"How about Keisha?" Raisa asked. "I'm still stunned. Did you see what she could do? I mean, I wasn't imagining it, was I?"

"I'm shocked too, but wow," Greg said. "I'm also impressed."

I was impressed and curious. I saw her eyes flashing—or I thought I did—right before she turned into Bruce Lee. *That* wasn't a natural thing.

Raisa grabbed her phone from her purse. "Great, no signal."

"What were you going to do?" I asked.

"Search about this mess online."

"Oh." Greg's eyes widened. He reached for a walkie-talkie radio on his belt and turned it on.

"... hundreds of them. Maybe thousands? I don't know." The voice coming from the speaker was shaky. "I've never seen creatures like these. They destroyed Central Park, Rockefeller Center, and Union Square. NYU is also in bad shape."

A new voice spoke. "Brooklyn is on fire." My stomach revolted. I had seen demons and fire in a vision once before, a vision that came true. Omi, the god of war, had been in that vision. "I would say eighty percent of Brooklyn is on fire."

"Same with the Bronx," another man said. "We have the creatures and fire. Fire coming from the sky."

Feeling sick, I leaned against a pile of heavy wooden crates. Fire coming from the sky. Oh, God, Omi really was in New York City.

"Fire from the sky?" one of them asked.

"I'm not kidding," answered the one in the Bronx. "Wait. Dude!" A huge boom came from the walkie-talkie. "Helicopter down! It was like ... like the fire was sent directly to it.

From above." He paused. "Holy shit!" A second explosion boomed. "Two other helicopters down."

Greg spoke into the walkie-talkie. "Is this happening to any other city in the world?"

"Not that I know of," the first man said. "But then, we're stranded with little communication, under attack, and we have no idea what's happening."

"They entered the building," one of them said. "I've ... I've gotta run."

He probably ran, leaving the radio turned on and his channel open, because we heard the demons advancing on him, growling, breaking everything, and then his screams. His screams fell silent; we could only hear the shuffling of the demons among what sounded like breaking wood, probably furniture.

The radio stayed muted for a long time.

Raisa looked at me with tears in her wide eyes. I took her hand and squeezed it.

"God be with us," the first man we heard said.

"It's not clear," Keisha said, opening the door. The three of us squealed and jumped. She looked at us as if we had gone nuts. "What?"

I told her what we learned from the walkie-talkie, which was now silent.

She frowned. "I didn't see fire up there, but it may be a matter of time."

"So we need to move now?" I asked.

"I don't know. There are many monsters up there. I can't take them all alone. We wouldn't make it ten feet out of the alley."

Greg let go of his axe and crossed his arms. "That's not good."

"What do you propose we do?" I asked.

"I don't think anyone will find us here for now, so I say we stay here for the next thirty minutes. Then I'll check outside again. If it's clear, we go; if it's not, we stay. Deal?"

Raisa looked at her. "You're the samurai here. Whatever you say goes."

4

____

THIRTY MINUTES PASSED RATHER QUICKLY WHILE I WALKED around the room and browsed the items hidden in here. There was nothing like the Mona Lisa or any valuable Ancient Greek statue, but I liked it anyway. However, my mind wasn't really on what I was looking at.

The demons were here. Omi was here.

Why were they here? I remembered those two demons looking straight at me and shuddered. Omi couldn't know about me, could he? We had been careful. Brock was dead. Nobody knew who we were.

Even if they weren't here because of me, they were here now and could find me if they got too close and sensed my aura. We couldn't stay here much longer, trapped in a basement. We had to leave the city. The question was, how?

I eyed Keisha. She sat on the floor, her back against a wall near the door, playing with her sword as if she did that every free minute of her life. When I first laid eyes on her, she looked like an elegant teacher or law student. Determined, yes, but also ladylike and delicate, even with her tall, strong body. Then her eyes flashed—I wasn't imagining things again, was I?—and she transformed into this brave warrior who didn't care about losing a pair of expensive pumps or ripping her skirt so she could fight better. It was almost as if she had changed right in front of us.

Keisha and her mad fighting skills were probably our only way out of here.

Directly in front of our precious personal ninja, Raisa sat on a wooden box. She rummaged in her bag, but I could see her hands trembling from here. Oh God, how I wished Raisa hadn't been here. How I wished she were at her parents' house as they wanted, unharmed.

I frowned. I didn't know if the entire country was under attack. My stomach twisted into dozens of knots. Oh God, no, no. I couldn't bear to think about what could be happening to my family right now.

I took a deep breath and pushed those troubling thoughts aside. One problem at a time. First, we get out of town. Second, I send Raisa to her parents. Third, I somehow get to my own parents.

In the corner, Greg kept messing with the walkie-talkie trying to listen for more details and find out what was going on, if this was a random attack, what the creatures were, and which places were safe. However, the voices and the stories grew gorier by the minute, and it didn't seem as if anyone would leave New York alive.

Not even us.

I shuddered.

Keisha shot up to her feet. "I'll be right back," she said, before slipping behind the door. Not even a minute later she was back. She opened the door wide. "I think we can make it now."

Greg pushed away from the wall, Raisa jumped up from the crate, and I made my way back to the door. We picked up our stuff from the floor, and Greg checked his gun.

"Counting my second cartridge, I should have about twenty-four bullets," he said.

"Make them count," Keisha said. She glanced at the daggers Raisa and I were holding. "Be careful with that."

As opposed to what? Not being careful? I was actually trying not to think about how I was holding a weapon capable of killing a person.

Raisa shook her head. "Are you sure we can't stay here longer? Maybe we can wait for a couple of hours. Perhaps by then they will have left the city."

Keisha took a deep breath. "I don't think they will leave the city with anyone alive in it. They'll scour inch by inch, even if it takes weeks."

"How do you know?" I asked.

"I don't. It's just a hunch. It's like they are looking for something, and they will keep killing and destroying until they find it."

I swallowed. Damn.

Doing the noble thing crossed my mind. Surrendering myself. But ... they were demons. They wouldn't back out of destroying the city and killing everyone in it just because I had given myself up. And there was my family to consider. If I surrendered, who would take care of them? Who would send them money every week? Who would make sure they were okay?

Although now with NYU and the entire city destroyed, I wasn't sure how that would work anymore. I shook my head. One problem at a time. First, getting out of here.

Greg turned off his radio. "Let's do this."

Keisha opened the first door. "Okay, we'll go up to the alley. Try to stay in the shadows along the walls and make no sound. As far as I can tell, these monsters are dumb but they have good ears and noses. We'll approach the street and make our way out of the city, sticking to the shadows and hiding in alleys or courtyards."

"You do realize we'll have to cross a bridge or a tunnel to exit the city, right?" I asked.

"Yes, but I'm trying not to think about that yet. One problem at a time," she said, repeating what I had been telling myself. She looked at us pointedly. "Ready?"

We exchanged glances, and my grip tightened around the hilt of the dagger I was holding.

Keisha led the way. Raisa was second, I was third, and Greg was last. Once I stepped into the dark corridor, I felt sick to my stomach. Oh God, we were going out among the demons.

Without ceremony, Keisha reached the top of the stairs and opened the door. She put her finger over her lips and beckoned us out. Following her lead, we plastered our backs to the wall of the dark alley, and I had a hard time staying calm.

I couldn't see the demons because of the darkness and the fact that we were trying to stay hidden, but I could hear them. Shrieks and grunts reached our ears, and I could only assume it came from demons crossing the street at the end of the alley.

I slowly breathed in and out, concentrating on staying calm.

The alley was wide and long. There were boxes and litter spread on the ground from an open garbage container, and it smelled almost as bad as the demons.

"Come on," Keisha whispered. Tiptoeing along the wall, she pulled the bow and an arrow from her back. "Be prepared."

"P-prepared for what?" Raisa asked.

"Anything," Keisha responded.

Raisa whimpered, and I reached for her hand. It seemed to have helped before, and I was in need of some reassurance right now too.

A gust of wind surged into the alley bringing a chilly breeze around us. I shivered. If I knew we would spend a long time outside, I would have worn warmer clothes. Jeans, a dark green sweater, knee-high brown boots, a brown trench coat, a scarf, and gloves weren't cutting it. But what else would I have worn? A blanket?

Crap, where were my thoughts going?

Eight feet from the alley's exit, Keisha raised her hand indicating for us to stop. Still plastered to the wall, we didn't dare to breathe.

Grunts and screeches grew louder, and my heartbeat rose with each taloned footfall scratching the concrete. My palms became sweaty, and I closed my eyes willing my fear and nervousness to back away. The alley was wide, which meant whoever crossed by its entrance had a good chance of looking in and seeing us. There was enough light coming from the entryway to illuminate our position. I just prayed the boxes and garbage hid us well.

I didn't believe we would get out of the city without engaging demons, but the less attention we attracted, the better it would be, especially because Raisa and I didn't know how to fight or even how to wield a weapon.

The first demons appeared through the alley's opening, and Raisa squeezed my hand. Two demons jogged across, no problem. A third walked slowly. He stopped and howled to someone or something behind him. Two more showed up, and the third one grunted at them. The three of them resumed their walk. Five others ran past us. Then two others came by. One of them stopped, eyeing the alley. He sniffed the air and grunted. The second one stopped and smelled the air too.

Raisa let go of my hand and clamped her mouth.

One of the demons pointed to the wall on the other side of the alley. Three human bodies laid there. Blood dripped from the gashes across their faces and chests.

Raisa swayed to my side, squeaking.

The demons' attention turned to us.

"Shit," Keisha muttered. She pulled the string of her bow and let the arrow fly. The arrow pierced the demon's forehead, and it fell back.

With a loud growl, the second one darted to us. By then Keisha had another arrow poised. She let it go, and the arrow ripped through its chest. The demon stumbled and fell.

Holding our breath, we waited. The others had heard us. There was no way they hadn't. Ten seconds passed. Twenty. Thirty.

A full minute later, Keisha exhaled loudly and turned to Raisa. "What the hell?"

With her back to the bodies across the alley, Raisa crouched, one hand still over her mouth the other on her stomach. "I'm sorry."

I rubbed her back. "It's okay. Just breathe in and out."

"It's not okay." Keisha paced in front of us, her eyes hard. "There are hundreds of demons out there. Maybe thousands. I would rather hide quietly than fight them all, and that means you can't whimper or squeak or gasp."

"Hey!" I glared at Keisha. "She has a sensitive stomach, okay? This isn't easy for her."

Keisha turned to me, her eyes hard. "Do you think this is easy for me?"

"You're the one who just took some swords off a table and used them as if you were a knight out of a medieval tale. It does seem easy for you."

"Are you insane?"

"Enough!" Greg muttered, though I could see he wanted to yell instead. "We can't argue among ourselves, and we can't waste time." He turned to Raisa. "Please, can you try to take this all in so we can keep moving?"

"You gotta do it," I whispered. "It's the only way to get away from here."

She looked into my eyes, terror visible in them. She had always been sarcastic and free-spirited, yet now she seemed scared to her bones. Well, she never thought she would fight in a demon attack and see bloodied, dead bodies.

I helped Raisa up. She pressed both hands over her stomach.

"Please, all of you, try to bottle your feelings up and let's do this." Keisha grabbed a new arrow from the quiver on her back. "All right. Let's move."

"Do we know which tunnel or bridge we are going to cross?" Greg asked, putting the safety of his gun back on.

"The Holland Tunnel is the closest one," I said.

Keisha gave a curt nod. "Then that is where we're going."

She spied out of the exit and gestured for us to come to her. We crossed the street with hurried but muffled steps, looking side to side to make sure no one was coming, and hid under a store's entrance. I recognized Houston Street. We were close to Sixth Avenue and closer to the tunnel than I first thought. We could do this. Finally, I had a glimmer of hope.

Bat demons soared through the sky every couple of minutes, and wingless demons rushed down the streets even more often.

"How about that car?" I asked, pointing to an abandoned car thirty yards from where we hid.

"That would attract more attention," Keisha said.

"If we can outrun them, who cares about attracting attention?" Greg said.

Keisha thought it over for a moment. "All right. Stay here. I'll see if it's working."

She checked the street for demons and then rushed to it. The door was unlocked, and she was able to slip inside before a group of demons hurried by. She waited until they were gone and tried the engine. It worked! She tried driving it, but it rolled like a beaten wagon for ten feet, and then stopped. Keisha opened the passenger door and spied out. With a disappointed expression, she came back to us.

"Two flat tires," she said. "And almost no gas. It wouldn't get us far anyway."

Still, if it could have gotten us through the tunnel, it would have helped.

We walked three blocks without any problems—two south on Sixth Avenue, and one west onto Spring Street. Closer to Hudson Street, the sounds and movements increased. Shrieks echoed through the air, and more demons ran past our hiding spots.

"There's something going on," Keisha said, pulling us into an alley two buildings from the corner of Hudson Street.

We took in as much as we could, trying to find out what was happening. After a couple of tense minutes, I gave up looking out and leaned against the alley wall. I was tired. I was hungry and dirty. I hadn't felt like this in three months, and I had hoped I would never feel this way again.

"If I didn't know better, I would say the monsters are gathering for a parade," Greg said, peeking around the corner of the alley.

It did look like that. But why would demons get together for a parade?

A bat flew by right when Greg was retreating into the alley.

"Fuck," he swore, aiming his gun at the coming creature.

The bat landed in the alley's entrance and shrieked. The creature was tall, taller than a human, with a bony body covered by viscous gray skin. It bared its sharp teeth and recoiled its large and bristly wings.

Its putrid stench of rotting flesh reached my nose, and I breathed through my mouth before I puked.

"He's going to call more monsters!" Raisa yelled.

The bat took two steps into the alley, scratching its talons along the concrete and screeching. Keisha pointed her bow at him, but Greg was faster. He shot the demon twice—between the eyes and in the chest. Trembling, the bat fell to the ground, and green liquid poured out of its wounds.

Beside me, Raisa doubled over. I rubbed her back, thinking she would throw up, but she only gagged. I gagged too.

With a lethal expression, Keisha pointed an accusing finger to Greg's gun. "If the demon's scream hadn't been enough, I'm sure your shots were."

"What did you want me to do?" Greg said, his voice rising. "It's what I have and what I know how to use."

"You brought an axe!"

"I don't know how to wield an axe!"

"And what do—?"

Keisha stopped yelling once we heard *them*. The shuffling of wings, the screeches. Bats appeared in the sky, close to the ground, as a new group of demons rushed to our alley. Even if we had time to hide, it wouldn't matter. They knew we were here.

I couldn't count fast enough, but there were easily eight wingless demons coming toward us and about five bat-like demons hovering above us.

Holy shit.

"What do we now?" I asked.

"Charge!" Keisha shouted.

She shot two arrows at the bat-like demons. Both fell to the ground dead. Then she unsheathed her long sword and engaged in battle, while I stared amazed at how warrior-like she was.

At once, the demons spread out and hovered around her. Two demons charged at the same time. Keisha stepped aside and ducked while they stumbled into each other. Taking advantage of the two seconds of confusion, she swung her sword and slashed open the back of one of the demons causing it to fall on its stomach, shrieking. Before she could even blink, the other demon was on her. Keisha parried a strong blow and dodged another. The demon kept coming, and Keisha kept stepping back, avoiding it.

The demon swung its claws toward Keisha's chest, but Keisha was able to deflect it. With a low growl, she kicked it back using as much force as she could. The demon staggered back, and taking advantage of its confusion, she lunged at it. But the demon had already recovered and waited for her. It stepped aside and lacerated her left shoulder with his sharp claws.

I gasped and she sprang at it, as if nothing had happened. It parried her attack, and after she landed a blow that made it raise it arms to ward the weapon off, she spun around and cut its stomach open. Gooey blood gushed out of the wound as the demon fell on the ground writhing.

She barely had time to catch her breath as more demons came at her, and one of the bats dove at Raisa and me. Greg shot it, and Raisa yelled when it fell at our feet, swiping its claw one more time before dying.

A wingless demon was able to weave past Keisha and Greg, who were deep in combat—Keisha with her sword, Greg with his fists and attempting to use the axe. The demon snarled at Raisa and me. Raisa hid behind me, and I raised my dagger trying to remember how I had fought against this kind of demon before, when Brock had Morgan and me as prisoners at that abandoned school.

I inhaled deeply. I could do this. I really could.

The demon charged, and I stepped aside, pulling Raisa with me. Because of their bulk, these demons were slow, and if I wanted to win this fight, I would have to play the speed game. I just hoped I was fast enough.

I pushed Raisa to the side, and she stepped away and fell flush against the wall. I adjusted my grip on the dagger. The demon came at me. I stepped aside again, but this time it saw my move. It reached with its arm and pulled me to it. I yelped as my back pressed against its chest, and it snapped its teeth near my neck. I was sure it would bite me and rip my throat out. I elbowed its stomach. That didn't do anything. So I did the next *natural* thing. I turned the blade of the dagger around and pierced its stomach. The creature screamed in my ear, and I thought I would faint from its fetid breath. Its hold on me loosened enough for me to elbow it again, push against it, and set myself free.

I turned to it with the dagger high and aimed at its chest. The demon growled. Advancing, it swiped its claws toward me, but I ducked and stepped back until I had my back to a wall. With what sounded like a growling laughter, the demon lunged at me. I kept my dagger high, stabbing the air and hoping the demon was dumb enough to run toward it. But it just swatted its hand at mine. What looked like a simple slap forced me to stumble to the side. The dagger went flying, and I fell to my knees. The demon grabbed me by my shoulders and yanked me up. It opened its mouth, and I closed my eyes and waited. It howled and let me go.

Wide-eyed, I leaned against the wall so I wouldn't fall again and looked at the demon, wondering why it hadn't taken my head off with its big mouth. Then its body fell forward with my dagger buried in its back.

A guy stood behind him.

"Hi, darling. Did you miss me?"

5

———

Dark jeans, black T-shirt, black leather jacket, and a smug grin. As stunning and strong as I remembered him, Micah stared at me with his deep, dark eyes.

My heart almost jumped out my open mouth. My throat felt dry.

"Ah ..." I didn't know what to say.

I hadn't heard anything in three months, and then I met with Victor, the Fates, and now Micah in a matter of two days. And let's not talk about the demons running around New York City. Oh, and my suspicion that Omi was in the city.

Micah took a step toward me, and I held my breath. "Too stunned to say hi. I know I'm good-looking, darling, but I thought you were used to that by now."

I shut my mouth and glared at him. God, he was cocky and petulant, but I had missed his incredibly sexy accent. I would never admit that to him, though.

A demon jumped at him, but Micah ducked as if it was the simplest thing he had ever done. He whirled around, grabbed my dagger from the other demon's body, and when the demon came at him again he simply cut its throat. Blood spilled from the cut, splashing all over my pants, and the demon fell back, making a terrible gurgling sound.

One of the winged demons turned to us. It looked at Micah and hesitated. It seemed unsure about attacking him. Micah, on the other hand, looked sure of what to do. He stepped forward and killed the demon, piercing the dagger into its chest.

Two other demons fought Keisha. Maintaining his regal pose, Micah struck one of them, and Keisha killed the other.

She looked at him confused, but only until the sound of metal rattling caught our attention. I glanced around. Raisa was still where I left her, shaking with fear, and Keisha was now stepping over the bodies of a few demons walking toward Greg, who had fallen over a garbage can, his hand over his chest.

"Oh no," I whispered.

Keisha knelt beside him. "What happened?"

Greg closed his eyes for a second. "I-I couldn't keep them off."

I approached the scene, Micah by my side.

"Let me see," Keisha said, pulling his hand from over his wound.

I gasped and clamped my hand over my mouth. Blood oozed from what look like ten thick holes, as if a demon had buried its claws in Greg's chest.

"I know it's bad," Greg mumbled.

"No, no. You can make it," Keisha said. She looked around as if asking for help. Unfortunately, I couldn't do much. I wasn't a doctor yet, and we had no supplies. I didn't have materials to stitch him up, and he was losing blood fast.

Taking off my scarf, I knelt beside him and applied pressure to his wounds. It was the only thing I could think of, but I knew it wouldn't be enough.

Raisa rose and stood beside us, avoiding looking at the scene.

Greg chuckled, but it sounded wrong. "Yeah, right." He took in a labored breath. "I'm glad I was able to help a little though." He grunted in pain. He clasped Keisha's hand and looked from her to me to Raisa. "I ho-hope all of you make out of here safe."

He closed his eyes, and Keisha pursed her lips.

We watched over him, until his chest stopped moving.

I checked his pulse. "He's gone." I took his hands and clasped them together over his chest. "Thank you," I whispered, wishing I had said it while he was still alive. Sighing, I stood and turned to Micah. "Hey."

His grin faded. In fact, he looked tense with a deep frown. His hands shook terribly, and he looked as if he was in pain.

Without thinking, I reached for him and took his hands in mine. The cold jolt shocked me, but only for a moment. He gasped, his head lolling back a little, as the energy rushed from me to him. My knees wobbled. He was taking much more from me than Victor had, which meant he was in worse shape, though he disguised it better.

I didn't mean to, but it was hard not to stare at the sharp angles of his face framed by his unkempt black hair, the strands a little longer than the last time I had seen him, his smooth skin, his inviting lips, and his black eyes now staring back at me.

I swallowed, realizing the healing was complete, and pulled my hands away.

"Thanks," he said, still ogling me.

"You took a lot from me."

"Sorry."

"That's okay. But why didn't you come before?"

He glanced at the ground, his jaw ticking. "Because I didn't want to attract demons here." The same thing Victor said. Boys! He gestured to the demons at our feet. "However, now that seems irrelevant."

"So you endured it?" He nodded. "And you would have kept enduring if they hadn't attacked the city?" He nodded again. "That's insane."

"No. Insane would be coming to you. The demons would sense my aura and be here in no time."

As he had done, I gestured around us. "Like that worked."

"Well, *someone* brought them here."

I put my hands on my hips. "Are you implying that—?"

"Nadine," Keisha called. "Who is your friend?"

I looked around. "Just ... a friend. Micah, this is Keisha. Keisha, this is Micah."

He narrowed his eyes at her. "Hey," he said, his voice normal. It was odd, because normally every time Micah spoke to a female, his voice was sugary and he acted all charming and smiling. Then Raisa stood beside us, and he barely glanced her way. "Hi, Raisa."

Wiping the unshed tears from her eyes, Raisa nodded in acknowledgment.

"We should keep moving," Keisha said.

Micah shook his head. "I'm not sure if you saw it, but there's a bunch of demons half a block from here. And by a bunch, I mean—"

Raisa's eyes widened. "Demons?"

Micah and I exchanged an oh-shit look.

I wasn't sure how the world would explain what was happening, what they would call these creatures, or if they would get a glimpse of what was really going on, and I wasn't sure Keisha and Raisa should know about it.

Micah cleared his throat. "Well, it's what I've been calling them."

"It suits them," Keisha said.

If only she knew.

Keisha knelt beside Greg's body and covered it with my scarf as much as she could. Then she dragged the demons' bodies to the back.

I lowered myself to help Keisha, but Micah put a hand on my wrist and pulled me back. "They are too heavy," he said.

What the hell? Keisha could carry them. I could too! I hooked my hands around one of the many demons' bodies, trying not to throw up from their nasty stench and nastier look, and pulled. It didn't budge. The damn thing *was* too heavy.

"Told ya," he said, with a knowing smile. I could hit him. After he carried three bodies back, he stood beside me. "Who is she? How and when did you meet her?"

I looked at his face, ready to snap at him for already being interested in a girl. He was serious, though. "I don't know. I mean, we were hiding and she was too. She looked elegant, like a fancy businesswoman, until the demons charged us, then she grabbed a sword from the museum and killed them as if she had wielded swords since birth."

"Did she explain how she knows how to fight?"

"No. Why? Should there be an explanation?"

"I don't know." He squinted, observing her. She was dragging the bodies as if they were dolls. "Her aura is different."

"Really? How so?"

"It's odd." He looked at me, his eyes sharp and intent, and I had to focus on breathing. "You know yours changed after

Ceris took the Destiny Gift from you, right?" It had? I shook my head. "It's not as strong right now, but it's still way stronger than a human's. Hers is like yours was. Strong, but not quite deity-like."

"What does that mean?"

"That she's not ordinary."

Seriously? And here I thought I would be able to turn my back on all of this after we were done escaping the city.

Micah went back to helping Keisha, and Raisa scooted closer to me. "What do we do now?" she asked.

"I don't know," I said, my voice low.

Keisha wiped her hands on her ripped skirt. "Wait here for a bit. Hope they don't find us. Then try to find another way out of the city if they don't disperse."

She turned her back to us, watching the street that intersected the alley, with her hands on her hips and her chin raised, like a badass security guard. Like someone who would get us out of the city.

I leaned against a wall with Raisa's head on my shoulder, but with Micah standing in front of us, I barely felt her.

He was here. Holy shit, he was here.

And he was staring at me with an odd look and his arms crossed.

Just like that, the anger and the resentment from when he left me alone on that island, the same anger and resentment that had built up these past months, surged back into me.

There was much I wanted to tell him, so much I wanted to yell at him. Why the hell did he leave me alone? Why defend me back then? Why send Rok after me? Why show up now?

I opened my mouth to ask all those questions, but his head snapped to the side, a big V between his brows, his shoulders tense.

"Oh fuck," he cursed.

"What?" I asked, stiffening.

He grabbed my arm and pulled me halfway down the alley. He leaned to me and paused. What was he doing?

Then he shook his head. "There's a god here, and he's coming this way."

I pursed my lips. "Omi."

"What? How do you know?"

"The radio ... a police officer reported seeing fire being hurled from the sky. I saw that before when Omi decimated that small village in Switzerland."

"Fuck," he muttered, raking his hand through his hair. "This isn't good."

"You said he's coming our way, which means he'll be able to sense us. You especially." He nodded. My eyes narrowed. "We should run, just run, the opposite way and pray we make it."

"It won't be enough. Besides, we're too far away from any other tunnel or bridge. We'll probably face the same odds if we go another way."

"Wait. Shouldn't you be attracting them now?"

He grinned. "Since recovering my memory I've been practicing how to hide my aura. Actually, it's more like trying. I can fade it but not for long."

The corner of my lips tugged up. "That's good, I guess." I lost the grin a second later. "What do we do then?"

He looked at the other girls. Keisha was seated beside

Raisa, holding her hands, probably telling her some lie like "we're gonna be fine". In this world? That was as far from the truth as it got.

"We'll bring them back here, and I'll try to fade all of your auras with mine."

I nodded. Trying to keep my exterior confident and steady, I walked to the girls. I was sure they could see past my facade, but it was probably better to see I was trying to be strong than to look like a desperate woman. Because on the inside, I was probably as afraid and nervous as Raisa.

I was able to convince Raisa and Keisha to join us in the middle of the alley. We crouched on the dirty ground, and Micah stood beside us. He closed his eyes, focusing on whatever it was he did to try and fade our auras.

His eyes shot open. He glanced to the alley's opening, as if he had sensed a powerful aura close.

I stood beside him. I slid the sleeve of his jacket up and put my hand over his wrist, skin-to-skin, trying to help him. A little of my energy seeped into him, and he sighed as if it was easier now.

The demons' screams and cheering came from afar.

Micah walked to the alley's opening and looked around the wall. I scooted close to him.

"You shouldn't be here, darling."

"Neither should you." My eyes settled on the mass of demons, and I was sure I had gone pale. "Oh my God ... there are too many of them. There are more wingless ones than winged ones."

"The winged ones are called Akuma," Micah explained. Akuma were on the ground, gathering in the center of the lane, as if they were ready for a parade. "And if you observe well, you'll see there are two types of wingless demons. The

Ornek and the Arak. The Ornek are right behind the Akuma, and the Arak are in the back. If you compare them, you'll see that the Arak have smaller ears and not as pointy. They have a little hair on the back of their necks, their arms are longer, and their stomachs are more pronounced."

I narrowed my eyes at him. "That's disgusting." He smiled. I took a sharp inhale before looking back at the demons. "Right. So, what are they waiting for?"

"For ..."

He didn't have to say it.

Omi appeared near the corner, floating a few feet above the ground on some kind of black cloud.

I gasped placing my hand around Micah's wrist again, and he tensed.

Omi wore his usual white crumpled suit. His hair could use a trim and a comb, and maybe his face needed a razor too. But he did look powerful.

As Omi got closer, we were able to make out his words. "... here somewhere." His voice boomed through the air. "Search every corner, under every stone, inside every sewer. Break into every house, kill everyone, but find her." My grip around Micah's wrist tightened. "I want her. I *need* her." I looked up as another dark cloud followed Omi, but this one was high in the sky and fire danced around it. "I want her alive!"

Omi raised his arms, and the fire bolts fell from the sky. The demons cried before turning around and running like lost rabid dogs.

"Fuck." Micah grabbed my arm and dragged me to the back of the alley again.

Keisha was already up, with her sword ready in her hand. Damn, the girl looked badass.

"What was that?" she asked.

"Omi—"

"Bad stuff," I said, cutting Micah off. "We need to run. Now."

Micah glanced around to the few doors in the alley. He marched to one and kicked it twice, three times. When it seemed a little loose, he grabbed the dagger from his waist and used it to pry it open.

"Come on!" he shouted.

Keisha, Raisa, and I rushed inside.

As Micah closed the door behind us, I looked around. We were in a mailroom of an office building.

Keisha stopped. "Here." She offered him one of her swords. "You probably can make good use of it."

Micah gripped the sword as if he owned it. "Keep moving. We need to find another exit, preferably far away from the demons."

We entered a long corridor, and I let the others pass in front of me.

I came close to him and looked him in the eyes. "It is about me, isn't it?" He pursed his lips. "Micah, Omi was talking about me, right?"

"I guess so," he said through gritted teeth.

"But how? How did he find out about me? Oh my God, what about my family? If they know about me, they know about my family."

He clutched my shoulders. "Hey. He didn't say your name. They are probably looking for a girl your age with a similar aura, and that's it."

"But how did they know to look for a girl?"

He shook his head. "I don't know. Just ... don't worry yet, okay?"

"You're asking me not to worry? I'm the queen of

worrying."

He smiled. "I know." He ran his hands down my arms. It was almost comforting. "But I'm here, darling, and I won't let anything happen to you." He looked at me as if he meant it.

I swallowed my tears. "After three months away you think you can waltz in here and use your charm to save the day? Think it'll work?"

With that smug smile of his, he tugged my hands. "I don't know. You tell me."

"Jerk," I muttered, shaking my head.

"What?" he asked, an amused tone on his voice.

I ignored him as we walked down the corridor following the others.

At the end of the corridor we exited to a large room with lots of tables and computers. There were doors labeled with exit signs across the room.

In the middle of the room I stopped and pointed to a corner. There were a few people hiding under some tables.

"We can't leave them," I whispered.

"We can't save everyone," Micah whispered back.

Ignoring him, I turned to the people. "Hi, hmm, you should leave. It's not safe here."

A man stood up from under a desk. "But there are mo- monsters outside."

"Yeah, and they are breaking into the buildings now. It's only a matter of time until they break in here."

"A-are you sure?" the man asked.

"Yeah, she's sure," Micah said. "Like she said, there's not much time. So, goodbye and good luck."

Once more, Micah grabbed my arm and pulled me toward the exit.

"What's the matter with you?" I hissed.

"What's the matter with me? I'm here trying to save your pretty little ass, and you're trying to save every stray we find."

"Excuse me?" I stopped and stared at him. "You came to save me? Let me tell you, I didn't ask for any saving."

He groaned. "Oh, really? Because you looked like you were about to be eaten by a demon when I arrived and saved your skin."

"Holy ... can you be any less infuriating?"

"Look who is talki—"

"Hey, you two," Keisha said. "Stop that right now."

"Nah." He had that mischievous grin of his on. "Nadine likes our banter, don't you, darling?"

His eyes shifted from my face to over my shoulder, and the grin disappeared from his face. I followed his gaze to a desk. He reached around me, grabbed car keys from a desk, and jiggled them in front of my face. "I have an idea."

6

____

"Not here," Micah said, pressing the button on the car keys as we walked through the second floor of the parking garage.

He was paying attention to the cars. I was looking at the concrete walls, at the large spaces they had every few feet, just like a window, but without any glass. Demons flew too close to those in my opinion, and the fire falling from the sky was even closer. It would be too easy to spot us or set us on fire.

We turned a corner and kept climbing the ramp toward the third floor.

Please let the car be here. Please let the car be here.

The car couldn't be on the fourth floor because the fourth floor was open to the sky, and then there was no escaping the demons.

Micah pressed the button, and the car beeped.

We all stopped and looked around while Micah pressed the button nonstop.

"Here," Keisha said.

We ran to her and found an old black Nissan GT-R.

"Now, that's what I'm talking about," Micah said with a big grin. He leaned into me. "Come on, darling, let's cruise."

I elbowed him in the ribs. "Please, spare me."

He opened the passenger door for me. "But you love it."

"Do you guys have something going on?" Keisha asked from the other side of the car. "Like ex-boyfriend and girlfriend, or just ex-lovers, or whatever?"

My cheeks heated. "What?"

Micah laughed.

"He used to follow her around a couple of months ago," Raisa told her, her voice still shaky.

I elbowed her too. She just shrugged and slid to the back from the passenger side, while Keisha did the same from the driver's side. I sat in the passenger seat, and Micah closed my door.

"Fuck," Micah muttered, before running to the other side.

"What is it?" I asked when he entered the car and slammed the door.

He put the key in the ignition and turned on the engine. "Don't look to your right."

"Why?" I asked, looking to the right. "Oh my God." My stomach dropped.

Winged demons flew into the garage, followed by huge balls of fire that rolled down the ramp from the fourth floor.

"We're dead," Raisa whimpered, recoiling in the backseat.

"Go, go, go!" Keisha said.

Micah backed the car from the spot then floored it, slamming us back in our seats.

He drove down to the main level. The garage exit was right before us, and I braced myself for what would come once we exited.

Micah turned west onto Spring Street, even though the street was a one-way going east.

The demons had broken into stores, offices, and restaurants. Glass and metal bar doors cluttered the sidewalks. I just stared. Were they that strong? My attention shifted up, where orange waves licked the tops of the buildings, lighting up the dark sky.

"Hold on!" Micah said, through gritted teeth. He yanked the car to the left as a balcony fell from the top of a building, missing the car by a few inches.

My heart stopped. I clutched the sides of my seat.

Keisha leaned forward. "They see us."

I looked ahead. Demons rushed at us, their claws drawn and teeth bared.

"Oh my God," I whispered, sinking into the seat.

"Let's just hope Omi doesn't see us," Micah said, shifting gears and stepping on the gas.

The car lurched forward. Just two blocks to the tunnel and yet, it seemed too far away.

"Who is Omi?" Keisha asked.

Micah and I exchanged a glance. Before we could think of anything to say, the demons swarmed at the car. One punched at my window, and I flinched to the middle of the car. Repeatedly the demon hit the window, fracturing the glass before being thrown from the vehicle because of Micah's driving.

"Darling," Micah said. "As much as I like you close to me, I'm trying not to kill us here." He nudged my leg, trying to reach the gearshift.

I scooted back a little. "Sorry."

He flashed me one of his smug grins before running over three demons.

The car bumped and I thought we were going to roll over.

Glass shattered, and I whipped my head back. Two demons had broken the back window, but Keisha slashed at them with her sword until they let go and fell.

More demons came at us. They scratched the sides of the car, broke windows, and tried to hold on and flip us over. I wished I still had that vial with the fountain water from the Clarity Castle so I could wish on it and take us out of here like I had done before when escaping that school with Morgan and Micah, but with Keisha's weapons and Micah's heavy foot, we were able to finally outrun the demons.

We reached the tunnel, and I took a long, calming breath.

"Micah," Keisha said, her voice holding a warning tone. "You might want to speed up."

Micah glanced at the rearview mirror, and I turned back.

A wave of fire entered the tunnel on our tail. Raisa was low in the seat, eyes closed, her ears clamped, and she sang one of the songs Olivia had composed to try and calm herself. Perhaps I should sing too. It had always helped my wacky nerves.

"Fuck," he muttered, speeding even more and bringing my attention back to the fire.

"More." Keisha's voice rose. "Faster."

"I'm trying." Micah shifted gears, and the car lurched.

Oh my God. I wouldn't die being devoured by a demon. No, instead I would die in a car crash in a dark tunnel.

The flames illuminated more than the car's headlights did, and I could feel the heat closing in on us.

We wouldn't make it.

We exited the tunnel and demons formed a wall in our way.

"Hold on!" Micah yelled.

He didn't stop; he didn't reduce speed.

We collided with the demons as they charged us. One dove at the window, right in front of me. He smashed through the glass on the passenger side, sending shards flying everywhere. I screamed, throwing my arms up to protect myself, but big claws pushed my arms out of the way, closing around my neck.

"Nadine!" Micah yelled, punching the demon's arm with one hand, while trying to maneuver the car free from the rest of the demons with the other. He had slowed down a bit, but I was sure he didn't mean to.

Keisha cursed behind me, followed by grunts and the clanks of a sword.

I wanted to glance back and make sure the girls were okay, but the demon pulled me forward, its hand tightening its grip on me.

I choked. I fingered the seat for a weapon, any weapon, but couldn't find anything. I couldn't do anything other than stare at its ugly, terrifying face, with its yellow, hungry eyes, sharp teeth, and nasty drool.

"Oh, Lord," Raisa muttered, her voice teary.

"Hang on!" Keisha shouted. I could hear slashing and growls, which meant she was still fighting in the back.

I held on to the seat, but the demon was stronger than I was, and it dragged me forward a little more. It was worming itself out, and then it would pull me out too.

"Oh, no, no, no." Micah's hand clasped my upper arm.

My vision dimmed.

"Take this!" Keisha said to Micah.

Two seconds later, Micah lowered a short sword over the demon's wrist, cutting its hand off in front of my face. The demon screamed and I gaped. Micah took advantage of that moment and swerved the car, sending the demon flying off the car.

I unlatched the demon's claws from around my neck and yelped as I threw it out the window.

Keisha pushed the last demons from the top of the car with her sword. "Demons and fire gone."

Micah kept driving on I-78 south.

"Are you okay?" he asked, stealing glances at me.

"Yeah. Yeah." I leaned back in the seat, feeling as if I had been through a war. Well, this was somewhat like it. I touched my neck where the demon's claws had sunk in. I brought my hand back and stared at it. Blood. Not much, but there was blood. I hid my hand before Micah could see it. "Just pay attention to the road."

The slashes didn't hurt much yet. I knew the shock would soon wear off, and then they would probably hurt. Until then, I could pretend I was fine.

I glanced back at Manhattan. The island had transformed into a giant mountain of fire. It reached the sky and lit the world with orange lights.

My eyes watered.

My classmates, my teachers, my residence, my colleagues, my job, my scholarship, everything I owned burned with the island.

At least Raisa was with me—shrunken and trembling in the backseat, but alive.

Keisha rested her elbows on the back of my seat and looked at me. "Are you okay?"

Wiping my tears, I nodded and faced forward.

Without looking at me, Micah reached over and took my hand in his, entwining his fingers with mine. Under normal circumstances, I would have yelled at him for being such a

Casanova, but right now ... right now, I welcomed the comfort. I rested our hands over my thigh and squeezed.

I let my eyes wander. The chaos was a normal level here. Destroyed roads and buildings, a couple of bats here and there, but no fire, no Omi.

"So, what do we do now?" Keisha asked. "Just drive south and that's it?"

"At the moment, the only thing that matters is to get as far from New York as we can." Micah let go of my hand and shifted gears. He didn't return his hand to me and disappointment burned in my chest.

"Did you have friends or family in New York?" I asked in a gentle tone. This wasn't an easy subject.

"No," she said. "I'm from the Chicago area. I came with the exhibition."

"Exhibition?" Micah asked.

"Yeah, the ancient weapons exhibition at the university gallery."

"Speaking of which, where did you learn how to use those weapons?" I asked.

She shrugged. "I don't know. I never had any training."

One of Micah's eyebrows rose. "You just knew what to do with them then?"

"I know it sounds crazy, believe me, I think it is, but it's the truth. I just took them and used them."

Regaining a bit of herself, Raisa took a deep breath and wiped her eyes. "She was kind of badass back there."

"Hmm." Micah returned to his attention to the road.

"I have a question. That guy, on the dark cloud ..." Keisha paused and shook her head. "I still think I hallucinated him. Anyway, he was talking about a woman. A girl." She turned to me. "Was he talking about you, Nadine?"

Micah looked at me, and I was sure his hard expression meant: *don't tell her anything.*

"I don't know," I said, not too happy about lying.

A pop song started playing, saving me from having to say more.

"It's my phone," I said, looking around. "Where's my tote?"

"Here," Raisa said. She handed it to me.

I grabbed the phone from inside my bag and glanced at the screen. My eyes watered again. "Hi, Mom," I answered.

"Oh, good Lord, please tell me you're okay. Please, tell me you were able to leave the city."

"I did. I'm out of the city." She whispered a thank you, and I heard her sobs. "Mom, I'm okay. Are you okay?"

"Yes," she mumbled through sobs. "This is just a relieved cry."

Micah's cell phone rang, and I tried to ignore it.

"Is there anything like that happening there?" I guessed I knew the answer, but I had to confirm it.

"No, dear. Only New York City." She cleared her throat, probably trying to rein in the tears. "You're coming home, right?"

I hadn't thought much about that yet. If I went home, I could attract demons there. However, I did want to see my family. "Yes," I said, not sure if I was telling the truth or not, but it was the answer she wanted to hear.

"Good, good."

We talked nonsense for about two more minutes, then my sister called her and she had to go. By then, Micah was off the phone too.

We all remained in silence for about ten minutes, until I couldn't take it anymore.

"Who was it?"

He glanced at me with a raised eyebrow. "Jealous, darling?"

I stilled. "You wish."

Keisha laughed. "See what I mean? You two act like a couple. In the middle of a break-up or a fight, but still a couple."

Micah winked at me, and I rolled my eyes.

"Hey, wait. Was there anything between you two?" Raisa asked, sounding more composed, more like herself. "I always thought your thing was with Victor."

"Who is Victor?" Keisha asked.

Micah lost the amused expression. "A nobody."

Raisa told Keisha all about Victor, Micah, and me. Everything she knew about, which wasn't much. Not wanting to hear even a simpler version of that mess again, I tuned them out.

"You're not gonna tell me where we're going?" I asked Micah, crossing my arms.

His knuckles turned white around the wheel. "You'll see."

7

<hr>

AFTER ALMOST TWO HOURS OF NONSTOP DRIVING AT A HIGH speed, Micah exited the interstate and took us down a side road. At first I thought he was searching for a motel, but there was nothing out here. No buildings, no hotels, no gas stations. It was just the broken road, the dying trees, the darkness, and us.

When he turned onto a dirt road, I began to worry.

"Please, tell me where we're going."

He was tense. I could see it in his strained neck, the way his jaw popped and his hand tightened around the steering wheel. More than that, I could feel it.

He didn't answer at first, and I thought he wouldn't.

"We're here," he said.

The tires made a crunching noise, rolling over dirt and rocks as Micah slowed the car to a stop in a clearing.

"What's here?" Keisha asked the question on my mind.

Without answering, Micah exited the car. I opened my door, and before I was completely out, he was by my side. Rok flew into the clearing and perched on a low branch, well in sight. I smiled at the bird, though my smile vanished when I looked up at Micah. He was staring at me, his eyes ... worried? Micah was worried? No. It couldn't be. I must have misread it.

He averted his eyes and clenched his fists.

I followed his gaze and almost fell back.

Ceris and Victor appeared from behind the trees.

"Who are they?" Keisha asked, sliding out of the car. Raisa was right behind her.

"People I would rather not spend time with," Micah said in a low, hard tone.

Victor's eyes met mine, and my heart squeezed. Even dressed casually—in jeans and a sweater that fit his long, lean form—he looked too handsome.

However, Ceris was a vision from another world.

With each step she took, her white dress and her white-blond hair floated behind her as if she was a model on a catwalk with those giant fans for wind effect. Her skin looked silky and her clear blue eyes shone.

I glanced from Ceris, to Victor, and back to Ceris. God, they were soulmates. Like husband and wife. For thousands of years.

Since the beginning, I never stood a chance against Ceris, but I hadn't known about her. I hadn't known who Victor was. I hadn't known my feelings had been messed with against my will.

"Same here," I whispered.

Keisha shot me a what-the-hell-are-you-talking-about look, and I shook my head.

Frowning, Ceris halted and pointed to Keisha. "Who is she?"

Keisha straightened. "I'm Keisha Cross."

Raisa stood by her side. "I'm Rais—"

Ceris waved a hand at Raisa. "I don't care about you." She squinted at Keisha. "I didn't mean your name." She turned to Micah. "Her aura …"

Micah sighed. "I know. It's different."

"What? My aura …" Keisha asked, looking around herself.

"Hey," Raisa called. "What about me?"

Nobody paid attention to her, and I pulled her to stand behind with me.

"I don't really know who she is," Micah continued. "She was helping Nadine when I got there."

"What are they talking about?" Keisha asked me in a low voice.

Ceris narrowed her eyes. "Helping Nadine?"

"Yes, ma'am," Keisha answered, dropping her head. After all she had fought against and all she had seen, always standing tall and proud, she now seemed afraid of Ceris. And calling her ma'am? What was the deal?

Ceris scoffed. "You could have done better."

What the hell did she mean by that? More importantly, who cared what she meant? Not me. I gathered my courage. "Okay, enough of that. What are we doing here? Why did Micah bring me here?"

"I called him and asked him to meet us here," Victor said.

"Why?"

He straightened his back like a commander about to give an order. "I think we have to stick together. All of us. These past three months have been hard on each of us, and I believe part of that is because we insist on being separated." Wait, what? He was separated from Ceris? "We can only win this if we do this together."

Raisa leaned into me. "What is he talking about?"

"Ditto to that question," Keisha whispered.

"I'm not sure you want to know," I muttered.

Victor eyed Keisha. "How strong is her aura?" I had forgotten he couldn't sense auras.

Micah nodded a little. "Stronger than Nadine's."

"Then perhaps she's involved in all of this," Victor said.

"That's impossible." The words fell from my mouth before I could stop them.

"Is it?" he asked.

Not really, but improbable. If she was involved, who was she? *What* was she? Where had she been? And how the hell did I cross her path like I did?

Keisha kept her head lowered and said, "I don't understand what you're talking about."

"We have more important topics to discuss right now." Ceris waved her off. "I'm not sure I agree with Levi. We can't function as a group."

"Who is Levi?" Raisa whispered in my ear.

"I agree," Micah said, his tone absolute.

"Of course you agree." Ceris showed him one of her evil smiles. "You only think about yourself, Mitrus. What you want is to see us fail, so you can join Imha in her chaos party."

Teeth gritted, Micah took a step forward. I grabbed his arm and pulled him back. Not an easy feat considering his size and how much stronger he was than me.

"You have no idea what you're talking about," he snarled.

"I don't? You'll probably turn your back on us and go find Imha. Or you'll go make your own Black Thorn and finish what you started."

"Ceris," Victor said in a warning tone.

Micah clenched and unclenched his fists. "You think so

little of me?"

"*Think* so little of you?" Ceris snorted. "I know who you are, Mitrus. I know how you are. Imha might be evil herself, but you're not far from it. I know you're waiting for a golden opportunity to derail our plans, to betray us again."

"You ..." He lunged forward, but I held him again.

"Enough!" Victor shouted. "I won't tolerate this kind of behavior from any of you."

"You're not the boss of me, Levi." Micah spat at his feet.

Victor shot him an irritated look before taking a deep breath. He clasped his hands together. "True, I'm not. But I am what brings us together, what balances all of us. I am the centerpiece of our existence, and you have to respect that even if you don't respect me."

Micah jerked out of my grip. "With all due respect, I don't want anything to do with you." He gave me the keys to the car. "Don't forget to ditch it after a couple of days. Police might not be worried about a car theft right now, but I'm sure if you're caught, you'll be in trouble."

"What?" I glanced at the keys in my hand. "Where are you going?"

"I'm out."

He turned and walked away. Rok jumped up from the branch and flew after him.

"Mitrus!" Victor shouted. "Mitrus, come back here. We have to stick together!" He sighed when Micah disappeared into the shadows of the trees. "It's the only way we're winning this."

With my jaw hanging open, I watched as Micah walked away from me once more. The weight in my heart dragged me down.

"See?" Ceris smiled. "I knew he would walk out on us."

Victor glared at her. "You said you disagreed with me, that we shouldn't stay together." He gestured in Micah's direction. "There you have it."

"It isn't my fault," she responded. "We don't need his help. We can do this, the two of us."

Victor shook his head. "No, we need everyone. You know that."

Was he suggesting everyone as in me too? As nice as saving the world sounded, I couldn't stay with Victor and Ceris. I would pull my hair out and scream until I was out of air and passed out. No way.

Besides, what could I do? Heal them, yes, but nothing else. I couldn't fight. I couldn't sense auras. I wasn't part of their creed, and my visions were gone. They didn't need me.

I turned to the car. "I'm out too."

"What?" Victor approached me. "Why?"

Ceris sneered. "I knew she was weak."

Three months of anger and frustration and deception surged into me, and I exploded.

"Weak?" I glared at her. "You threw me into hell and watched as I struggled. I—"

"I didn't just watch. I was there. I helped."

"You lied. You deceived me. If you stop and think about it, you're not much better than Imha."

"Don't you dare compare me to Imha," she snarled.

"It's true," I said, looking into her eyes.

She advanced a step, but Victor rested a hand on her arm. "Don't, Ceris. You're not helping."

Ceris jerked her arm from his touch. "Are you defending her?"

Victor sighed. "I'm not defending anyone."

"It doesn't look like it. From where I'm standing, you're on her side."

"I'm on everyone's side."

Tuning them out, I marched to the other side of the car and opened the driver's door. "Raisa, Keisha, are you coming?"

Raisa rushed to the car without sparing a second.

Keisha looked lost for a moment. "Yes."

We entered the car, and Victor held my door before I could close it.

"You need to help us."

I sighed. "I know. But you have made it three months without me. You can make it another three. I'm sure you can find me when you need my healing again."

I closed the door, turned on the engine, and backed the car out of the clearing.

Once we were back on the road, Keisha turned to me. "What the hell was all that?"

THE DRIVE TO PITTSBURGH LASTED A LITTLE OVER THREE HOURS with no incidents.

The only problem was Keisha and Raisa asking me about things I wasn't sure I should talk about.

"You're not gonna answer any of our questions?" Keisha asked.

We crossed the Welcome to Pittsburgh sign on the interstate. It was broken and rusty and hanging precariously from a bent metal post. The city was still here, but in much worse shape than New York City had been before the attack. Half of it had been sacked and destroyed. The rest looked like a prison in decay.

I sighed. "I don't know."

"Humor me. After all I saw, you can't expect me to be surprised by much."

I laughed. "Yeah, right."

"I'm serious. Tell me."

I watched her. Why not? Soon the world would be at war, and by now, everyone probably knew what had happened to New York, who attacked the city. The creed wouldn't be able to hide for much longer.

After confirming that Raisa was sleeping on the backseat, I took a deep breath and blurted it out. "Micah is also called Mitrus. Victor is also called Levi. Ceris is ... just Ceris. The man we saw in New York is named Omi, and he works with a woman called Imha. They are gods, all of them. Their creed is called The Everlasting Circle. Thirty years ago Imha set up Mitrus to turn against Levi. She was experimenting. She wanted to see if she could kill a god. It turns out they can die. Mitrus killed Levi; however, Levi also killed Mitrus. Without all the gods, the world was thrown out of balance, and that's why we have been living in darkness and danger and destruc-tion. What nobody expected was, six years later, they were reborn as humans. Victor and Micah. Three months ago, Victor and Micah found out they are gods trapped in human bodies, and they need to become full gods again to restore the world to what it was before the darkness."

I glanced at her.

"So ... they are gods? Real, honest to goodness gods?"

"Yes."

Her eyes narrowed, but she watched me with attention. "All right. Give me a minute."

I nodded, expecting her to take way more than a minute.

"Wait," she said, after fifteen seconds. "Raisa mentioned a

Victor earlier. That Victor? You're telling me you had *something* with a god?"

"Hmm, after everything I told you, this is what you ask first?" I glanced at her, and she shrugged. "Yes, that Victor. At the time, he and I didn't know he was a god."

"Okay, now I'll need another minute."

I shook my head, wondering about her logic.

Before her minute was over, we arrived at a barrier of soldiers standing at the road.

"Shit," I muttered, bringing the car to a stop in front of them. Keisha turned around, making sure the weapons were on the floor of the backseat, and shook Raisa awake.

Two soldiers, holding rifles, came to my window. I pressed the button and slid the glass down.

"What's your business in Pittsburgh, miss?" one of them asked. The embroidery on his chest read Wilson.

"We want to get to the train station," I said.

"For?"

I frowned. "We are survivors from the New York attack. We just want to get to the train to go home."

"Survivors from the New York attack?" the other one asked, clearly surprised. His name was Flores, according to the embroidery on his uniform. He pulled his radio. "Sir, we have survivors from the New York attack at the southeast barrier."

"Let them in," a sharp voice said through the radio. "I'm on my way."

Wilson tapped the top of the car. "Go in, and stop your car by the large tent over there." He pointed to our right, but I couldn't see any large tents from here. "Let them in!" he shouted.

The soldiers forming the barrier stepped aside, and I drove in slowly. Now I could see the tent a few yards away.

"What now?" Raisa asked, yawning.

"They will probably want to know what happened," Keisha said.

"I know."

"What will we say?" Raisa asked.

"That we didn't see much? We saw a few figures assaulting the city, and everything was burning but we escaped."

"And how did we escape?" Raisa yawned again.

I parked the car before the big white tent. "With the car?"

"They won't believe us."

"Even if we tell the truth, they won't believe us." From the mirrors, I saw Wilson and Flores walking up to us. "Just play up being nervous and shaken."

They nodded, and we exited the car as an older man stepped out of the tent.

"I'm General Andrews," he said, halting in front of us. "What are your names?"

"I'm Nadine, and these are my friends, Raisa and Keisha."

"How did you escape New York?" the general asked.

We told them what we had rehearsed. It was far from being a confident lie, but it was all we had. The nervous and shaken thing was working, especially for Raisa.

"They said they want to get to the train station, sir," Wilson said.

"Yes, yes," General Andrews said. "How about you clean up first? We have an infirmary close by. The nurses can take care of your wounds, and I think they have clean clothes too."

"That would be great, actually," I said, relieved he wouldn't grill us to find out more.

"Wilson, accompany them. Make sure they are taken care of, and then take them to the train station. Come back once their trains have departed."

"Yes, sir." Wilson saluted before exiting the tent with us.

In the end, we left the car and the weapons there and drove with Wilson in a SUV to the infirmary. There, the nurses treated our wounds, let us shower in warm water, gave us clean clothes and tasty food. For those precious minutes, I almost believed we were in heaven.

After we were taken care of, Wilson drove us to the train station.

"Did you see what attacked New York?" he asked once we were on the road.

The "what" didn't escape me. "It was all a blur," I said before the girls could. I was seated in the passenger seat, and the girls were in the back. "Everyone was running and screaming. We were lucky to find the car and escape."

He gave me a sidelong glance. "With the reports we received from there, you were lucky indeed."

I remained quiet, and thank goodness, he took the hint and didn't ask more questions.

The security was heavy at the train station, but Wilson made it easy for us. He got a ticket to Chicago for Keisha, one to Richmond for Raisa, and one to Minneapolis for me.

Keisha's train left before ours. We walked to her platform, and when we stopped beside it she pulled me into a hug.

"I didn't think you were a hugger," I teased.

"I'm not. I just want to talk to you," she whispered. "What happens now? I'm supposed to just go back to my life and pretend those *gods* weren't talking about my *aura* and that somehow I'm supposed to be involved in whatever this is?"

"I think so," I whispered back. "If you're really supposed

to be involved, don't worry. The gods can find you."

"That sounds crazy," she whispered, before stepping back. "All right. Take care."

"You too."

She patted Raisa's shoulder, thanked Wilson, and hopped on the train. As soon as it left, Wilson walked us to Raisa's train. This time, the hug I got was real and tight.

"I can't believe we just went through that," Raisa said, stifling a sob.

"Me neither, but we made it. We got through. And you'll be all right, okay?" I kissed her cheek. "Be careful."

"You too." She pulled back, wiping her tears. "And please, keep in touch."

"I will."

With uncertain steps, she hopped on the train.

"Your turn," Wilson said, steering me to the other terminal.

"Thanks," I said, when we stopped beside my train.

"Good luck out there."

I nodded and entered the train. I couldn't believe I was actually going home, but I had to. I had to see my family and grab some of my things, the few things I had left behind when I had moved to New York, before leaving them again. I couldn't risk staying too long with them, though I had no idea where to go.

I reclined in my seat and sighed. That was a problem for another time. Now, I needed to relax a bit and be thankful for making it out of another battle alive.

The train moved, and I watched as the streets and buildings disappeared, giving way to the dark and dead countryside.

Outside my window, a raven followed the train.

8

———

THE TAXI STOPPED IN FRONT OF THE APARTMENT BUILDING MY parents had moved to after the farm closed about two months ago. I didn't know this new place yet, but goose bumps chilled the skin on my arms when I stepped onto the snow-covered sidewalk.

The building was downtown in one of the small towns around Minneapolis. It was four floors high, the balconies were gone as if they had just fallen off, the paint was peeling, and there was a metal security door over the wooden one, both looked old and weak. I bet I could punch and break them.

Holding my coat tighter with one hand, I rang the buzzer but nobody answered. Instead my mother showed up at the door with a huge smile.

"Nadine!" She unlocked the three thousand bolts on the metal door and pulled me into a hug. "Oh, Lord, it's so good to see you." Her smile turned into a sob. "I thought ... I thought you had gotten stuck there. I thought I had lost you."

I rubbed her back. It was good to see her after so long,

after what happened. "I got away, and I'm here now." I wasn't sure for how long though.

She pulled back and looked at me. She probably thought I was too thin, with not enough clothes on in this cold, and other things every mom thought. But she didn't say them aloud. As I didn't say how she had lost weight, how her once full and long brown hair looked dry and thin, how her skin was pale, and how her bright green eyes had lost their usual energetic shine.

She patted my cheek before taking my hand and guiding me inside the building. The hallway was as bad as the outside. She led me past the stairs, into a short corridor on the first floor, and pushed open the last door.

"Home, sweet home," she said in an uncomfortable voice.

The place was tiny. Too tiny. The orange fabric of the couch and the armchair was ripped and faint, as if it were fifty years old. Scratches covered the wooden center table. Worn patches stamped the brown rug. The floor looked like a second-hand toy land. It was a tiny, chaotic, falling-into-pieces place. There were three doors, besides the one we had just entered. One led to a patio, a second led to the kitchen, and the third led to a hallway.

A pang ran through my heart. Oh my God, it was worse than their previous house.

"Where's everyone?"

She grabbed my tote and turned to the hallway. "The kids are at school. They should arrive in about two hours, and your father is doing some job, I don't know where. I can't keep track of all he does."

I followed her into the hallway, noticing there were only two bedrooms and one bathroom.

"Sorry. We're going to have to rearrange." She entered a

bedroom with a bunk bed that clearly couldn't hold the weight of a cat, a twin bed in the corner, and a dresser squeezed between the beds. That was it. There was barely room between the furniture to turn around.

My parents' bedroom was across the hall, and it was worse. The queen mattress was on the floor against a moldy wall. Their clothes were folded on the floor, against another moldy wall. And once more, there was no space to turn around.

It was horrible. This whole place was horrible.

"I know it's not much, but after the farm was gone, we weren't left with much," she said, her voice low, embarrassed. "I'm sure things will get better though. Your father is working a lot, and I'm trying to find some other work instead of babysitting. We'll be fine eventually."

I didn't know what to say. If she had told me things were this bad, I would have sent more money. I would have abstained from the black coffees I bought everyday. I would have eaten a little less and not bought so many books. I would have taken fewer classes and worked more hours. I would have done something. Anything.

Mom pushed me inside the bedroom my siblings shared. "Why don't you rest for a while? I'm sure you're tired, and once Nicole, Teddie, and Tommy get home, they won't leave you alone, so you better take advantage now."

There was so much I needed to do, think about, to decide, but I was tired after spending the entire night on a train, and then the taxi ride from Minneapolis to here. I could use a little sleep.

I nodded, and she offered me a smile before closing the door.

I looked around, but there was nothing else to see. My

chest ached for them. Oh God, this was a terrible way to live, and the fact that I couldn't help anymore hurt too much.

I sat on the twin bed, feeling exhausted and miserable.

I had no idea if my things had been brought from the previous house to this apartment, and anything else I had of any value had been burned in New York City. The only thing I still had was my tote with a few books and my wallet with my bank card. I had a little money in my account I could give my mom, but that wouldn't help long term. She would be able to buy groceries for this month, and maybe a change of clothes for each of my siblings, but that was it. Nothing more.

The tears came without warning, and I let them fall. I was tired of trying to be strong—and failing. My life as I knew it was gone: my scholarship was gone, my job was gone, my colleagues and classmates were gone. At least Raisa had gotten out. But everything else was gone. Not to mention the precarious conditions my family was living in, and the fact that my perfect plan to save them was gone.

I lay down on the bed, hugging Nicole's pink pillow and savoring her sweet baby scent.

I had to be strong for them. I had to fight for them, but right now I just needed to get this terrible feeling of helplessness out of my system.

***

"ARE YOU DONE WITH THAT?" MY MOTHER ASKED.

"Almost." I chopped the last onion and passed the cutting board to her. "Done."

She took it and dumped the chopped onion inside the pot on the stove. She mixed the contents with a wooden spoon and reduced the heat. "Should be ready in twenty minutes," she said, putting the lid over the pot.

I turned around the kitchen, almost hitting my elbow on a cabinet. Everything was tiny in this place. Everything. Even the fridge looked more like a compact refrigerator than what it was supposed to be.

I sighed, trying not to think about that. "What else can I help with?"

"Hmm, you could set the table."

I frowned. The table consisted of a classroom desk-sized table in the corner of the kitchen. Four stools surrounded it, but there was no way more than two people could sit there at a time.

Keeping my thoughts to myself, I did what she asked.

I was grabbing the mismatching glasses when Nicole burst into the kitchen, dragging a pink stuffed bunny by the ear. I had given it to her when she was born. It looked old and dirty, but she never let go of Pinky. She even took it to school, and I was somewhat proud of it.

"Are you done helping?" Nicole asked, looking up at me with huge bright green eyes. She moved back and forth on her heels, making her pretty, curly hair bounce. She was my six-year-old angel, and I couldn't help but fall in love with her all over again each time my eyes met hers.

I ran a hand on the top of her head. "Almost."

"That's okay, Nadine," my mom said. "I cook every night alone. I can do it tonight again. Give them some attention."

I didn't argue. I hadn't seen them in so long, and I was dying to experience how much they had grown and changed, and to play with them.

Nicole grabbed my hand and pulled me to the living room, where Tommy and Teddie were wrestling. Teddie was ten and a lot taller than Tommy, who was eight, but he played it down, letting Tommy win some rounds. There was no TV at home to keep them entertained, but my mom kept a radio on in the kitchen at all times, broadcasting news and music.

When he was born, Teddie looked exactly like Troy. I remembered the first day, when it was odd looking at him. It was as if Troy had come back to life, though I knew it couldn't be. I had no idea how Troy would have turned out since he died before he was six months old, but Teddie was cute. He would break many hearts when he grew older. All of them would.

Sighing, I sat down on the couch, and Nicole climbed on my lap. I squeezed her, wishing with all my soul the world would stop getting worse so my siblings had a chance to grow up, to build less miserable lives. Way less miserable.

God, I couldn't really stop and think about the future. It hurt too much. And I had no idea how to help anymore. Without NYU, my scholarship, and my job, I couldn't help. I was actually a burden. Everything I vowed I would never be.

I had to think and come up with a plan. I couldn't stay here and make things worse.

"Sing for me," Nicole said.

I smiled. I would leave the thinking and planning for after they had gone to bed.

"What do you want me to sing?"

"Don't you have one of your own songs?"

"Hmm." Not really. I had never had time to write songs down, though lyrics of several pieces of my own were stored in my memory. "I know one."

Nicole jumped off my lap and went into her bedroom.

"Hey, where are you going?" I asked, confused.

She came back, dragging Pinky and my old Spanish guitar.

"Where did you find this?" I asked, taking it from her hands.

"It was under my bed. I grabbed it for you when we left the other house. I thought you might want it."

My heart squeezed a little. After everything, she still thought of me.

I pulled her into an embrace. "I do want it. Thanks, Nikkie."

She sat beside me and nudged the guitar.

I took it, cleared my throat, and sang an old song written before I was born, one that I had sung to them every night when I put them to bed, when I still lived with them. *Lullaby* by Dixie Chicks.

After the first verse, Teddie and Tommy stopped wrestling and sat down at my feet, swaying with the tune.

"I missed that song," Tommy whispered between verses.

My eyes filled with tears, and I noticed Mom was leaning against the doorway, watching us with a smile on her face. I fought so my voice wouldn't crack and I wouldn't cry in front of them.

"More!" Nicole yelled, as soon as I stroked the last chord.

Mom took three steps to the couch and kissed my forehead. "I'll never get tired of listening to you sing."

Tommy and Teddie argued about which song I had to sing next. I didn't wait for them to decide before I played another. They quieted down immediately.

"Wow," Mom said, her eyes wide. "If you can calm them down that easily, I will ask you not to leave us ever again."

I almost missed the right chord. I knew she was joking, but it didn't change the fact that I should leave them sooner than she expected me to. I still hadn't made up my mind about how many days I could stay, but I had decided that more than a week would be too much.

One more thing for my after-the-kids-go-to-bed to-do list: to decide when I would leave and where I would go.

DAD ARRIVED JUST IN TIME FOR DINNER. HE SEEMED SURPRISED to see me, and he hugged me tight. Under my arms, I noticed how weak and thin he was.

"Glad to have you here," he said, pushing back and looking at me.

While he had lost weight, his face had gained a few wrinkles since the last time I had seen him.

"I'm glad to be here too."

He leaned down and kissed the top of Teddie's, Tommy's, and Nicole's heads. They barely paid him attention as they played a board game on the floor.

"Come on, dear," my mom called him. "Dinner is ready."

The kids had already eaten. Mom had insisted I eat too, but I preferred to wait for Dad so we could eat together, even if we had to squeeze around the tiny table.

Mom served us, and then sat down with us. As I predicted, we were crammed and our plates touched each other on the table.

To keep my mind off that, I started a conversation. "So, Dad, what were you working on?"

"I have been working for the mayor," he said.

"Really?"

"With all that is happening, the mayor wants to build a wall around the city, keep guards at the gate, and supervise everyone who comes and goes. So, I've been helping. I've been building the wall."

A wall like NYU had. A wall that had done nothing other than delay a major attack for about five minutes. There had not been enough time to run and find shelter, especially when the city burned to the ground.

However, I didn't mention that to my parents. If the wall brought a little internal peace to the townspeople, then so be it. Besides, this heavy work had probably given jobs to many unemployed adults.

My mother touched my hand. "Nadine, will you tell us what happened to New York City? What did you see, and how did you escape?" I stared at her. "I'm sorry, honey. If you don't want to talk about it, that's okay. It must hurt, I know."

"It hurts, but I guess I can tell you."

I opened my mouth, and the words I had rehearsed with Keisha and Raisa rolled off my tongue. It was easier than telling the truth.

I thought of the girls for a second. I wondered if they made it home, if Chicago and Richmond were still intact. Then I thought about what I had told Keisha, if she believed me, or if now that she was safe at home she thought I was insane and everything we had been through had been a nightmare.

I wished.

"You're blessed for escaping," my mom whispered. Wiping her tears, she stood up. "Go play with the kids. I can clean up here." She grabbed our plates and put them in the sink.

I stood. "I want to help."

"I can help your mom," Dad said.

"But—"

My phone rang, and Mom smiled at me. "Answer it," she said.

I excused myself, walked into the kids' bedroom, and fished the phone from my pocket while closing the door.

Unknown number.

"Hello?"

"Nadine, hi."

"Victor? What happened?"

"Nothing," he said. I sat down on Nicole's bed, not sure what else to say. "Look, I need to see you."

"Oh, you're in pain."

He didn't answer me right away. "Yeah." He took a long breath. "But I don't want to go to you because I don't want to risk having demons follow me there."

Good point. I didn't want that either.

Wait. He knew where I was? Well, thinking about it, it wouldn't take a genius to figure out where I could have gone. One more reason to leave soon.

"What do you suggest then?" I asked.

"You could take a taxi to Minneapolis and meet me in a public place. Or maybe not, considering what happened to New York City. You could take a cab to a gas station or motel outside of Minneapolis."

Out of habit, I grabbed a thick piece of my hair and twisted it around my finger. That would mean a twenty- to thirty-minute drive. In a cab. Paid. With money I shouldn't be spending because I had to buy groceries for my family.

"Victor, I can't."

"I just looked online and found a taxi company. I'll send one to pick you up. You just need to tell me a time."

He would pay for it? I knew he was loaded as a human,

and I couldn't imagine how rich a god could be. I wouldn't argue with that.

"I'll walk my siblings to school at eight thirty tomorrow morning. The taxi can pick me up right after."

"Okay," he said. "See you tomorrow."

He ended the call before I could answer. I stared at the phone confused. "See you tomorrow."

9

———

THE TAXI SHOWED UP IN FRONT OF MY PARENTS' BUILDING AT 8:45 a.m.

"Ms. Sterling?" the driver asked through his lowered window.

"Yes," I said, skeptical.

"I'm here to take you to your meeting."

I nodded and entered the taxi. He drove toward Minneapolis but turned south before we entered the city.

Forty minutes into this awkward drive, the driver exited the interstate. He took us down a back road for about five more minutes, and then stopped at an abandoned motel.

I opened the door. "Thank you."

"Thank the guy paying for this trip because if it wasn't for the ridiculous amount of money, I wouldn't drive here. Ever."

I ignored his comment and exited the car. Pulling my coat tighter around me, I looked around. The place was creepy and reminded me too much of the school where Brock had kept Morgan, Micah, and me.

The motel didn't only look abandoned; it looked sacked.

Vandalized. Torn down doors, walls covered with graffiti, broken lamps, and the sign, once hanging from a post, was now in pieces on the ground.

Victor wanted to meet here? Seriously?

And where was he? I wouldn't stay here, in the dark and in the middle of nowhere, for long. I grabbed my phone and was about to call him when he appeared out of the darkness.

I held my breath.

His sea-green eyes were hard on mine, ensnaring me.

And he didn't look sick.

"I thought you said you needed my healing," I said as he approached me.

"Yeah." He ran a hand through his hair. "Not really."

Frustration built in me. "What? You brought me to this motel out of a horror movie for nothing?"

He halted four feet from me. "Not for nothing. I think we need to talk."

"Talk? No." I turned to the taxi, but he held my arm.

"That day at the hospital, I wanted to talk to you, but you just left. You're not leaving again."

"Who do you think you are to tell me what I can or cannot do?" I raised a finger. "Don't answer that."

A smile tugged at the corner of his lips. "Please, talk to me."

Talk about what? The past? He was dreaming if I was going down that lane again.

"Victor, I didn't sign up for this. I don't want to be involved in any of this. I know I can't escape healing you or Micah, but this doesn't work." I gestured around us. "I can find a way of coming to you when you need healing, but other than that? Please, leave me alone."

"I'm trying," he said in a low voice. "I'm trying to leave you alone, but after all that happened between us, I think we should talk."

I crossed my arms. "About what?"

"Us. We obviously felt something for each other a few months ago."

I stared at him. The expression on his beautiful face reminded me of a lost puppy. "Like you said, a few months ago. It's in the past."

"Is it?"

I took a deep breath. "You want to know what I think? Okay, I'll say it. I think my feelings for you weren't real, as yours weren't for me. Ceris planted those feelings in me. She steered me to you, and she pushed us together. It was her plan. Every little thing, especially my feelings. Whatever I felt for you wasn't real."

"Felt," he repeated.

"Yes. In the past. And I'm sure if you stop and think about it, you'll realize your feelings for me weren't real either. Or maybe you felt something because you thought you were alone. You wanted to feel something for someone, and I was there. Which was not a coincidence since it was all in Ceris's plans."

He frowned. "She said the same thing."

Wow, that was unexpected. I tried pressing my lips together, but the words rushed out of my mouth on their own. "I take it things aren't good between the two of you."

Victor laughed, and it wasn't an amused tone. "Aren't good? They have been terrible." He paced. "First, she takes me off that mountain without my permission and leaves you alone with that demented Mitrus against hundreds of demons. After all the bad things she had done and the people she killed, I was sure I could have included that act to the list. But then the Fates found us and said you were okay."

I snorted. "No thanks to them. I was lucky Micah and Morgan were there with me."

"I'm sorry about leavin—"

I raised my index finger. "Don't go there."

He stared at me, and I averted my eyes. "Anyway, Ceris and I talked—well, argued really. We can only argue—and we decided to start working toward finding my scepter. That's what we've been doing for the last three months."

Of course. Finding the scepters was priority.

"No success?"

"None. We have no idea where to look for it. In addition, we had to deal with the demons and run from Omi and Imha more than once. Ceris can fade her aura completely, but only lessen mine. The demons pick up my aura often, and that makes it hard to look for the scepter because we can't stay in one spot for long."

"Unfortunately, I know nothing about The Everlasting Circle's lore and power or whatever. I can't help with that. I also don't have visions anymore and can't lead you where you need to go. What I can help with is healing, which isn't what you need right now." I turned to the taxi. "Please, only call me when you need my healing."

He rushed toward me. "Nadine—"

"I beg you, Victor. Don't involve me in this mess more than I need to be involved." I slipped inside the taxi. "Good luck."

"Ready to go, Ms. Sterling?" the driver asked.

I closed the door and turned my back to the window. "Yes, please, take me back."

THE REST OF THE DAY WAS UNEVENTFUL.

I returned home in time to have lunch with my mother. Then she asked about my plans, and I said I didn't have any. Which wasn't a complete lie. After the kids had gone to bed last night, I had thought about what to do, but my mind kept going to Victor and his call, and I lost my train of thought. Now that I had seen him, I was in a bad mood because I had been away for two hours for nothing and because I had seen him.

I told my mom I would probably try to find a job while applying for scholarships to other universities, preferably closer to home this time. That part of the plan was true, but what I didn't tell her was I would be leaving in two or three days. I wasn't sure exactly to where. At first, I had thought I needed to stay in a big city because they had more soldiers and protection, but my options weren't many. I wanted to stay no less than five hours from here. Minneapolis was too close to home, and Des Moines was only three and a half hours away.

However, now that I had talked to Victor and he mentioned having to move around because the demons could sense his aura, I wondered if that would happen to me too. I was afraid of attracting them here, wasn't I? So what would stop them from sensing me in Des Moines or any other place I decided to move to? Then demons would attack the city, and people would die because of me. I couldn't live with that.

The solution was to move around.

But how would I help my family if I didn't stay in a place

long enough to get a job and make some money? If I couldn't be in school?

At three thirty, Mom picked up the kids from school, and I went grocery shopping. Mom almost had a heart attack when I came back with more than I could carry, but it was the least I could do. Once inside the house, the kids surrounded me and we played on the side patio until Dad came home from work. After dinner, I put the kids to bed, singing the lullaby song for them, and then came back to the living room where my parents sat. My father cleaned his work boots, and my mother organized the kids' toys.

I knelt on the floor and helped Mom.

"Nadine," my father said. "Your mom and I need to talk to you."

I stopped and looked at him, worried. Could he know something? "About?"

"About you and your situation right now."

"Oh." I put the toys in my hands in a box, and then sat beside him on the couch. "I know things aren't easy and I'm sorry for being a burden, but—"

"A burden?" my mom asked, her expression appalled.

Dad shook his head. "You're not a burden, dear. On the contrary. You're the one that actually kept this family up for so long."

"I'll do it again," I said. I had to believe I would. There had to be something I could do. "I'm not sure how yet, but I will."

"You don't have to do this. It's not your responsibility."

"But I want to help."

"I know. But I think finishing your education is more important."

Honestly, I wasn't sure about that. Right now, I just had to work anywhere so I would stop being one more mouth to feed and maybe help with feeding the others. Regardless, I was convinced I couldn't stop in one place for long. How would I finish school like that?

"Yeah, but that is gone. I am thinking about going back to school, but I don't know where and how yet," I lied. Guilt filled me, but what could I tell them? They sounded so hopeful and thankful that I was here, that I would stay here. I couldn't break their hearts. Not yet.

My father narrowed his eyes. "If you're not in a rush, I could talk to the mayor and see if he has a job for you."

"Work on the construction of the wall?" my mother asked. "That isn't a place for a woman."

"I know," my dad said. "But I can ask him if he has anything else."

I pressed my lips together. My leaving would be hard on them, maybe harder than I thought it would be.

"Yes, Dad," I said. "Talk to him."

I probably wouldn't stick around until a job came up, but I couldn't tell them that. Not yet.

Dad patted my hand. "Good."

10

I ROLLED ON THE COUCH. SLEEPING HERE WOULD BREAK MY back, but there weren't many options. My mom had insisted on giving me their bed, or having Nicole sleep with them so I could have her bed, but I declined. I was already disturbing their lives and routine as it was.

I brought the comforter to my chin and tried adjusting the pillow. As if the couch being uncomfortable wasn't enough, the cold was bad too. The forecast was for three feet of snow tomorrow. Ugh, I wasn't happy about that.

At one thirty in the morning, I reached for a book in my tote. I might as well read and hopefully it would make me sleepy enough that I wouldn't feel the hardness of the couch.

I read two pages and felt my eyes droop. Hmm, this was working.

I was turning the third page when the siren of a fire truck blared outside.

What the hell?

I woke up completely, and I rushed to the window.

Despite the cold, I opened it and tried to spot the fire truck, not that I could see much from the first floor or past another three-story building on the side.

I gave up on the window and marched to the kitchen, where I turned on the radio and tuned it to the local news channel.

There was nothing. Only static. I changed to another news channel. Same thing.

The building shook and a loud boom sounded from outside, and I grabbed the counter to steady myself.

When everything stopped moving, I dashed back to the living room and unlocked the patio door. As I stepped out, the raven appeared by my face. I stepped back as it cawed desperately, circling my head. Added to the noise of sirens and screams, I could feel a headache coming.

I put my arms around myself, shivering in the cold. "Rok, calm down." He didn't. "I can't understand you. What is it?" He came at me again, and I jumped back. He wanted me to get inside? To run? "I'm trying to understand, okay?"

My parents appeared at the door. "Nadine, what is it?" my mother asked, her eyes sleepy, but her expression tense.

"The walls were shaking," my father said, pulling his robe tight around him. He stilled, watching Rok. "Shoo." He raised his arms to wave the bird away.

Mom rubbed her eyes. "What is that crazy bird doing?"

Rok soared around me once more before flying away.

Okay. Think Nadine. Based on the sounds and Rok's reaction, the city had to be under attack.

"Let's go inside," I said, pushing them past the door.

"You're scaring me," my mother said.

I closed the door behind us and leaned against it. They

watched me, waiting for a response. I opened my mouth but nothing came out. Because really, how could they have found me? I had just escaped New York City. They couldn't possibly have tracked me this fast.

More importantly, I was supposed to be far away from here when they came for me. I wasn't supposed to attract them here. Not here.

I shook my head. "I ..."

"I don't know if anyone is hearing me," a voice came from the radio in the kitchen. "But ... our town is under attack. I think it's similar to what happened in New York City. There are ... creatures, or whatever they are, entering the town from the east, and they are destroying everything in their path. If you can, run. Now."

Oh, God. Not again. No.

My throat felt raw, and I clutched my neck, having difficulty breathing.

My parents looked at me with wide eyes.

My nerves brought goose bumps to my arms. I closed my eyes for a moment and took a deep breath. I had gone through this before; they hadn't. They needed me and I had to be strong for them.

"Come on. Let's go." I rushed to my bag beside the couch, changed into jeans, and put on my boots. When I turned, my parents were still staring at me. "We need to go. Now!"

Whimpering, my mother ran to her bedroom. My father followed close behind. I grabbed my bag and slid it over my shoulder, then marched to the kids' bedroom.

"Nikkie." I tapped her arm. "Teddie. Tommy." I shook their feet. "Wake up, please. Wake up now." I found an empty duffel bag under the bunk bed and stuffed it with some of their clothes.

"What is it?" Tommy asked, rubbing his eyes.

"We gotta move."

"Why?" Teddie asked, sitting up.

"I'll explain later, okay? Right now, we gotta move."

I reached up, clasped Tommy's waist, and helped him to the floor.

"Where are Mom and Dad?" Nicole asked.

"Here, sweetie," Mom said, appearing at the door. She had put on pants and a heavy coat.

Coats. Holy shit, it would be freezing outside. I rummaged through their drawers, grabbed socks, beanies, sweaters, and coats, then pushed them out the door. I directed Teddie to Dad, Tommy to Mom, and picked up Nicole in my arms.

With Teddie's hand firmly in his, Dad walked to the front door.

"Dad, is there a way through the back patio?"

He frowned. "Yes, but it leads to a back road."

"Would that be to the west?"

He thought for a second. "Yes."

"Then that's where we're going."

As we exited into the chilly air, Nicole tucked Pinky between us, wrapped her arms around my neck, and buried her face in my chest. "It's cold," she whispered.

I rubbed my hands on her back, trying to warm her. "I know, Nikkie. I'm sorry about that, but there's no other way."

Nobody spoke as Dad led us through a long, narrow corridor between buildings. In the dark and with almost no lamps on the street, it was hard to see where I was stepping. I tripped a couple of times and almost fell.

When we reached the back road, Dad peered out.

"What am I looking for?" he asked.

I sighed. "Monsters. Really big, nasty monsters." Nicole whimpered in my arms, and my mother shot me an are-you-crazy look. "I'm serious. Sorry I skipped this part about the New York attack, but I know the same thing is happening here."

"How do you know?" my mother asked.

I pressed my lips tight. *Because they are after me.* Not a good answer.

"Please, just believe me. We need to get out of town ASAP. Not only out of town, but we need to get away fast."

"Nadine, what aren't you telling us?" my dad asked.

Once again, I opened my mouth and words didn't come. What could I tell them? I didn't want to get them involved in this. Too late for that. However, we didn't have the time to discuss this. We had to move.

I walked past my dad and out of the corridor. At the intersection, about forty yards from me, an Ornek ran by. With a gasp, I retreated into the corridor and plastered my back to the wall. My heart raced. I closed my eyes and squeezed Nicole, trying to calm myself.

"What is it?" Mom asked, going to the edge of the corridor.

I held her arm. "No. Wait." I shook my head. "One of them just ran down Magnolia Avenue."

Her eyes widened. "One of them?"

"One of the monsters," I whispered, afraid the kids would understand. Who was I trying to fool? They were too old not to understand.

"I want to see!" Teddie said, his voice too loud.

Dad shushed him. "Be quiet. They will hear us."

I looked at Teddie. "This is not a game. This is real. If they see us, they will kill us." Nikkie's arms tightened around my neck. "We'll be okay," I said, more to calm their nerves than my own. Because honestly, if I stopped to consider this situation, I wasn't sure I would believe me.

I peered down the street.

That demon walking down Magnolia Avenue was probably a patrol, sent ahead to check. Others would come via opposite streets and back roads.

What then? Wait for the demons to pass, or try to get ahead of them? Or follow the first one down Magnolia Avenue? I didn't know what to do, and each second that passed was precious because it meant the demons were advancing and getting closer.

What I wouldn't give to have Keisha and her weapons with me.

A loud boom shook the ground, and my ears rang. I leaned against the wall for support, my head spinning. When I recovered, my mom was pushing off the ground, and my dad was crouched behind us, his eyes wide.

I looked back and my heart beat heavy in my chest.

Fire engulfed the building we had just exited, the building where my family had made their home. The heat licked against us, and I had an urge to run.

"Oh, God," I whispered. If the building was on fire, the demons were around it, and Omi was close. "We need to move." I took a deep breath and went to the street. I looked left and right. Nothing. "Come on."

I ran to the other side of the street and hid in the shadows of a store's entrance, my parents following me.

"No short cuts through the middle of this block?" I asked.

"I think there is," Dad said. He and Teddie rushed to the corner of the store and turned at the driveway.

Mom and I trailed behind them. The driveway ended in a

parking lot behind the store. A short picket fence surrounded it, and there was another parking lot and building, its back to us.

Mom and I dropped the kids on the ground, helped them cross the fence, then crossed it ourselves and got the kids back once we were on the other side. I tried ignoring the fact that Nicole was heavy, and I knew I wouldn't be able to hold her for hours. Maybe not even an hour.

I shook my head. We made our way across the driveway of the building and slowed down once we got near the sidewalk.

It started snowing. Slow, fluffy flocks fell from the sky, sticking to our hair and coats, and covering the sidewalks and street.

The weight in my chest increased. "Now they will see our footsteps."

"Let's try to gain some distance from them before the snow covers the streets," Dad said.

He crossed the road and ran into the front yard of a house. Mom and I did the same. Once we were on the house's side, I looked back. Our footsteps weren't clear. Perhaps the dumb demons wouldn't notice.

A shriek filled the frigid air, and I almost dropped Nicole to clamp my ears. She stifled a cry, but sobbed in my shoulder.

"What was that?" my mom asked, her tone fearful.

"Bats."

"Bats? Here?" My dad looked at the sky. "We've never seen bats here."

"They have been spreading lately," I said, satisfied for not lying for the first time since I arrived.

Dad's eyes returned to mine. "How do you know so much about this?"

"It's a long story, and we should get out of here first." I marched to the back of the house.

With the Akuma, it would be harder to get out of here. They were probably hovering around the entire town, searching and maiming. Damn, this kept getting worse.

I looked around the backyard. There were trees lining the lot down the back, and then I could see the roof of a house, probably on the other side of the block.

"Let's keep moving," Dad said, walking past me.

I followed him to the trees. Mom was close behind.

We had just begun to weave through the trees when a shriek echoed through the sky. We all froze. The kids whimpered. The Akuma's screams sounded too close, but not right above us.

"Go," my dad whispered.

We moved again, but it wasn't the same. Any noise we made—crunching of grass or snow, sweeping leaves or branches aside—the demons would hear it and find us.

We finally reached the end of the trees, only to bump into a tall iron fence. It was approximately eight feet high with no horizontal bars we could use to step up and swing over the top. The tips had a blade-like appearance.

"No, no," I muttered. I released Nicole and shook the fence. "No!"

My father let go of Teddie, then ran a few feet to the side, checking the fence. "No openings, no weak points."

I looked up. An orange cloud approached, swallowing everything in its path. Omi would rain down on us soon.

"We can't go back." I looked around. "Let's check the

sides." I pushed Nicole and Teddie closer to Mom and Tommy. "Stay here."

Dad darted to the left, and I went to the right. My heart raced and my head spun as I shook the fence, trying to find some broken post or a gate.

This couldn't be happening. Oh my God, I had to stop thinking about this, or I would break down right here right now and curl up on the snow and cry out my desperation, exhaustion, and fear. That was all I wanted to do. Curl up and cry. But that wouldn't bring my family to safety.

However, I knew what would save them.

I sprinted back to my mom and siblings just as Dad did too.

"No way of passing," he said, out of breath. "I saw a few bats flying by, and I saw an orange cloud coming in this direction." He shook his head. "I must be out of my mind."

I took a deep breath. "I know a way of making it through this. We'll hide here for a while, maybe up in the trees. When we're sure we can run around the fence and keep going, we do that and we don't look back."

"How are we gonna be sure we can run around the fence and keep going?" my father asked.

"Just ... trust me."

A sequence of shrieks resonated through the air.

"They are getting close," my mom said. Fear laced her words.

"Okay. Hide. Now." I pushed them against the thicker trees. I stepped back and looked at them. With the dark and the shadows, I couldn't really see them, only if I tried hard. I hoped their auras were nothing and the demons would bypass them. "Whatever happens, hide, then run, and don't look back." I retreated one more step. "I love you."

I ran.

"Nadine?" my mom shouted at the same time my father asked, "What are you doing?"

I didn't stop. I just hoped they stayed hidden.

I ran to the front of the house and went toward Magnolia Avenue. I wasn't stupid; I wouldn't run toward the demons. They would catch up with me too soon, and I wouldn't have given time for my family to escape. I ran north, hoping to be able to run for a minute or two, enough to get some distance from where I hid my family.

The shriek of an Akuma reached my ears. My heart stopped, and I slipped on the snow. I regained my footing as the creature flew to me. I ducked and it rose in the sky again. The thing flew away for a few seconds, to call the others probably.

I kept running, even when my legs hurt, even when I knew I was marching to my death, even when the urge to curl up and cry ripped through me again.

Moments later, the Akuma was back with some of its friends. I didn't bother looking up and trying to count them. I was screwed anyway.

The grunts, growls, and battle cries of the Ornek and Arak surrounded me, followed by the sound of their heavy footfalls.

Oh, God, let me keep going for one more minute. Please, one more minute.

I gritted my teeth and pushed my muscles, my blood pounding in my ears. I turned slightly right onto the street that would become a ramp and lead to the road out of town.

Just a little more.

I could see the ramp, but I also could hear the footsteps and growls gaining on me.

Omi materialized in front of me in a mist of gray cloud. My shock made my muscles lock, and I slipped in the snow, falling on my knees at his feet.

I gasped for air, little clouds leaving my mouth as my rapid breathing froze in the frigid air, and I looked up.

He was smiling down at me, his eyes amused. "Finally, we meet."

11

<hr>

"ARE YOU COMFORTABLE?" OMI ASKED.

Holding his red-topped scepter, he stood before me in the middle of what looked like an Ancient Greek room. Thick pillars in the corners supported the high ceiling, torches attached to them, illuminating the interior with dancing shadows. I could see openings on the sandy walls behind some of those pillars. A rolled up tapestry hung from two pillars. The beige floor was rough, and there were several Persian rugs of orange and reddish tones spread throughout. The chaise I sat on looked like something out of Ancient Egypt with hieroglyphs carved along its simple wood, and the green cushion felt more like barbed wire.

I glanced to the cuffs made of bright red light around my wrists. Comfortable? Who cared about comfortable when I was panicking on the inside? I was somewhere in the world with the god of war, demons were probably outside the door, and I was sure Imha was close by. The only hope I was holding on to was the fact that I was here alone, my family had escaped the demons. I didn't know what would happen to them or how they would survive, but at least now they had a chance.

Tears stung my eyes. I didn't want to cry in front of Omi, or anyone else, but I couldn't help it. I honestly wasn't afraid of dying, but I was afraid of suffering before dying. And every time I thought about my family, I wanted to cry more. I would never see them again—not for many years, until they died from old age, I hoped, and met me on the other side. I would miss them so much ... At least I would have Troy in heaven with me.

Wait. Heaven? Or maybe it was the underworld.

A couple of tears rolled down my face.

Omi leaned over me and brushed his rough hand across my cheek. "Don't cry, beautiful. This will be over soon."

I flinched. If he noticed, he didn't show it.

My mind reeled at his words. What would be over soon? My life? This confinement?

"Where is she?" her voice echoed through the room before I could see her.

The flames of the torches grew brighter as she stepped between two pillars and strode to me. Her white dress hugged her perfect form, and the floating skirt belonged on a catwalk. Her black hair went down to her knees, and like Ceris's it looked like it had a life of its own. Her skin was too white; it was almost translucent, which was creepy when paired with her black eyes and red lips.

She had her scepter—a long crystal stave, topped by a orb emanating purple light—in her right hand.

Her eyes met mine, and my stomach dropped to my feet. Something like a whimper escaped my throat.

Oh, God. I was in the same room as Imha, the goddess of

chaos, the one responsible for our dark world and everything else going on with it.

Omi gestured to me. "This is Nadine Sterling."

With an evil smile, Imha halted before me. "Nadine, it's an honor to finally meet you."

I stared at her. I had never felt this small and helpless in all my life.

Omi paced behind Imha. "She hasn't said a single word since I found her."

If I had the choice, I wouldn't say a single word until they killed me.

Imha narrowed her eyes. "I thought you said her aura was stronger than this. Are you sure this is the girl helping Ceris?"

"Y-yes," Omi stuttered.

So fast I missed most of the movement, Imha whipped around and loomed over Omi. "Are you sure?"

He raised his chin and looked into her eyes. "Yes, Imha. I'm sure. Her aura isn't as strong, but I know it's her."

"Yes, I can feel her aura. Not too strong but different. And powerful."

What did she mean?

"Very," Omi muttered.

Imha paraded over to me. A chair matching my chaise appeared behind her, and she sat down. Her evil smile twisted her lips.

"Nadine, you will tell me all about Ceris. What is she planning, where is she hiding, what are you helping her with?" She tilted her head. "How do you help her? I mean, you're a mortal. Your aura is a bit stronger than most mortals, but still you're only a mortal. Why would Ceris need your help? With what?"

Pressing my lips into a thin line, I turned my head away.

Her cold fingers clutched my chin, and, using her power, she pulled my head toward her. "No, no, no. Don't be difficult, Nadine, because I can be more difficult than you'll ever be, and I guarantee you, you'll regret it." Her nails pricked my skin for a brief moment before she let go of me. "Tell me everything you know about Ceris."

I held her gaze, hoping the fear and panic weren't clear in my eyes.

With a loud growl, Imha slapped my face, making sure her nails scratched my skin.

A gasp robbed me of air as my head whipped to the side, and I almost fell off the chaise. Pain exploded on my cheek and spread through my face. I brought my shackled hands to my face, careful not to touch the red light anywhere other than my wrist, since it burned, and cradled my cheek.

God, this hurt!

Imha shot to her feet. "If you won't collaborate with me, I have no reason to treat you well."

Imha treating someone well? Was that a joke?

A purple energy ball sprang to life around the orb of her scepter. Before I could understand what she was doing, Imha pointed the scepter at me, flinging the ball.

I leaned back in a failed attempt of running from it, but the bolt burst on my chest. I gasped as a wave of dizziness and pain assaulted me. My vision darkened, and my muscles went slack. I blinked, trying to clear my vision, to clear my head, but it was like drowning. I paddled, trying to stay above water.

I slid off the chaise and everything went dark.

I was awake, but my eyes refused to open. My muscles were too stiff and rusty; my head was dizzy. Feet shuffled near me, muffled voices spoke, and growls and flaps echoed.

Growls and flaps?

My eyes shot open, and I sat up on the chaise lounge. The red cuffs still held my wrists together. Imha and Omi stood beside the rolled up rug, muttering what sounded like harsh words, and demons—holy shit, four drooling demons—stood around me, their eyes on me. One of them knocked its stave on the ground. At once, Imha and Omi stopped talking and looked at me.

"Nadine, you're awake," Imha said, approaching me with her evil smile. "Are you ready to talk now?"

I met her gaze, but I didn't say one damned word.

"She's still playing dumb?" Omi asked.

"She's playing," Imha said, looking at me. "But she's not dumb." She conjured another purple bolt, and I flinched. "I'll repeat my question. Are you ready to talk now?"

Omi muttered some more, then reached for the rolled up rug. He tapped it with his scepter, and it magically opened, reaching the floor. The tapestry—a brownish world map— was large, almost as large as five or six men standing side by side.

However, the size wasn't what caught my attention. What caught my attention was the fact that certain points on the map, at least two dozen, shone brightly. I squinted, trying to make sense of it. Cathedral Rock was one of those points. As was Stonehenge, the pyramids in Egypt, and many other known places. The white lights blinked and then shifted. What the hell?

The ball of energy in Imha's hand died out, and she

looked from me to the map and back to me. "What do you see?"

For a second, panic surged up. I willed my face to look as emotionless as I could and averted my eyes.

Omi turned his back to the map. "What happened?"

Imha didn't answer. However, the smile on her face wasn't only evil, but the kind of smile that said *I know what you saw.*

The lights blinked and shifted once more. When they settled, they expanded and I could see them better. They weren't only lights, but also symbols, though I couldn't exactly make them out.

Then the symbols danced around the map again. I fought the urge to look at them, but I couldn't resist. I could *feel* them. I stared at the symbols and tried to make sense of it. I noticed a couple of symbols moved along with the others, but they always came back to the same places.

Her creepy smile widened, and I turned my head away, forcing my eyes to focus on a crack in the stone floor. She muttered something to Omi, making his smile grow wide too.

Oh, God.

His eyes fixed on me, and he strolled forward, halting a few feet from the chaise.

"Nadine, tell us where Ceris is," he said.

I remained quiet because saying "I don't know" would be just as bad.

Omi pointed his scepter at me. "Last chance to see a nice version of me. Where is Ceris?"

Swallowing my fear, I raised my chin and met his gaze, without saying a single word.

"So be it," he said.

A red stream surged from the orb of his scepter. My muscles locked as it traveled to me. The red light twisted around me like an unending snake. Panic filled my chest, and I fought the urge to scream. The red snake curled around my arms, around the cuffs, and lifted my arms above my head, pulling me up. Up and away from the chaise. Pain shot from my wrists, and I whimpered as the snake stretched me in the air. It was like there was a rope holding me up by my wrists, and it *hurt*.

Omi seemed amused. "Where is Ceris?"

I whimpered because honestly I couldn't hold on without screaming a bit, but I still didn't say anything. I wouldn't say anything.

Omi looked at the four demons standing guard and gestured to me.

Baring their teeth, the demons attacked.

One of them raised its claws and swiped at me. I screamed, making Omi laugh while Imha looked bored.

Taking turns, the demons played with me as if I were a piñata. They clawed my legs, pushed me back, and twisted me around, causing more pain in my wrists.

After a few minutes, Omi raised his hand and they stopped.

He looked up at me. "Where is Ceris?"

I kept my gaze on my torn clothes. Blood trickled down my numb legs.

Shrugging, Omi walked away, and the demons growled, resuming their game.

I opened my eyes and recognized everything about this place and situation in less than a second.

I was in a dark, chilly, tiny room with gray stone walls and no windows. A cell in a dungeon. A thin strip of light coming from a torch illuminated the place.

My arms ached. I looked up. Metal chains wrapped around my wrists. My clothes hung in tatters, and when I moved, my back scratched painfully against a rough wall.

Just like the vision I had three months ago.

Imha walked into the room, her head high, holding her scepter. A black cloud followed her. I shuddered.

"Hello, Nadine," she said, an evil smile over her red lips. "How are you?"

I bit my lip as bile rose from my stomach. Oh, God, that vision. The torture vision. I had joked about it with Victor and Micah.

Approaching me, Imha tsked. "It is polite to answer questions addressed to you. Didn't your mother teach you good manners? You don't want me to call my friends, do you?" she asked, still smiling. "Be a nice girl and tell me everything I want to know."

I remembered this part. In my vision, I had asked her, "What do you want to know?" but this time, I knew what she wanted to know.

I grimaced but kept my mouth shut. I would change this vision. I didn't know how, but I would.

Imha laughed like an evil queen in a fairy tale, sending goose bumps over my skin. "Still playing the mute one, are we?" Her laugh died, and her eyes became hard. "Tell me everything, and I will end your suffering."

Suffering was a big fear of mine, but loyalty was one of my best traits. I wouldn't crack. Even if she spent ten years torturing me, I wouldn't crack.

"If you tell me about Ceris and her plans, I promise your death will be quick and clean." Imha came closer until her face was inches from mine, her eyes sparkling with pure vice. "On the other hand, if you keep up with this silence game, I promise you, you will regret ever being born." She kissed my cheek.

No, no, no. I braced myself as her icy lips touched my skin, cracking it, drying it out. The withering spread, sending searing pain through my face until it reached my throat, making me gasp and choke.

I tried to inhale the air that would save me, but it was in vain. The parching spread down to my lungs and chest. The world spun, and the room became even darker. Blood trickled from my wrists as I struggled against the cuffs, and my legs went numb.

Imha sent a purple bolt from her scepter to my chest. The bolt hurt as if it had opened my flesh and crushed my organs. I tried to yell but couldn't. However, a few seconds later—although it seemed like decades—the power of the bolt spread, and the drying sensation left me. I took a deep breath, not caring that my body weight dangled from my bloody wrists. I didn't have any strength left, not even to look at Imha while she laughed.

"That is just the beginning," she said, sauntering toward the dungeon door. With her back to me she added, "I'll give you a while longer. Choose wisely."

She left. The door closed behind her, leaving me in total darkness. Despite myself, I cried.

12

Nasty hands carried me out of my cell, but I couldn't keep my eyes open for long. I was tired. I was hungry. I was thirsty, and I was in pain.

I was thrown on the same hard chaise I had been on ... yesterday? Two days ago? Last week? I had completely lost track of time.

"Nadine, I have something to show you," someone said.

Nothing they had to show me could possibly interest me.

Hands clasped my shoulders and held me up.

"Open your eyes," Imha said. Against my will, my eyes fluttered opened. Imha flashed her evil smile. "Good girl." The bright symbols danced on the map behind her, but before I could pay attention to them, she gestured to the pillars to her right. "Bring them in."

Them?

The air fled from every cell of my body when demons brought my father, my mother, Teddie, Tommy, and Nicole in the room.

The floor—the world—was pulled from under my feet.

"No," I muttered. My throat felt raw, but I didn't care. "No, no!"

"Nadine!" my parents shouted as demons dragged them to stand before me by the shackles on their wrists.

"Nad!" Nicole cried, coming to me. The chains held her back, and she tripped.

Their clothes looked like mine, in tatters, and they appeared weak, too thin, too pale, and hurt. Oh God, they were hurt. My father and my mother had purple bruises on their faces and arms. I wondered how many more bruises their ripped clothes hid. The kids had bruises around their shackles and on their bare feet.

The demons tugged on their chains, making the kids cry more.

Oh, God.

My chest burned as the tears made their way out.

I stood and Omi pushed me back down. "Nu-uh. You play by our rules."

My parents looked at me. The dull shine in their eyes was relieved, as if they were happy to see me, but it was also sorrowful.

"How ... How—?"

"She speaks!" Imha laughed. The evil tone in her voice made my skin crawl.

"How ...?" I couldn't speak.

"How did I find them?" she asked. "Simple. I learned of your hometown and that your family still lived there. So after we got you, I sent a search party back to retrieve them."

No, no, no ... this couldn't be happening.

"Please, let them go." My voice broke.

Imha walked behind my family. "I will let them go once you tell me everything about Ceris and her plans."

I shook my head. "I don't know anything."

Imha raised her scepter and pointed it at my family. "I thought we were done with games."

"I don't know where she is. I swear; I'm not lying. I met with her briefly in the middle of nowhere before going to my parents' place, and I hadn't even seen her for three months before that."

"Her plans," Imha urged. "I know she has been up to something for quite some time now, and you're going to tell me everything."

Oh, God. How could I give her what she wanted without telling her the truth?

My eyes swept over my family. How could I not tell Imha the truth? This was my family, my blood, the reason I lived, breathed, and went on everyday trying to do my best. Who cared about the fate of the world? Who cared if Imha found Ceris, or if she found out Levi and Mitrus were alive? Who cared if the world plunged into more darkness, war overtook every corner, and demons ate every living person?

I should care.

The saying to sacrifice one life, or five, to save millions was true, but I didn't really care about it when it came to my family.

But I should care.

How could I think of keeping my family alive when there wouldn't be a world to live in?

My head hurt, and my thoughts zoomed by too fast. I couldn't make sense of anything.

New tears sprouted in my eyes.

"Tell me!" Imha's voice boomed, shaking the walls.

I cringed, the kids cried, and my parents whimpered.

"I ... I ..." I shook my head, willing the words to come out. "I ..."

Omi's grunt became a battle cry, and he pointed his scepter at me.

"No!" Imha pushed his arm away, and the red bright light shot across the room, blinding me for a second. I tried focusing past it, my heart racing.

The light receded, and I blinked. My family was on the ground.

My blood turned into ice, and I couldn't process what was right in front of me.

I watched them. Quiet and too still. Bright red blood seeping from under them.

My heart tightened. "No!" I cried, dashing to them. I knelt on the floor and poked at their shoulders, not sure whom to check first. I turned to Mom, then to Nicole, then to Tommy. They were too far away, and they weren't moving. "No, please, no, no." I turned Nicole around and screamed. Blood trickled out of her ears and her eyes. I pressed a hand to her chest and willed her heart to beat. It didn't. "No," I whispered. I pressed harder. Nothing. "Oh, God." I punched her chest.

It couldn't be. This wasn't happening. I grabbed Teddie's arm and pulled him to me. I reached for Tommy's sweater and dragged him over my legs. As much as I could, I scooted closer to Mom and Dad. We had to be together. I would take care of them. They would be okay. We would find a way out of this.

Their blood covered me, and I wished I could drown in it.

I brushed Nicole's hair from her beautiful face. A sob raked through me, bringing reality with it.

Tipping my head back, I screamed my rage and my pain away until I passed out.

THERE WAS A MOMENT DURING MY HIGH SCHOOL SENIOR YEAR when I thought I wouldn't make it. I thought I wouldn't be accepted into any good university; I wouldn't get a scholarship, and without it I wouldn't be able to pay for my studies. There was a moment I believed I would end up like my parents, working my butt off on the farm and barely getting through a day without any aches and pains, or complaining about not making enough money to buy food for my siblings.

When the NYU letter arrived with one of the best scholarship options they offered, it was like a rich person's Christmas. After that, I just needed to get a well-paying job, and I would be able to lessen my parents' burden.

The week before I moved to New York, Nicole had been in a crazy mood because she was upset with me. I didn't blame her. I was sad about leaving them too.

I was packing what little I had when she stormed into my room and threw Pinky at me.

"I don't want it!" she yelled. "You gave it to me because you said you loved me. You're leaving, so you don't love me anymore, and I don't want anything from you!"

I stared at her.

Was she really just five years old? Sometimes I believed she was closer to ten than the boys were.

With a loud huff, she marched out of my bedroom.

I picked up Pinky from the floor and gave a step toward the door but stopped myself. Going after her now would only cause her to yell at me more. She needed to calm down, and then I would try to talk to her, try to explain to her why I had to go. I just hoped she would listen to me with the maturity of a ten-year-old girl.

"She's going to be all right," my mom said, appearing at the door.

I offered her a small smile. "I know. It's just hard. This is hard for me too, and she's making it harder."

"If it's hard, why are you going?"

"Mom, I already told you why, and you agreed."

"The logical part of my brain agreed, not the emotional one." With a sad grin, she sat on my bed. "You're the one she looks up to, and I think she can't imagine not seeing you everyday."

Tears burned behind my eyes. "The truth is, I can't imagine not seeing all of you everyday either."

Mom patted the bed beside her. "Don't break down now." I sat beside her, and she put an arm around my shoulder. "You're strong, determined, and I'm proud of you. Even if you tell me you don't want to go anymore because you'll miss us, I'll kick you out of here and ship you to New York"—I chuckled—"because I won't let you waste this opportunity. Something like this won't come knocking at your door again. You must grab it with both hands and feet and teeth, and you can't let go." She kissed my cheek. "I know you're going to make me even prouder of you, if that's possible."

Only a mom would know exactly what to say and what a daughter needed to hear. I wiped a tear away and turned to her, winding my arms around her.

Something heavy fell on us, and then Nicole's small arms embraced Mom and me.

"I'm sorry," she whispered, burying her head on my shoulder. "I don't want you to go because I love you."

I pulled her close to me. "I love you too, Nikkie."

I hugged her tight, wishing I could protect her and care for her—for them—forever.

A tug on my arms suddenly erased the memory from my mind, and I opened my eyes.

I was back in my cell, but I wasn't hanging from my wrists anymore. I was lying on the cold floor, metal shackles around my arms, linked by a chain screwed to the wall in front of me.

Another tug jerked me forward, and I groaned as my arms scratched the rough floor.

Omi knelt before me.

Omi ... the red explosion ... my family ...

Panic swept through me, and a dull pain squeezed my heart. It had all been a dream, right? Oh, God, it had to be a nightmare. I looked at my clothes and arms. I was covered in blood—not only my blood.

A sob shook me, and I closed my eyes willing the pain, the hurt, the mourning to consume me, to destroy me, to kill me.

If I had any strength left, if each of my nerves and muscles and senses didn't protest in pain, both physically and mentally, I would have jumped at Omi's throat. I didn't care that he was a god and couldn't die, not without a Black Thorn. All I cared about was hurting him, hurting him as much as he and Imha had hurt me.

Omi shook the chains, trying to lift me up.

"She is as good as dead now," Imha said from somewhere. "After what you did, she really won't talk."

Omi shot up and turned to where I thought Imha was. "What? Now the fault is mine? She wasn't talking before, and we would have killed them either way."

Oh God, I felt sick.

"But she didn't know that!" Imha said, her tone chilling the cell, chilling me.

"What will you do with her now?"

Imha didn't answer right away. "Use her to lure Ceris to us."

13

Even when I tried, I couldn't keep track of time. I wasn't sure how many hours—or days—went by while I remained on that dirty floor, going in and out of consciousness, praying to whatever god would listen to me to take my life and let me be with my family.

Oh God, my family.

I closed my eyes, unable to stop the image from bursting in my mind. Nicole, Teddie, Tommy, Mom, and Dad around me, their blood smeared across my clothes, arms, and face.

I shuddered as new tears sprung from my eyes. By now, I should be completely dry from crying so much, but there was nothing else I could do. My throat was too raw for screaming to be an option anymore. Yet I did want to scream.

The single torch in my cell went out, and I welcomed the darkness, hoping death waited for me behind it. However, my hope faded when a woman came in carrying a new torch and a plate. She wore brown robes and a veil over her head. She looked like a servant, but there was something else about her.

She turned and her eyes met mine.

Cheryl. As in ... Cheryl.

My stomach turned as I quickly realized it was Ceris disguised as Cheryl. Her skin wasn't as pale, her long white-blond hair was now in a neat yellow-blond bob, and her blue eyes were silver.

"Quick," she whispered, dropping down before me. "We don't have much time until they find the real servant locked in a closet."

I scooted away from her, pressing my back to the wall.

She put a hand over the shackles. Pink light shone from her palms, and the shackles fell to the ground. I sighed in relief, shocked by how much the damn things weighed and how quickly I was getting used to it.

She stood and offered me her hand. "Come on."

I narrowed my eyes at her outstretched arm. "But you hate me."

"I don't ..." She sighed. "I don't hate you. Besides, this isn't for me. I'm doing this for Levi."

Of course.

The door opened and I froze.

Keisha popped in her head. "What's taking you so long?"

"What are you doing here?" I asked, my voice raspy.

She looked different with her long dark hair in a ponytail and black clothes—leather armor like clothes, combat boots, and lots of weapons.

"We can talk about that later. Right now, we have to move."

I let my body fall slack on the floor. "I don't want to go."

Ceris—or Cheryl—grabbed my shoulders. "I don't care. I'm taking you."

I slapped her hand away, and she slapped me hard on the

cheek. My face whipped to the side. Stars exploded against my vision, and pain burst on my cheek.

"Bitch!" I yelled, pressing my hand over my throbbing skin.

"Did that wake you up? Because you looked like you were under some kind of self-pity spell."

I glared at her. "You're seriously sick."

She shrugged. "Sick, but alive."

Alive. Unlike my family.

I shrunk into myself. "I don't care about my life."

"Well, unfortunately, I do." She gripped my arms and pulled me toward her until my nose was an inch from hers. "Your parents would be really disappointed in you right now."

I pushed her away. "Don't you dare talk about my parents." New tears choked me. "It's your fault. You put me in this situation. You chose me to play this game. If you had never messed with my life, they would still be alive."

She sighed. "Can we please discuss this someplace else? We really need to go."

Holding a long sword, Keisha knelt beside me. "Nadine, please come with us."

I looked into her chocolate eyes. Confidence and strength rolled off her in waves. I wished I were like her. Maybe my family would be alive if I had been strong, if I had known how to fight, if I had been determined enough.

Still alive ...

I closed my eyes as a new sob rolled through me.

Ceris was right. My family would be disappointed in me. They would want me to escape and live, even if I didn't feel like it. I couldn't imagine a life, even if for only one day, without them, but they would have wanted me to go on. I wasn't sure what to do with myself. For now, I would honor my family and leave, but only because it was better than the alternative of curling up here and waiting for Imha to come play with me whenever it pleased her. The last thing I wanted was to be her toy. I would rather she killed me and be done with it.

I leaned against the wall, cringing when my muscles pulled and my injuries protested. I used the wall to support myself and stood.

Keisha grabbed my wrist. "Let's go."

A wave of dizziness assaulted me after the first step, and Ceris hooked her arm around my waist. All my nerves screamed for me to push her away, but I couldn't afford it. Not right now.

"How did you two get here?" I asked.

A slow smile appeared over Ceris's features. "One of the servants is enchanted to report to me. She told me Imha is planning on using you to lure me here tomorrow."

"Why tomorrow?"

"Imha's joke for Thanksgiving."

Tomorrow was Thanksgiving. Already? And my family wouldn't be here to celebrate with me.

A pain like a knife twisting in my gut ripped through me, and I took a deep breath.

"She's sicker than you," I muttered.

Ceris laughed, and it sounded *almost* as evil as Imha. "So we hurried things and came today."

Besides her evil laugh, her words made her sound as if she cared, which I knew for a fact she didn't.

Keisha opened the door and peeked out. "It's clear."

Millions of questions whirled in my mind. How was Keisha with Ceris? Where were Victor and Micah? I still didn't know how exactly Ceris and Keisha got in here without being seen, being sensed.

One question clouded my mind. "How long has it been since I was taken?"

"Six days," Keisha answered, ushering us out of the cell.

The corridor was clear, if we didn't count the three dead demons on the floor. Their reek filled my nostrils, and the gooey, green blood oozed from their wounds. I pressed a hand over my mouth to keep from throwing up.

Down here it didn't look like the Greek building I had been in before. It looked more like a medieval dungeon with gray stone walls and steps and torches lighting the corridors.

Keisha stopped before the stairs and turned to us, gripping her sword tight. "Things are about to get crazy."

I held her arm as she was about to turn back. "Wait. What is the plan?"

"To get away from here."

I looked at Ceris. "Can't you just *poof* us out of here?"

"Not here," Ceris said. "We have to step out of the protective circle, and then I can *poof* us."

"Okay," Keisha said, sounding annoyed. "Are we ready?"

I took a deep breath, and pain rippled through my wounds. "Not really, but what choice do I have?"

We rushed up the stairs and paused before a wide, heavy wooden door. Keisha put her finger over her lips before poising her sword.

She flung the door open and stabbed the first demon before it could turn. The second growled and swiped its claw toward her. Keisha parried it with her sword, cutting its flesh. Then, as it pulled the other arm back to land a new blow, Keisha whirled around, gaining momentum with her sword and cutting the demon's throat. The creature fell on the ground, making guttural sounds.

Keisha stepped over the body and pulled out her bow and an arrow as more demons appeared at the end of the corridor.

She hit three in the forehead, and Ceris took out two more with her pink bolts. The others were too close, and Keisha let go of the bow and pulled out her sword again.

A wave of demons rushed toward us, but Keisha didn't seem affected. She actually met them halfway, brandishing her sword with elegance. She was like fire, forcing them apart, cutting a path through the gore.

If I forgot the fact that she was killing demons and we were trying to escape, it was kind of enchanting. It was as if she was dancing with her weapons, and she was a hell of a dancer.

"She's a hero," Ceris said.

I stilled. "What?"

"You know, like Achilles and Hercules."

That information took a minute to process through my brain. "Are you telling me she's the daughter of one of you and a human?"

Oh, God.

"No. That's Grecian and Roman legend. The real version is different." She stared at me, probably enjoying this too much. "Heroes are created, chosen really, by the Fates in times of need. They chose Keisha and gave her special abilities like her knowledge of fighting, her strategy skills, her faster healing, and her increased strength, agility, and stamina."

"Oh."

"Are you two coming?" Keisha spoke up from the middle

of the corridor, one of her hands on her waist and her lips pressed thin.

I looked around. A dozen demons lay dead at our feet, and I did my best not to throw up.

Ceris and I skirted around the bodies—I held my breath so the stench wouldn't make me puke—and met Keisha in the corner.

"So, there's the exit." Keisha pointed to the door on the other side of an empty medium-sized room. "If I'm correct, the outside will be swarming with demons. I'll do everything I can to hold them back, but we can't stop moving or they will overrun us."

"Moving where?" I asked.

"To the right," she said. "There's a path between two buildings, a hill, then a wall. We cross the wall, and Ceris can *poof* us out of here." She put emphasis on the word poof, and Ceris rolled her eyes. "Ready?"

It was my turn to roll my eyes. "Do you have to ask?"

"Here." Keisha threw me a dagger.

I caught it, glad my hand closed around the hilt, not the blade. "What am I supposed to do with this?"

She shrugged and ran. Ceris and I followed her, and we sprinted across the room just as the doors burst open and the first wave of demons emerged.

"Oh, God."

Ceris raised her hand and flung pink bolts at them, and Keisha engaged them in battle.

"Don't stop moving!" Keisha yelled, pushing through the demons.

Ugh, easy to say.

Ceris brought up a pink shield before us and pushed a few demons back. We made it through the doors, and I inhaled deeply. The air wasn't fresh, but it was crisper than in the dungeons.

A new wave of demons came crushing down on us. Ceris tugged me, and we ran to the right. Each step brought pain shooting through my wounds, but I gritted my teeth and kept going.

We were running along the path between two Persian-style buildings when right in the middle of it Ceris gasped and faltered. "I can feel Imha and Omi. They are coming."

Her hold on me tightened, and she rushed our steps.

More demons came barreling down from both buildings, snarling, their talons ready.

Keisha ushered us past her. "Go!"

Ceris didn't hesitate. But I did. "No!" I tried fighting Ceris, but she used magic to make me come with her. "She can't take them all."

"It's her choice."

"You can't be serious."

She didn't answer.

I whipped my head to the side, but my wound pulled and I cried out. Disheartened, I focused on the sound of the swords clashing and the grunts of fallen demons. The sound never really lessened. I hoped Keisha was able to keep up with us.

We reached the hill. Ceris rushed down, dragging me along, but each hurried step was more unsure than the next, and soon we were sliding down the hill. Ceris lost her hold on me as we toppled into a roll. I raised my arms to protect my face, and my side scratched against a stone.

More wounds. More hurt. More exhaustion.

I stopped rolling and lay on the grass, trying to catch my breath and remember what we were doing. I blinked several times at the dark sky. The clouds closed in on me—thick, dirty, and suffocating.

Then the shrieks echoed through the darkness and vibrated over my skin.

I shuddered and pushed up on my elbows. The Akuma were coming at us. Fast.

Ceris was on her knees about twenty feet from me. We both looked up the hill where Keisha landed blows on the Ornek, as she slowly retreated. However, she couldn't contain them all. Some sensed Ceris's aura and bypassed Keisha.

"No!" Keisha screamed, running down the hill after them.

There were too many. Dozens on the ground. Dozens in the sky.

We would never make it.

Keisha would never make it.

"Come on." Ceris grabbed my arm and tugged me back. She dragged me to the wall. "Climb."

My muscles locked, and my gaze was glued to Keisha as she hurried down in large, graceful jumps, landing blows left and right, like a warrior on a battlefield.

Ceris tightened her grip around my wrists, letting her long nails graze my skin painfully. "Climb!"

When I didn't move, she used magic to hurl me over the wall. It wasn't too tall, only about five feet. I fell face-first on the other side, but I used my hands to break the fall.

She climbed over next, but stayed on top of the wall. "Come on!" she called.

I watched her, my eyes narrowed. There was a moment when I thought Ceris didn't care if Keisha made it or not, but now she was waiting for the girl.

"Oh, by the Everlast," Ceris muttered.

I opened my mouth to ask what happened, but words

failed me when I saw what she meant. Omi and Imha were on the path between the buildings, gliding on black clouds in our direction.

Miserable, painful cold took hold of me, and I gasped. Suddenly, there was no air in the world.

"Seize them!" Imha shouted.

Growls, roars, and heavy footfalls filled the darkness.

"Keisha! Now!" Ceris extended her arm.

I couldn't see what was happening on the other side of the wall, but the noises weren't good. Grunts, growls, shrieks, yells, thuds, clashing, and things I couldn't identify.

I stepped on a loose stone and looked up the wall. Like a ninja, Keisha hurled herself in the air, flipped, and landed on her knees by the wall. She clasped Ceris's hand. A demon threw itself at her and weighed her down on the opposite side. I propped myself up on the wall and grabbed her other arm.

Ceris shot a pink bolt at the demon and it let go.

We helped her up, but then something grabbed my shoulders, and flung me down the wall. Air escaped my lungs, and pain shot through my back as I hit the ground. A demon hovered over me. It lifted its sharp claws. Fear erupted in me, and I prayed death didn't hurt much. I shut my eyes, and clenched my fists. The dagger. I had forgotten about the dagger in my hand.

The demon scratched my shoulder as I plunged the knife into its chest. It opened its mouth, its razor-like teeth too close to my face, and it growled. I winced, holding my breath.

Its lifeless body fell over me, its weight squashing me like mashed potatoes until Keisha and Ceris tossed it aside.

"No!" Imha yelled from the other side of the wall. She raised her scepter toward us.

A purple bolt flew from the orb atop her scepter just as Ceris held our hands and transported us to safety.

CERIS BROUGHT US TO SEVEN DIFFERENT LOCATIONS BEFORE actually arriving at our destination.

"To make sure they can't follow us," she explained.

On our penultimate stop, somewhere in the middle of a forest, Ceris pulled out a bag from a hollowed tree trunk. Meanwhile, I leaned against another tree and, not being able to hold on any longer, I slid to the ground.

"Nadine." Keisha knelt beside me. "No, no. Hang on."

My eyes were heavy, and all I wanted to do was curl up and sleep. "Just a minute," I whispered.

"Ceris, she needs healing."

"Not here. Put this on her, then grab one for you. Quick."

Keisha lifted my arms as something heavy fell over my shoulders, and I felt suffocated and hot.

"Hang in there. Just a minute more."

Then it changed. The sky was dark, but everything around us was bright. And it was cold. Too cold.

My eyes fluttered open. Snow. We were somewhere with lots of snow. I wanted to look around, but my energy was at its last drop.

Arms surrounded me.

"What took you so long?" a deep, rough male voice asked. I knew this voice, though I couldn't match a face to it.

"Don't start," Ceris said. "Just take her inside."

The arms folded my body against a hard, warm wall. I snuggled against it, wishing it could take away the pain.

"You'll be fine," the voice said. "You'll be all right."

14

I FELT A DAMP CLOTH ON MY FOREHEAD, THE SOFTNESS OF A mattress under me, and the warmth from a comforter tucked around me.

"Darling." Micah's rough voice penetrated through my dizziness, and I focused on it. "Are you waking up?" he asked. I took the cloth off and blinked the blur from my vision. My eyes met his. "Hi there." A corner of his lips curled in a sympathetic smile.

I turned my head away, desperate to focus on something other than the sympathy in his eyes and his voice. I couldn't take that. I scanned the place. I was in a twin bed in a small bedroom with white walls and no windows. The door was made of metal and looked thick.

"You've been out for a day and a half," he said. The noise of the metal chair he sat on being dragged closer to the bed rang in my ears, making me cringe. "Sorry," he muttered. "How are you feeling?"

I thought about it for a moment.

I was okay. I could feel my legs where the demons had cut

me, the side of my stomach where I had grazed the stone, and my left shoulder where that last demon had slashed me, but none of these injures hurt too much. Physically, I was okay. I would be okay.

What hurt was the emptiness inside me.

My family was gone.

All I did for them, all I tried doing, all in vain. In the end I couldn't protect them; I couldn't save them. In fact, I put them on the path of danger.

If I had stayed away, or if I only had stopped by for a couple of hours, the demons wouldn't have followed me there, and my family would be safe. My family would be alive.

Oh, God.

I tried curling into myself, but my injuries hurt too much. I gave up and pulled the pillow from under me instead and hugged it, hiding my face.

A sob choked me, and I prayed to die too. Why? Why hadn't Omi killed me too?

I spied from under the pillow, thinking Micah had slipped out of the room while I ugly-cried until my eyes hurt, but he was still there seated on the same chair. As usual he was dressed in black. This time it seemed almost as a joke. I guess I should dress in all black too from now on.

If I had any clothes left, because I didn't. Everything I had was gone. Everything. Every piece of clothing, every book, every picture, every document, every person I loved and lived for.

A tear rolled down my face, and I quickly wiped it away.

Micah's eyes fixed on mine with a sorrowful shine. The sympathy from before and the sorrowful expression on his face made me angry with him. Why was he sad? Out of pity? I didn't need his pity, and I didn't need his help.

"Talk to me, darling. How are you feeling?"

How do you think I'm feeling?

Pain sliced through my chest, and I closed my eyes, hugging the pillow tighter.

I didn't want to answer. I didn't want to think about it because if I thought about it, if I remembered it, it hurt more. The memory, the image of their bloodied bodies around me, burned inside, twisted my soul, and it ached more than my injuries. Much more. If I thought about my family, I wouldn't do anything else other than cry.

Who was I kidding? I didn't want to do anything else other than cry.

"Darling," Micah whispered. His voice carried a tone I had never heard from him. His hand caressed my arm, and I felt like crying more. "I have something for you."

I didn't want anything from him, or anyone.

He gently clasped my wrist and turned my arm around so my palm faced the ceiling, then he dropped something there, something soft, fluffy, and almost weightless.

Realizing what it was, I flung the pillow aside. The air fled from me when my eyes fell on Pinky, Nicole's stuffed bunny.

"Oh, God." I pressed it to my chest, and a sob shook my core. Micah's hand slid up my arm and squeezed my good shoulder. "How?"

"Rok told me your hometown was under attack, but I wasn't fast enough." He looked down. "When I got there, Omi was taking your family. There were too many of them. If I tried to save your family, I would have been captured too and that would make everything worse." He dropped his hand.

"Forgive me for not fighting for them right there. I thought I would be able to fight for them later."

At a loss of what to do or what to feel, I did the only thing I could think of. Ignoring the ripples of pain that shot through my body, I knelt on the bed and embraced him. He was stiff at first, as if I had surprised him, but then his arms were around me, pressing me tighter. He buried his face on my neck and sighed.

"Nicole dropped that bunny, screaming that it was a gift from you and she couldn't be without it. That's why I grabbed it."

Another sob ran through me. I inhaled deeply, trying to calm down. His vanilla and sandalwood scent washed my senses. In the past, I had felt lust whenever I had taken him in, but this time it brought me only security and comfort.

"I'm sorry, darling. I wish there was something I could do to ease your pain."

"You could kill me," I whispered without hesitation. He was the god of death, the dead, and the underworld, wasn't he? He could kill me.

He grabbed my shoulders with a gentle grip and pushed me away. He stared at me with wide, hard eyes. "Don't you ever kid like that, you got it? Never."

I didn't reply.

Hugging Pinky, I lay down on the bed turning on my side, my back to Micah.

I was being serious, even if he didn't want to hear me. The best thing that could happen to me right now was to die, because the only thing I had to live for was gone.

OMI CIRCLED MY FAMILY AND ME, POINTING HIS SCEPTER AT each of us.

"Eeny, meeny, miny, moe," he sang. His eyes sparkled red, sending fear crawling up my spine.

Desperate, I turned to my family and huddled them in my arms.

"No, Omi," I mouthed. My voice didn't come out, and I didn't understand why. "Please, no," I tried again, but the words were only in my mind.

"Tell me, Nadine, where are Levi and Mitrus?" Omi asked.

"I don't know." I shook my head, trying to emphasize my answer since my voice was completely gone.

Nicole's arms tightened around me, and she buried her head in my chest. "I'm afraid," she said.

"I won't let anything happen to you," I tried to say, and once more, there was only silence.

Omi turned his scepter to me. "I'll give you one more chance to tell me."

"I don't know!" I mouthed, but he didn't hear or see me.

He clicked his tongue. "What a shame."

The red light shot out of his orb. I screamed. My family screamed.

The light became fire burning everything around me. Everyone. Except me.

I ran around my family, crying, trying to help them, to put out the fire, to get them out of there, to ease their pain.

My family writhed, screaming, jerking, their skin wrinkling and darkening. Burning, Nicole threw herself in my arms.

"It's your fault," she croaked before her skin peeled away. She shrunk and became dust in my hands.

I screamed.

"Nadine," a voice seeped through my mind. "Nadine, wake up!" A strong hand clasped my arms and shook me. "Nadine!"

I opened my eyes and stopped screaming when my eyes settled on Micah's worried face.

"It was just a nightmare," he said, his grip easing around me. "You're okay now, darling. It was just a nightmare."

I looked around. We were still in the same place—some research bunker, I heard the others mentioning. I was in my room in my tiny bed, and we were safe. But my family wasn't. My family was gone.

Whimpering, I hugged Pinky.

Micah let out a heavy sigh, ran a hand through his hair, cursed under his breath, then knelt beside the bed.

My eyes widened.

"I'll stay here until you fall asleep again." It wasn't a question. It was a statement, apparently not open for discussion.

However, I couldn't lie. I didn't want to be alone right now, and if Ceris had offered to stay with me during the night, I would have let her. At least Micah was nice to me—some of the time.

He sat on the bed beside me, his back to the headboard, arms crossed. I scooted closer, but turned on my side, my back against his leg, and faced the wall.

Micah's heavy hand rested on my arm, caressing me from my elbow to my shoulder and over my back. Almost like a lullaby.

I barely got out of bed for three days.

They came and went all the time. Micah, Keisha, Victor,

and even Ceris. They tried to convince me to eat more, to walk around, to breathe fresh air, to explore the bunker ... anything. But I didn't move. That didn't stop them from telling me about everything that was going on.

Apparently Micah had found this shelter years ago when he was still a god. He had scared the researchers away and used it whenever he wanted time for himself in a place where no one could find him. He never told anyone about this place, so we were safe here.

The bunker was supposed to be huge, with three underground levels—the first two levels were comprised mainly of labs and technical rooms, and the third level, where we were, had dozens of bedrooms, conference rooms, a cafeteria, and a kitchen.

Keisha seemed to like it here. Victor, on the other hand, hated it. However, I guessed that was mainly because he had to put up with Micah. Well, he had been the one to suggest they stick together, and after what happened to my family and me, they decided it was time to push past the childish loathing and stand together. For what I could gather, it wasn't going too well.

Victor came to visit me a couple of times each day.

During the second day, he sat in a chair beside my bed, took a deep breath, and burst. "I think I'm responsible for what happened to your family. For what happened to you. My aura is stronger, and the demons probably followed me. Once we were together, they separated and followed us both. I was able to disappear, but you couldn't. They found you and ... I'm so, so sorry."

I didn't know what to think of this. Was he responsible for my family's deaths? I wasn't sure. Even if what he said were true, in the end I would have gone to him at some point, healed him, and caused the demons to follow me back. The demons would have found me sooner or later.

Still, I couldn't help the disheartened feeling smothering my chest. It was easier to blame him than myself. Easier to be mad and frustrated at him than me.

I also had learned the residents of the bunker had meetings where they discussed where the scepters could be, because that was the most important task right now—to find the scepters so Victor and Micah would be able to become full gods again, and be strong enough to wage a war against Imha and Omi.

However, Ceris also wished to look for allies. According to her, there were many powerful deities out there, and they would need any help they could get for the upcoming war. Victor seemed reluctant about it. He thought they should do that after they were full gods again because if they attracted attention now, Imha might find out about them and have them killed easily since they were still in human bodies. The group argued more than actually decided anything. Not that I saw any of that. Keisha was the one telling me.

"There are times when I think Lord Levi and Lord Mitrus will start a fist fight right then and there," she told me once, extracting a small smile from me.

On the third day, I had a huge surprise when someone I wasn't expecting entered my room.

"Morgan!" I yelled, sitting up on the bed.

"Hey, girl!" He came to me and hugged me tight. "I'm so sorry."

Oh, God. New tears sprung to my eyes, and I couldn't help but sob. Whenever someone said they were sorry, my helplessness and guilt returned.

He rubbed my back, and whispered comforting words. After a long while, I took a deep breath and sat back.

"I'm glad you're here," I muttered.

"Me too. Someone needs to kick that pretty butt of yours and get you up."

I smiled. "You sound like Micah."

He made a face, scrunching his nose. "I know, right?"

"Hey. What happened to you? I mean, we were in Victor's car and you spilled the fountain water around us, but when Micah and I made it to the other side, you weren't there."

"The Fates sent me back to the temple in Jacksonville. I was confused, but they sent me a message later telling me you both were safe and I shouldn't worry."

"And how did you end up here this time?"

"Lady Ceris is all about connecting with allies. I guess I'm one of them."

"Oh. Good. You're a good asset to their quest."

He squinted at me. "You know, I arrived here a couple of hours ago, and all I have heard since is that you have barely eaten or moved." He took my hand in his. "I know you must be hurting, Nad, but you can't stop living. Your family wouldn't want you to do this."

"I know," I whispered, a little ashamed.

"If they knew about your ability to help the gods, to keep them going so they can restore the light to the world, your family would want you working hard on that."

I groaned, hating to hear these truthful words. "I know."

"Then what's stopping you?"

I closed my eyes for a second. "It hurts."

"I know it does, but use that hurt. Channel it. Do something about it. Use it to fuel your motivations."

"How?"

The door opened, and Keisha stepped inside.

"Hey," she said with a tight smile. "Hi, Morgan." Apparently they had already met. He waved at her, and she turned to me. "How are you?"

"The same," I answered. She had her long black hair in a ponytail and wore gym clothes. "Where are you going?"

"To train," she said. "Micah transformed one of the big conference rooms into a gym."

A gym inside a seventy-year-old bunker. That was interesting.

"So, you just run on a treadmill?"

She laughed. "That too, but mostly I train with weapons and punch a pretty mean punch dummy." She looked at her cell phone and pouted her lips. "I should get going. I have only two hours before the next meeting. I'll stop by later."

She left the room, and I stared at the closed door.

Somewhere in this bunker, she would train. Landing punches and swinging weapons. Skills that could be useful in battle. A battle against Imha and Omi. A battle I could participate in. My family would support that; they would approve of me helping in this war.

It was like a burst of energy shot through my veins. The sorrow, the sadness suddenly became rage and hunger for revenge. But I needed more. Just fighting wouldn't do it. I needed a bigger reason than just revenge against Imha and Omi.

Morgan raised his eyebrows at me. "What is it?"

I almost told him I probably found a reason to get up from this bed, but I didn't want to get my hopes up yet. I only averted my eyes and answered, "I'm not sure yet."

15

———

THE NEXT DAY, I WENT TO THE IMPROVISED LIBRARY. IT WAS ONE of the bedrooms, filled with hundreds of books Morgan insisted on bringing with him. Good for me because I was hoping to find what I was looking for in one of them.

I sat down on the floor with a few books I thought could have the information I needed. The first one was called *The Gods and Goddesses of the Everlasting Circle*. This should be interesting.

I flipped through the pages. There were drawings of each god and goddess, but they didn't look like the real thing at all. They looked more like Greek gods with those round faces, white robes, and the leaves on their heads. So odd.

A sentence from the introduction caught my attention.

No god or goddess or any deity of The Everlasting Circle is fully good or fully evil. They fight for their beliefs, which may change as the world changes, even if their foundations do not.

I thought of Imha and Omi. They weren't fully evil? Of course they were. Look at what they were doing!

Shaking my head, I continued flipping the pages. That wasn't what I was looking for.

My fingers stopped by Levi's page.

He's the balance, the sole force that keeps the Circle strong and tied together. He'll always stand on the neutral side and try to bring others to an agreement. He'll put his needs after the needs of his brothers and his people.

So far, human Victor hadn't been that unselfish.

Ceris's page was next.

The goddess of love and family will do anything for her family.

No argument there.

She's the strength behind Levi's balance. Without her, his equilibrium will tip over and The Everlasting Circle will crumble.

A pang shot through my heart. I pushed the feeling aside, because who was I to feel jealousy if there was nothing there to be jealous about? I knew she had created my feelings for him so I could do whatever I had to do to help them.

Even so, it was hard to shut my emotions down. Despite what I wanted, I still thought of him, of the kiss we shared, of the feelings behind that kiss, and sometimes I wondered if those feelings could truly be false.

Pushing that aside, I flipped to Omi's page.

Besides being bloodthirsty for war, Omi is a great strategist, and he finds himself useful when planning the balance of the world with Levi. He oversees any war going on in the world, keeping an eye on the wounded and lost, along sending help their way. He also tries to judge which side is right and wrong, if any, and help them win the war, so not many lives will be lost in it.

Whoa. No, this couldn't be.

Omi seemed cruel and bloodthirsty like the passage said. And just that. Bloodthirsty. Nothing else.

He had killed my family, and I refused to accept any other image of him.

Irritated, I continued my perusal. Next was Imha's chapter.

She may be the goddess of chaos, but even she can get tired of eternal chaos. In the past, whenever she threw the world into chaos, she confessed regretting it.

What?

Imha had thrown the world in chaos before? And she regretted it?

Why did nobody tell me that?

The next paragraph, though, made me sick.

Though Imha doesn't have a true mate, as Ceris and Levi are, there are recordings in history of short relationships with Omi and with Mitrus. Although fleeting, events indicate these relationships are recurrent.

What?

Holy shit. To imagine her with Micah ... I felt like throwing up.

Seriously? This book couldn't be half-right. It had been written by humans who hadn't had any contact with the gods. Of course, it wasn't right.

Then I flipped the page and found the chapter on Mitrus.

The god of death, the dead, and the underworld cares about his people as if they were family. Sometimes it may seem as if he cares more about the dead than the living, but that's a misguided perception.

I shuddered. Good thing he was still in a human body and without his full powers, otherwise I would have to worry about upsetting him and him killing me in his head. Not that that would be a bad thing. I wasn't afraid of dying anymore, and until yesterday, I had wished Micah would kill me. I just didn't want to die yet—not without knowing I could do something, anything. There had to be a solution for my pain, for my suffering, in one of these books.

Then the next paragraph changed it all:

He has the power to overrule death and bring anyone back to life.

He could? I mean probably not now, but once Micah became a full god again, he could bring anyone back to life. That got the wheels in my head turning. I could use this, but I needed more ...

Taking deep breaths, I flung the book down and picked up another book titled *The Everlast Energy*. Nothing I wanted in there. Hours passed. I flipped through at least thirteen books, and I found nothing.

"What are you doing here?" Morgan asked, entering the door. He carried six thick books in his arms.

"Sorry. Just trying to learn more about the creed, that's all."

He smiled. "That's good." He set the books on a bed. "If you have any doubts about what you read or, any general questions, you know where to find me. I like talking about it."

I opened my mouth to ask him about what I was looking for because, if there was anything like it, he would know about it for sure, but I decided against it. He would suspect my intentions and give me an earful about it. No, thank you.

"Thanks," I said.

"All right." He turned to the door. "I need to go to another meeting with Lord Levi, but I'll be back in a bit."

"Okay."

Smiling, he left the room, and I tensed. I hoped I found whatever I was looking for before he came back because I honestly didn't want any of my questions answered by him.

I glanced over the books he had brought in. One of them was titled *Magic in the Everlast.* Oh, this could be it.

I grabbed the book and flipped through it with intent.

There were all kinds of spells in the book, from how to ward a house against demons, to speculations on how to make a Black Thorn, and how to become a lesser deity—which brought to mind Brock and the Crimson Dagger. Then I found it.

The Soul Oath.

Once more it was all speculation, but that was better than nothing. I read the entire chapter three times to make sure I didn't miss anything. It wasn't complicated; it just warned there was no way of undoing it.

For a moment, I wondered if I really should do it. Then I remembered the Fates had given me my soul back because I would need it.

I knew this was why.

I searched for him throughout the bunker, which wasn't the size I would imagine a bunker to be. It was huge. Really huge, and surprisingly warm. I had no idea how, but there was electricity and heat here.

I was about to give up on my search when I found him in a conference room, one much smaller than the one turned into the gym, but still a conference room.

Micah sat in a chair, leaned back, his feet on the oval table and crossed at the ankle. His eyes were fixed on the plain white wall, his mind clearly somewhere else. He looked focused and stern, unlike his usual nonchalant and sure self—a side of him I only saw on rare occasions.

I leaned in the doorway and tried to fight the urge to stare at him. I could only try, because really, who wouldn't want to stare at him?

The dark jeans hugged his legs, especially in the position he was in. The black shirt didn't hide his muscles around his chest and shoulders. His black hair was longer than before, framing his chiseled face. Too handsome for his own good.

"Like what you see?"

And too cocky for his own good too.

I straightened. "I need to talk to you."

He put his feet down and pulled the chair in, resting his elbows on the table. "Hmm, you need to talk to me? That's new. What can I do for you?" Before I could speak, he continued, "I know. Cuddle some more. Darling, I'm all up for that."

I shook my head, and the idea of marching out of the room without talking to him crossed my mind. However, I needed to talk to him. I wouldn't be able to go one more day without resolving this issue and putting my mind to rest.

"Speaking of cuddling, I found out you have a history with Imha."

He shot me one of his award-winning smiles. "Are you jealous, darling?"

I scoffed, but chose not to comment on that. "I can't ... I can't imagine you and her."

"I can't imagine it either." He lost the smile. "It seems too long ago. I guess it was. We never took our hook ups seriously, and honestly, I can't really remember the last time we were 'together.'" He made air quotes with his fingers. "Maybe two hundred years ago? Something like that. It never lasted. We were never like Levi and Ceris. We didn't belong together; we weren't soul mates. Imha and I simply had fun together." He shook his head. "Living as a human made me realize how pathetic my affairs with her were. I regret them now."

His unexpected confession crumbled my tough facade. Unfortunately, regret didn't make everything right.

He was right, though. I was jealous. Too damn jealous, and I was fighting not to show it. I was trying to hide it even from myself, because honestly, I didn't know what feeling that meant.

Jealousy aside, I also wanted to ask him about the other times Imha inflicted chaos on the world, but I was already pushing my luck.

I cleared my throat. "Remember you said you wished there was something you could do for me?"

"Yes."

"Well, I know what." He stared at me with his cryptic black eyes, and I took that as a cue to continue. "I want to strike a Soul Oath with you."

"What?" He stood—tall, large, and powerful. I fought the urge to cringe. "How do you know about the Soul Oath?"

"Morgan's books."

He narrowed his eyes. "He showed that to you?"

"No. He doesn't know about it." I paused, thinking of the best way to approach this. "Please, hear me out."

"Only a handful of Soul Oaths have been struck in this world, and most of them didn't do any good."

"This isn't about doing good or bad. Just listen to me."

He sighed. "I don't see why."

"Please," I begged, sure I had sad puppy eyes, even though it wasn't a conscious act.

He sighed. "All right. Tell me."

I inhaled deeply before blurting it out. "After all this shit is done, when you're a full god, and we defeat Imha and Omi and restore the world to order, I want you to bring my family back to life."

He crossed his arms. "And what do I get from it?"

"My soul."

His eyes widened. "What? Of course not!"

"Yes. Yes. You will do—"

"Even if I wanted to strike a Soul Oath with you, the Fates have your soul. You can't give it to me."

"They gave it back to me."

He stared at me. "What?"

"Back in New York, a few days before the attack. They visited me and gave me my soul back. They said I would need it." I took a step in his direction. "This is why they gave it back to me. I know it."

He shook his head. "It doesn't make sense."

"But it does," I said. "You will strike this Soul Oath with me, because if you don't do it, you might as well kill me right now." Trying to be bold, I walked around the table and halted before him, the tip of my shoes touching his. I reached to the neck of his shirt and pulled the necklace from under it. He tensed. "I ... I'm not sure how you feel about your human family now that you remember who you are, but try to think of what it was like before, of what you would have done for your parents. That's how I feel. I will do anything for my family, and this is the only thing I can think of. They are my reason to live, my reason to fight. I need you to accept this, to do this for me."

It took him a full, tense minute to answer. "One soul for five?"

"Six."

He raised his eyebrows. "Six?"

"Yes. Since you'll bring them back to life, I want Troy to come back too."

"That's even worse. One for six."

"It's what I have to offer."

He watched me, thinking. "And your soul will be mine?"

"Yes. You can send me directly to the underworld or whatever you call that, I don't care."

His jaw tensed and he took a step back. "No."

A punch in my stomach. The air leaving my lungs. That was how his response felt. "What? Why not?"

"You didn't think this through. You will die. Don't you realize that? Die, as in never be alive again. You don't want that."

Tears sprung to my eyes. "I do! That's exactly what I want."

He turned his back to me. "No, Nadine. I won't do it."

"But—"

"I won't change my mind."

I pressed my lips into a thin line and clenched my fists, holding back from jumping on his back and punching the hell out of him.

If he wouldn't strike the Soul Oath with me, then I had no options left, nothing to reduce the pain, to feel like I could do something. Oh, God. Sorrow replaced the anger and a tear rolled down my cheek.

Defeated, I ran back to my bedroom, threw myself on my bed, and hugged Pinky.

"I'm sorry," I whispered. "I'm so sorry I couldn't keep you safe."

16

———

"You have to get up," Keisha said. She placed the plate on my nightstand and sat on the metal chair beside my bed.

She came to check on me at least five times a day for the last four days. During her visits, she tried to convince me to eat and then get up.

"Think about what your family would want," she said. "They wouldn't want to see you like that."

I just put the pillow over my head, hugged Pinky, and ignored her.

Who cared about what my family wanted? They were dead. They had no say in my life anymore. Ugh, a life I didn't want anymore, a life I wanted to end, though I wasn't brave enough.

Knowing this shelter had a gym with weapons, I hashed out plans of sneaking in there, grabbing a dagger, and piercing my heart. However, I wasn't brave enough. I wouldn't be able to hold the dagger still and stab myself. I needed someone to do it for me. Unfortunately, asking the others for help was out of the question. They would never agree to it.

So I stayed in my bed, praying to wither away in my sleep before any nightmares came to me because they hurt too much. They made me feel more guilty, more hopeless. They increased the dull ache in my chest until it was too difficult to breathe, and all I could think of was stop. *Stop breathing.*

Victor and Morgan also visited me at least once each day, but there was no sign of Ceris or Micah. Micah had no excuses, other than the fact that he wanted distance from me. Which was true, right? He had left me alone on that island, and he refused to strike the Soul Oath with me, proving to me he didn't care about my feelings and didn't want any association with me. This dismissal only added to the pain in my chest, making everything worse.

As for Ceris, I suspected she was still out, searching for the scepters because, if I knew she was here, I would go to her. I would ask her to bind the Soul Oath with me. However, whenever I thought about it, I knew it wouldn't work. For one, Ceris didn't like me and wouldn't do me any favors, even if in the end it meant she would be rid of me. And two, she wasn't the goddess of death and the dead. She couldn't bring anyone back to life.

Killing myself was the only solution to end this pain and reunite with my family. The plan came to me during a nightmare.

Enfolded by fire, my mom grabbed my hand in her smoldering ones. "You have to save us," she said, her voice croaking.

I held on to her, even though the heat scorched my skin. I gritted my teeth and endured the pain that ricocheted through me. "I want to. I want to save you. All of you," I said between sobs.

My father appeared on the other side and slapped my

mother's hand away from mine. I gasped, not expecting such action.

He glared at me. "You are poison. You're poison to us. You're poison to anyone around you."

Desperation gripped my heart. My father hated me. He hated me because I couldn't help. Because they died and I did nothing.

"No!" I cried, reaching for them.

The fire bellowed higher, stronger, brighter, and engulfed them. I raced to them, screaming when the heat wrapped around me and the fire charred my skin.

Panting, I jerked awake. My hands shook and my tee clung to my sweat-dampened torso.

I took a few deep breaths to calm my racing heart, and then shut down my conscience, the part telling me this plan was insane and I shouldn't do it.

But I had to. I couldn't go on like this anymore. I pushed those thoughts away, and a weird mix of desperation and numbness settled in my heart.

Feeling like a robot on a mission, I threw the comforter aside and jumped out of bed. I pulled a jacket over my tee and shorts and exited my bedroom, hoping everyone was asleep at this hour of the night.

I tiptoed to the bathroom, grabbed the medicine box from the cabinet, and then tiptoed to the kitchen. I emptied the box of medicine over the counter and sorted through it. Tylenol Cold, Tylenol pain reliever, aspirin, Benadryl, Robitussin, Zyrtec, Anacin, and several others. I opened them all and dumped the contents in a bowl. Now I need some liquid. Water maybe, but I would prefer something a little stronger. I opened the fridge and found beer. Hmm, if I didn't find anything else, it would have to do. I searched the entire kitchen until I located a tall cabinet housing hard liquor. I grabbed a vodka bottle, a glass from the drying rack, and filled it to the brim.

I glanced at the bowl with at least fifty tablets and the vodka glass before me.

My conscience wanted me to listen. It banged on the walls I had built around it, asking me to listen, asking me to think better about this, to give up on what I was about to do—but I refused to hear it. Clinging to the numbness in me, I pushed my conscience away, making it stay locked behind my walls.

Swallowing pills and drinking would be far less painful than trying to pierce myself with a dagger—and hopefully easier. I wouldn't feel anything while taking them, not until it was too late. I shrugged. I would probably pass out before feeling real pain and dying, and that was all fine by me.

Shaking, I held the glass with one hand, took a handful of pills in the other, and popped them in my mouth.

"What do you think you're doing?"

My heart racing, I jumped and choked on the pills. The glass slipped from my hand and crashed to the floor. A coughing fit shook my body.

Micah rushed to my side. "Nadine," he said, his voice strained.

He held my torso up and smacked the heel of his hand, not too gently, on the middle of my back. I spat the pills and took a long breath, which started another coughing fit.

He turned me around and helped me lean against the counter. The cough subsided and I glanced at him. His brows were furrowed, his lips pressed together, his jaw flexed, the muscles in his neck tense, and his eyes ... were filled with hate? Disgust? No, but I couldn't figure out what it was exactly.

He ran a hand through his disheveled hair. "What were you thinking?" The tone of his voice carried such disappointment I winced. "I don't ..." He exhaled through his nose. "Why?"

I averted my eyes and said nothing. I wasn't sorry about what I had planned to do; I was only sorry that he got here in time to stop me.

"Are you this unhappy? So miserable you're willing to take your own life?"

There was an open bottle of vodka, a broken glass, and medicine spread over the counter and on the floor. The answer should be clear.

If I had my way, he would forget what he saw and walk away so I could fill another glass with vodka and grab another handful of pills.

He shook his head. "What can I do, Nadine? How can I help you feel better?"

Oh, now that was one question I wanted to hear from him. I lifted my chin and stared at him. "A Soul Oath. I want a Soul Oath from you."

He cursed under his breath. "I can't believe this."

"If you do this, if you strike a Soul Oath with me, I won't try to kill myself. I will make every effort to stay alive, to help you find the scepters, to defeat Imha, until we can honor the Soul Oath."

"I don't see any advantage. You will die either way."

"Not true. If I die now, I'll just end my misery. But with the Soul Oath, I'll die for a good cause. I'll help you and the others in this war and then I'll die to save my family. There's nothing I want more." He shook his head. Despair rippled through me, and I punched his chest. "Then get out of here because I want to die! If you won't help me, then leave!"

He grabbed my wrists, stopping me from hitting him again and watched me with hooded eyes for a long time. I couldn't read his look, but I was sure he wouldn't help me. I didn't care what he thought; I just wanted him gone from here.

A new wave of despair hit me and a sob shook my body.

Letting go of me, he retreated a step. His eyes were hard on mine. My knees buckled and I leaned back on the counter for support, taking a deep breath. This wasn't working. Micah would never understand my desperation. I thought of giving up for tonight, telling him it was a moment of weakness, and it wouldn't happen again. Then I would come back here another time.

"Okay," he finally said.

My heart skipped a beat and I gaped. "Okay?"

He raised an eyebrow. "Wasn't that what you wanted?"

"Yes, but I thought you would say no."

He sighed. "All right. We'll do it tomorrow. Let's clean this mess up and go back to bed."

"No," I said, taking a meat knife from one of the drawers. "I want to do it now, before *I* clean up this mess."

I thought he would argue again, but he ended up nodding.

He took the knife from me. "There is no way of undoing a Soul Oath. Are you sure about this?"

I held my hand out to him. "I'm sure."

He prickled my finger with the knife, drawing blood, and then pricked his. He took my palm and smeared his blood on it, then did the same with my blood and his palm. Next, he placed my bloodstained palm over his heart and his blood-stained hand on my chest.

"Ready?" he asked.

"Yes."

"By the Soul Oath, I swear to bring Nadine's family back to life once the war is over and the world is safe again. In return, she'll give me her soul."

"By the Soul Oath, I swear to give my soul to Mitrus if he brings my family back to life once the war is over and the world is safe again."

Instantly, the blood in my palm stung my skin, and I almost jerked away. Micah reached to my wrist. "Hold it there," he said.

A cold rush replaced the stinging, and it spread out of my hand and into him, just as a wave of coldness reached me, from his hand to my chest. When the energy was gone, he recoiled. I pulled my hand away and stared at it. The blood was gone.

Micah looked down at me. "Done."

17

I THOUGHT I WOULD FEEL DIFFERENT, AS IF THERE WAS AN internal clock ticking the seconds away, counting how long it would take me to die. However, nothing changed. Not really. The only two things that changed: A tense cloud began circling me, reminding me the others didn't know about the Soul Oath and I didn't want them to know, and the despair and helplessness in me changed into hope and purpose. I had a mission now, a mission that wouldn't completely absolve me of my guilt, but it would fix at least everything in the end.

After the Soul Oath, Micah helped clean the kitchen. Neither of us said a word, and I couldn't help but notice I had never seen him so tense, so unlike himself. Since he had entered the kitchen, he hadn't been cocky once, hadn't called me darling, hadn't joked or teased me.

"First things first," Keisha said, bringing my mind to the present. She stood before me in the center of the mat. Again, she wore workout clothes, and her hair was pulled into a tight braid.

When I pulled her aside this morning and asked her to train me, she had sounded ecstatic. Nevertheless, she warned me she was going to be hard on me since I didn't have years to master whatever she was going to teach me, and because of that, we met at the gym thirty minutes later.

The place really looked like a gym except for the large, oval table squeezed along a wall and a white board hanging over it. There was a mat in the center, weight lifting equipment to one side, treadmills and ellipticals to the other side, and punching dummies and weapons hung on the wall to the far back.

"We begin with stretches." Keisha showed me what to do, where to pull, and where to bend.

I was rusty but at the same time relieved to be moving. Not because I was in need of exercise—I liked being lazy—but because I needed to occupy my mind. I needed to focus on my current purpose in life.

After stretching she showed me how get in a stance to deliver punches and how to clench my fists so the punches didn't hurt as much. It was tiring. Really tiring. Yet, it still made me feel useful.

"So," I said, during one of our three-minute breaks, "how was it to find out everything I told you was real?"

She snorted. "I still think I should pinch myself sometimes. For real, though, it's ... awesome. This feels right. I mean, being here, helping, getting ready to fight. I feel like I waited my entire life to find you in NYC and be led here."

I wished I had those same feelings. "Is your family okay? I mean they didn't mind that you left them and came with us?"

Her toned shoulders squared. "I told them I needed to leave. My mother didn't take it well, but my father noticed something was up and helped me with her." She wiped her forehead with her towel. "Lady Ceris gave me an untraceable cell phone to give to them so I can call them in case they need to run. Hopefully, I'll never have to use it." Her eyes widened. "Shit. Sorry. I ... I forgot about your ..."

"It's okay," I said, offering her a tight smile. "I was the one asking. I'm glad you have a way of reaching them."

"Me too." She threw her towel back on a chair and marched to the center of the mat. "Come on. Time to get this really going."

I perked up—until she explained I was supposed to stand there, ready for a fight, with my legs apart and arms raised in front of my body. She would throw punches at me, and I was supposed to block her. Simple.

However, simple ended up in her connecting her fist with my shoulder, upper arm, and stomach at least ten times each. Each time she hit me, the air flew out of me, and I knew she wasn't even packing her entire strength in those moves. By the end of the day, I would have purple bruises all over.

She lifted her fist, and I raised my arms to block it.

"What are you doing?" Victor's irritated voice cut through my focus.

My arms went slack, and Keisha landed her fist on my chin. Pain shot through my bones, and I yelped falling on my side.

"Sorry!" Keisha said, trying to hide her laughter.

I touched my chin, afraid my jaw was broken. I knew it wasn't, but still, it hurt.

"It's not funny." I groaned. Speaking hurt too.

Victor knelt beside me. "Are you okay?" He tried to reach for me, but I stood up on my own.

Micah was in the doorway, his arms crossed and an amused grin on his face. His eyes met mine, and if I didn't know better, I would say I had imagined the events of the previous night. He was back to his old cocky self. Better this way. I didn't want anyone knowing what he had seen or what we had done.

I looked from Micah to Victor, ensnared by their beauty as always.

Victor narrowed his eyes. "What are you two doing?"

I placed a hand on my waist and stared at him. "What does it look like?"

He sighed. "Nadine ..."

"Since I have no choice but to stay here because of your situation, I want to be useful when the time comes. I asked Keisha to teach me how to fight because I'm tired of cowering and running away."

"You never cower."

"But I was never able to really fight either."

He pressed his lips into a thin line. "I'm not sure I like this."

"You don't have to like anything. All you have to do is search for your damn scepter and leave me the hell alone." I whirled on my feet and took my stance before Keisha. "Again." She looked past me with worried eyes. "You don't need their permission."

"They are my gods," she whispered. "I kinda do."

"You gotta be kidding me."

"I approve," Micah said. The satisfied tone in his voice didn't escape me.

"Stay out of this," Victor hissed.

"Why? I think Nadine is right. Since she's here and she'll probably stay until the end, she might as well be able to help."

Wait, back up. Micah thought I was right? About fighting?

Victor cursed. "You can't be serious? What if she gets hurt?"

"She has a better chance of that happening if she doesn't know how to defend herself or how to fight."

"Exactly," I said. Though that wasn't the real reason I wanted to learn how to fight.

"So, what is it?" Keisha asked, clearly afraid of over stepping *her* gods.

"Train her. It's what she wants." Micah leaned closer with his smug smile, and I tensed. "Besides, chicks fighting? It's hot."

I HAD TROUBLE SLEEPING THAT NIGHT BECAUSE EVERY GODDAMN muscle in my body hurt. When I finally fell asleep, images of Nicole, Mom, Dad, Teddie, Tommy, and Troy burning invaded my mind.

Nicole reached to me with her bony fingers. "Help," she croaked. Her eyes dulled, the skin on her face darkened until it became gray, then crumbled to dust, and she was gone with the wind.

Heart racing and shaking, I sat up on my bed, fully awake.

I tried, but it was impossible to go back to sleep. I felt restless, as if I could run a marathon, as if I *should* run a marathon to burn all my energy, to burn all my guilt.

I threw the covers away, put on jeans and a loose sweater over my sleeping shorts and tee, added another pair of thick socks to my cold feet, and sauntered out of my room.

At first I walked aimlessly. I had no idea where to go, just that I wanted to keep moving and exploring, occupying my mind so it wouldn't return to the nightmare.

I turned a corner and walked by Morgan's room. Light seeped from the open crack. Smiling, I was about to knock and pull the door fully open when I saw Morgan knelt in the middle of the room, the circle with the symbols drawn on the floor around him. By the way he was chanting, he seemed to be performing a ritual. He had his back to me, but his arms were tight around his chest, as if he was holding something there, something dear to him.

Curiosity swelled in me, but I knew better than to interrupt a ritual. He was probably praying for the gods—the ones here and the ones that had gone into hiding after Imha took over.

Thinking maybe I should ask him to let me participate sometime in one of these rituals—I could use some praying—I tiptoed away from Morgan's room.

My stomach growled. A healthy snack might be a good idea. Perhaps I would be able to go back to bed once my belly was full.

The cafeteria looked like a tiny version of a school lunchroom. A narrow room with two long tables and benches, white walls, a bar on one of them, and the kitchen behind it. However, there was no lunch lady. We had to walk around the bar and prepare our own food.

I entered the cafeteria and stopped. The kitchen's lights were on.

"Hello?" I called.

Two seconds later, Victor peered out from the window connecting the bar to the kitchen.

"Hey." He disappeared behind the wall again. "I'm making mochaccino. Want some?"

"No, thanks."

Again his pretty head peeked through the window. "No?"

I shook my head.

With a frown, he went back to his business. I sighed and joined him in the kitchen.

"I prefer black coffee," I said, opening the fridge. "But it wouldn't be wise to drink it in the middle of the night since I hope to go back to bed in a few."

He picked up his mug from the counter and looked at me. "Oh. I didn't know you liked black coffee."

For eleven months, I had liked mochaccino. But after knowing of Ceris's influence on my life, I thought it was best I stayed away from it.

I grabbed cheese, ham, lettuce, tomato, and mayo from the fridge, bread and a plate from one of the cabinets, and knife from one of the drawers, then set everything on the counter on the other side of the kitchen to work on making my sandwich—all the while aware Victor's eyes were on me.

"How are you?" he asked.

Still in pain. Frustrated. Hurt. Heartbroken. Disappointed. Did I mention hurt?

"I'm okay," I muttered.

I finished preparing my snack, then returned the items to the fridge and washed the knife, all in silence. Honestly, I didn't know what to say to him. Sometimes I thought I really had nothing to talk to him about. Why pretend to have nice conversations?

I picked up my plate with my sandwich, grabbed a bottle of water, and went back to the cafeteria. I sat down on a bench, and Victor emerged from the kitchen, his mug in hand.

Determined to keep my cool, I bit into my sandwich.

He sat down across the table from me. "How's training going?"

Well, I might believe I had nothing to talk to him about, but I wasn't about to be rude.

"It's going well." I stared at my plate. "Apparently I'm better at fighting than I thought I would be. That's a nice surprise."

He sighed. "I still think it's dangerous."

I pressed my lips together before a couple of nasty words flew out of them. He had no right to think anything about what I did or didn't do.

To keep my mouth busy, I took a big bite of my sandwich, and Victor kept staring at me. It was making me incredibly uncomfortable. Why did he have to look at me like that? His *wife* wouldn't like it.

I couldn't keep quiet anymore. I swallowed and blurted out. "How are things with Ceris?"

His eyes widened. "I never thought you would want to know about that."

"Well, not really. I'm just making conversation."

He sipped from his mug before answering. "Since you asked, things are complicated."

Shit, I didn't think he would actually answer. "Complicated might not be that bad, right? I mean, you two have been together forever. Things will work out, right?"

He narrowed his eyes at me. "Is it me, or do you sound hopeful that Ceris and I will work things out?"

"I read one of Morgan's books the other day. It said something about Ceris being your strength. Without her love, your balance won't be the same and the creed will crumble." I watched him as his gaze flickered to his mug and back to me, probably a bit embarrassed. "So, even if I wanted to, there's no chance. You two are meant to be together. Forever."

"Even if you wanted to? You don't—?"

"Victor, I told you. I *know* Ceris created my feelings for you. And yours too. There wouldn't be anything if Ceris hadn't put it there."

"You can't be sure."

"No, I can't. But I think I'm right."

"Nadine, I—"

"Please. Just let this go. It's easier this way." I held his gaze, hoping he saw in my eyes the determination I wanted to have, the determination I wanted to feel. Another topic I had read in the books came to mind, and I thought it would be a nice icebreaker. "I was planning on asking this during the next meeting, when Ceris is back, but I'm curious. In that same book, I read that this isn't the first time Imha has brought chaos to the world."

"True."

"How did you defeat her, or control her, before?"

"Well, for one, Mitrus and I were gods, with our full power. It was easier to overpower her when all of us were together and in full force. Second, Imha never did anything this big. She had never killed deities before, and she had never messed with the entire world at once. Some of her mischiefs are what humans call the Ten Plagues of Egypt, the Black Death, the eruption of Vesuvius, and any major earthquake in populated areas. But you see, always within an area."

"The Black Death could have spread to the entire world."

"It could and I think she was expecting that, but thankfully it didn't." He swirled his mug, looking at it as the liquid splashed side to side, but not really seeing it. "Anyway, we're in a different situation this time."

Not exactly what I was hoping to hear, but it made sense.

"So, no secret weapon or spell or whatever that will save us?"

He chuckled, and a pang zapped through my heart. God, even though I didn't want to feel anything for him anymore, I couldn't help but notice how handsome he was, especially when he was smiling.

"Unfortunately, no," he said, already in a more serious note.

"That's a shame."

"I agree."

Our eyes locked and images of our time together flashed in my mind. It felt like too long ago, almost as if it didn't happen at all. Like it had been a dream. A vision.

I knew he felt the same. I could see it in his sea-green eyes.

Clearing my throat, I stood. "Well, Keisha likes to start training early. I better go back to sleep."

I grabbed my plate, but Victor reached across the table and took it from me.

"I'll wash this," he said.

"I don't mind doing it."

"Me neither," he said, standing. He held his mug in one hand and my plate in the other.

"Are you sure?"

"I am."

I retreated a step. "All right, then. Thanks."

"Good night, Nadine."

"Good night."

I walked out to the hallway and inhaled deeply, as if the air inside the cafeteria had been too dense to breathe properly.

Walking back to my room, I realized Victor and I might

not have been in love as I first thought, but I could never wish anything bad for him, as a god or human. In fact, I wished him the best. I wished he would find his scepter, restore his powers, defeat Imha, and forgive Ceris.

How stupid of me. Wishing Victor would forgive Ceris when I was sure I would never forgive her myself. However, he had to spend eternity with her. I just had to endure her for a few months, or however long it took us to defeat Imha. Then Micah could honor the Soul Oath, and I would be free of this pain that scorched me on the inside.

18

———

"Wʜᴀᴛ's ᴜᴘ?" Kᴇɪsʜᴀ ᴀsᴋᴇᴅ ᴛʜᴇ ɴᴇxᴛ ᴍᴏʀɴɪɴɢ ᴅᴜʀɪɴɢ breakfast. She sat across the table from me and sipped from her coffee as if nothing was wrong with the world. "You look tired. Didn't sleep well?"

"I'm not tired," I said a little too harshly. I busied myself by stuffing my face with a forkful of boiled eggs.

What could I tell her? That I had barely slept all night because I had another nightmare with my family dying around me? That I woke up and had a conversation with Victor in the middle of the night? She didn't know the whole story of what happened a few months ago, and I wasn't in the mood to fill in the blanks for her.

"... if we have time," Keisha's voice cut through my thoughts. She frowned at me. "Did you hear what I said?"

"Yeah, something about training."

"Sorta. I was saying training will have to wait because Lady Ceris is back, and we have a meeting. Where is your head?"

I shrugged. "When did she get back?"

"About an hour ago. She called the meeting as soon as she stepped foot in the bunker."

Twenty minutes later, we huddled in a conference room. I sat in a chair near the middle of the oval table. Keisha sat at my right side; Morgan sat to my left.

Victor entered the room and our eyes met. He nodded at me then at the others.

"My Lord," Keisha and Morgan said together.

Sometimes I wondered if I should be calling them Lords and Lady too, but I always decided against it. It felt awkward treating them that way. Almost as awkward as I felt looking at Victor right now, as if we had done something wrong, like sneaked out in the middle of the night to make out.

Victor took a chair at one of the heads of the table as Micah stepped into the room.

"Morning," he said.

"Good morning, my Lord," Keisha said at the same time Morgan said, "Morning, my Lord."

I didn't say anything as his eyes breezed past me. His expression was bothered, as if he had gotten out of bed too early.

He offered me one of his smug grins, his black eyes shining with mischief. My cheeks warmed, and my heart skipped a bit. I looked down at my hands, embarrassed by the way my body reacted to a simple look.

Keisha nudged her elbow on my arm. I glanced at her, and she raised an eyebrow at me. What? She couldn't possibly have noticed that. She stole a quick peek at Micah then stared pointedly at me.

Oh, God.

Shaking my head, I sunk into my chair.

Micah took the chair at the other end of the oval table.

Edgy silence occupied the room the entire two minutes it took Ceris to burst through the doors. Her white dress and long hair trailed behind her, making her look every inch the goddess she was, but what intrigued me was her expression. Tense and worried.

As if we weren't even there, she paced.

Three minutes passed before Micah leaned back in the chair and rested his heels on the edge of the table. "Ceris, are you going to tell us what's up, or do you prefer to just leave a mark on the floor?"

Sighing, she stopped and looked at him. "I ... I've never seen anything like it. Imha and Omi declared full war. They attacked Chicago, Los Angeles, London, Paris, Rome, Dubai, Hong Kong, Shanghai, Sydney, and any other major city you can think of."

"But ..." I couldn't process it. "That's millions of people."

"Yes." She avoided my gaze. "All dead."

"By the Everlast," Morgan whispered.

"And they aren't hiding anymore," Ceris continued. "People have seen them. News shows, where they still have one, recorded them. Humans have seen them, with their powers and all. Humans are going crazy over it."

"They know about us?" Victor asked.

"Yes, and the creed fanatics are acting up too. Some are sided with Imha, and they are performing her crazy acts on their own, be it with their neighbors, at schools, at churches, and so on."

"That's horrible," Keisha whispered.

"It is," Ceris said. "And I've never seen this many demons before. There are too many, everywhere. I couldn't stay in one place long, or they would have found me."

"Okay, okay," Victor said. "We get it. It's terrible and because of that we have to do something."

"Exactly." Ceris smiled. "Which is why I looked for allies. I didn't approach them; I just watched them. I wanted to know where they are hiding, or fighting from, which ones seem to be on our side. Things like that."

"And?" Micah asked.

"I couldn't find the other gods, but I found some deities that are fighting against Imha. In particular, a forest protector, Zelen. His forest is the only one still green and abundant. He's doing a fine job, and he would be a great addition to our team."

Team? That was the first time I had heard Ceris call us a team. Thinking about it, I guess she was right, though the word still sounded foreign to my ears. Us, a team? The way everyone seemed ready to jump at each other's throats? It was almost a joke.

"Good." Morgan nodded. "A forest protector is a powerful deity. If he and his accolades join us, we'll have better chances."

Keisha spoke up. "Is it possible there's more than one hero out there? I mean, if there is, we could bring them in too."

"It is possible," Morgan answered.

"How do we find them?" Keisha asked, sounding eager.

"We don't," Ceris said. "It has to happen organically. He, or she, has to find us. Just like you found Nadine."

I stilled. Ceris had said "us," and then my name in the same reference. She would never put me, a mortal, on the same level as her and her beloveds. I watched her, but she acted normal, as if she hadn't said anything out of ordinary.

"Oh." Keisha's shoulders sagged.

"I know who else we can contact," Micah said, looking pointedly at Ceris.

She shook her head. "I told you, I don't think it's safe."

"And contacting the other gods or deities would be? They are my kin. I know them."

His kin? "Who are you talking about?" I asked.

Micah turned to me, his expression business-like. "My Death Lords."

"Who?"

"Death Lords are—" Morgan started.

"Soon, this bunker will be too small," Victor muttered, interrupting Morgan.

Micah glared at him. "I bet if I was talking about any other deity, you would give up your own bed. But my Death Lords?"

"Mitrus, it has been thirty years," Ceris started. "You don't know how they turned out."

"We have a chance here," Micah said, resolute. "Would you rather we didn't contact them and confronted Imha on our own?"

Victor held his gaze with the same venom. "I should let you confront Imha on your own. You're the one that started this whole mess!"

Micah punched the table. "I was tricked!"

"That's bullshit!" Victor stood up. "You knew exactly what you were doing. You killed me because you wanted to."

"And you killed me, bastard."

"It was self-defense," Ceris protested.

"And that excuses him, how?" Micah asked.

"You're such a hypocrite," Ceris mumbled.

Micah laughed. "And you're not? Look at all the shit you have done the past few years. You're as evil as Imha."

Ceris turned red. "Don't you dare compare me to her."

The same words she had said to me when I compared her to the goddess of chaos. Apparently she really didn't appreciate it.

"Why not? You killed, you lied, you tricked, you—"

"Mitrus, shut the fuck up!" Victor shouted.

Micah stood, ready to charge Victor or Ceris. Or maybe both. I stood too and rushed to his side, grabbing his arms and holding him back. "Stop! All of you. My goodness, you don't sound anything like powerful gods right now, jeez!"

Micah stopped pulling against me and looked at my hand around his bicep. Self-conscious, I let go of his arm and stepped back.

Morgan cleared his throat. "I hate to say this, my Lords, but Nadine is right."

"I understand what you went through, sort of," I said. "I know it's hard to get past it, but you have to. Like Victor said before, we'll only win this war if we stick together, if we stop bickering and hating each other and actually do something."

With annoyed pouts and frowns, Micah stood by my side, Victor sat down, and Ceris took a few steps back.

"We're doing something," Ceris said. "I was looking for allies, and I'll go after them as soon as we decide which ones we want on our side."

I frowned hoping she wouldn't blast me for speaking up. "I don't think allies are the most important thing right now. If the scepters aren't found, what is the point of having allies? We need Victor and Micah with their full power during this war."

"I know," Ceris said. "But we can't find the scepters, and I don't know where else to look for them. I would rather do something useful, like gathering allies, than sit here and wait to find out where the scepters are."

I nodded. "I agree, but I feel like you're wasting all your energy on allies. It should be at least fifty-fifty. Look for scepters while trying to contact allies."

Ceris crossed her arms. "I am the only one who can come and go. I am powerful, but I still can't be in two places at once."

"I know. I know. And that's why I think you should take us with you next time."

"What?" Victor and Micah said together, the same astonished tone in their voices.

I didn't let their stances intimidate me, though. "Ceris can drop us somewhere. We can look for the scepters while she goes and tries to contact whoever she wants to, and a few hours later she comes to pick us up."

"And what if something happens while I am away? What if demons attack you?"

I smiled. "Then we fight."

I GRABBED A ONE-AND-A-HALF SWORD FROM THE WALL AND tested its weight in my hand. When we moved on to train with wooden swords, Keisha gave me a full lecture on them. One-hand swords were used with shields or another one-hand sword. Two-hand swords were long and meant to be used alone, with both hands around the hilt. A one-and-a-half sword had a hilt and blade long enough to be used alone, or with a shield or other sword. I liked these because they weren't so short I needed another weapon, but they also weren't too long and heavy for someone of my height and weight.

"Darling, you're crazy."

Not in the mood to argue, I kept my back to him and swung the sword. It was on the heavy side, but I needed to get used to it.

"You're going to ignore me," Micah said, sounding closer. On purpose I turned around, swinging my sword at chest level. He jumped back. "Whoa there, darling. Don't damage the goods you love so much."

I rolled my eyes. "Can you be a little less cocky?"

His smug grin spread over his lip. "Why would I? It's not like I'm lying."

Seriously?

I took a step back and focused on testing the sword. In the end, this one was too heavy. I reached for another one, but Micah was faster. He appeared before me with a one-and-a-half sword made with a darker metal that he had taken from the other side of the wall. I would probably have skipped it, but well, he had lived for too many years and probably understood swords.

He extended it to me, and I reached for it. My hand ended up closing over his because he didn't let go of it.

Attracted by a force stronger than me, my eyes met his. The air in my lungs whooshed out. I could jump into those endless black pools and live there, lost forever.

Then cold bit my palm, and my energy slipped away. I narrowed my eyes at him. He was shaking. Slightly, but he was shaking.

Letting go of the sword, I stepped into him and cupped his cheeks.

The cold bit my skin again, but I welcomed it. My healing

kicked in, and the extra energy transferred from me to Micah. With eyes closed, he tilted his head back, relishing in what I believed was a nice sensation.

I didn't think he noticed when he raised his left arm and clasped my wrist. In the same unconscious manner, he put his right arm, the one holding the sword, around me, pulling me closer.

The energy intake reduced until I knew he was fully healed. I let my free hand fall to my side, but Micah held the other one to his cheek. He straightened, took a deep breath, and with eyes still closed, he leaned into me, resting his forehead to mine.

"Thank you," he whispered.

His scent washed over me, and I inhaled deeply welcoming the comfort it brought me.

"Why didn't you ask for it?"

His eyes fluttered open. "You're not an object to be used like that."

"But that's the only reason I am here."

With his jaw set, Micah let go of me and retreated a step.

What was it with him? A few months ago, I would have accused Victor of having insane mood swings, but he was actually behaving lately. Who inherited the mood swings? Micah. He was driving me insane.

With every intention of being upset with him for another week, I took the sword from his hand. Instantly my frustration faded away. "It's light. I mean, as light as a sword can be."

"Test it."

I thrust it into the air, amazed at how perfect it was. "I love it."

"I knew you would." I lifted my eyes to his. He had a half-smug grin on, and even like that, my heart skipped a beat. "I still can't believe Ceris is letting you come with us."

Of course he would kill the mood.

My sword and arm froze mid-swing, and I gaped at him. "Wait a minute. You're the one who supported me when I wanted to learn how to fight."

Micah took two giant steps and halted right in my face, looking into my eyes. "It is one thing to know you can defend yourself if danger comes to you, but it's another thing to go looking for it."

"Oh, so now you think I'll be a problem?"

He groaned. "I don't want to see you risking your life."

I refrained from snorting. "My life already has a timer. I don't care about the rest."

"But I—"

"Hey, there you are," Keisha said, stepping into the gym. Micah stepped back and looked at my feet. Keisha looked from me to him and back to me. "Oh, sorry, my Lord." She bowed to him. Micah looked annoyed by the gesture. "Am I interrupting something?"

"No," he snapped. Without looking back, he marched out of the room.

Keisha raised an eyebrow at me. "What was that about?"

I focused on the sword in my hand. "Nothing."

"Okay." She didn't sound convinced, but let it go. She extended a large brown bag to me. "Well, then I brought you these."

I stared at it suspiciously. "And what would that be?"

She dropped the bag on the floor and showed me she had another for herself. "Gifts from Lady Ceris."

19

———

Following her weird protocol, Ceris transported us to several places before arriving in the right location. In the first place, coincidently a forest, she pointed to a tree where Rok was perched on a low branch.

"The trunk is hollow. Leave your snow stuff there," she said, shrugging out of her coat.

I slipped my coat off and looked down at my clothes. I felt badass in the armor Ceris had gotten for us. Suede pants with patches of intricate leather on the sides, a white fitted thermal tee, a leather vest with the same intricate pattern, and a belt to hang our weapons. Everything in beige, even the combat boots, and everything with some kind of endurance spell, also supplied by Ceris. The guys wore similar clothing, and I had to restrain myself from peeking at Micah and Victor every few seconds because, good Lord, they looked incredible in those tight tees and vests. And totally badass with their swords hanging off their belts.

Morgan seemed uncomfortable in those clothes. "I would rather have my own shirt on," he said, tugging the thermal.

Micah caught my coat from me, his eyes fixed on mine. "I knew you would look hot when ready for battle, but damn, darling, I wasn't ready for this."

Heat surged up my cheeks, and I averted my eyes. Why did he have to do this? First, he acted like a jerk and pushed me away, and now he was sweet-talking me. It didn't work that way.

We stashed our coats, gloves, and beanies in the appointed place, then Ceris held our hands and let her magic envelope us. The air shimmered around us making my skin tingle. In one quick blink we were somewhere else.

Four or five stops later, we stood at the border of Zelen's forest.

I pointed the flashlight I was holding around us, and my mouth fell open. Green. Green everywhere. Tall, rich trees. Thick grass and bushes. And flowers. Mainly yellow and orange, but I had never seen anything so bright, so alive.

I knelt beside a flower bush and smelled them. Such a sweet scent.

"Come on," Ceris said. "The pylon is a little over two miles from here."

In the end, the forest that Zelen protected was also where a sacred pylon was hidden—the Antar Pylon, a place of power. I wondered if Ceris had purposely chosen this place for our team's first outing together since here we wouldn't need to divide into groups.

Micah frowned. "Why didn't you take us there?"

"Because I can't," Ceris answered. "The pylon is protected by a shield. We'll need to walk from here."

Imha's place had a shield, our shelter had a shield ... everything in their world had a protection cast around it. I thought it was a little odd because I always thought I would see the shield, feel it, but it was invisible to me.

We marched. Ceris took the lead with Victor by her side. Keisha walked right behind them, then Micah and me, and Morgan was way in the back.

Rok flew past us and disappeared between heavy trees.

"What is he doing?" I asked.

"He's keeping an eye on things," Micah said. "If anything looks strange, he'll let me know."

He was close, too close. If he took half a step to his left, his arm would brush against mine, and that thought alone brought a wave of heat to my core.

As usual, I tried focusing on something else, something of importance to our mission, to our war, because there was no point in thinking of him like that. He was a god, and I was a human doomed to die. There was no future with us. Why bother enjoying these feelings?

"So. About the Death Lords," I said, needing another topic to occupy my mind.

He raised an eyebrow at me. "What about them?"

"I have no idea who they are or what they do."

"Well, they are sort of like me. Think of them as less powerful versions of me. And less handsome too." He winked and I shook my head. "They are like my employees. Deities that help me bring souls to the underworld."

"Like reapers?"

"Sorta. Each culture has their own idea of reapers. The Death Lords can only take lives; they can't give life back like me. I can't ... couldn't do it all alone. It's a big world and too many people die at the same time." A knot appeared between his brows. "I wonder how they do it now, with so many deaths."

"How many are there?"

"Not as many as I would like. Only eight."

"Still, that's a lot."

"Yes. And they could be good allies in this war."

"I noticed you discussed this with Ceris at the meeting. Why is she opposed to contacting them?"

"She thinks I can't be trusted, so, in turn, she thinks even less of them."

"That's not fair."

He frowned but didn't say anything. I would have given my left pinky nail to find out what was on his mind. I wanted to help him, to help release whatever pressure he felt. And there my mind went, back to issues I shouldn't think about, to the feelings I shouldn't feel. I berated myself and clamped my mouth shut.

A couple of minutes passed in silence as we marched through the forest. I was impressed by the green around us. I had never seen anything like it.

An orange flower appeared in my line of sight. I almost tripped from the surprise, and my heart hammered when I took it from Micah. Hadn't I just decided that I wouldn't fall for this? For him?

"I wish you could have seen how it was before," he said, causing my heart to skip a couple of beats. "The blue sky, the clean oceans, the colorful birds. You would have loved it."

Oh God, it was impossible. There was no way I could fight this, not now.

Closing my eyes, I smelled the flower and tried to picture the blue sky and the birds.

Morgan cursed under his breath, and I opened my eyes. He tugged on his shirt. "Damn it. This thing is suffocating me, you know?" He took a deep breath and slowed his steps. "I guess I don't have a choice but to wear this. Or take this shirt off?" He wiggled his eyebrows at me.

I laughed and, from over Morgan's shoulder, Micah smiled.

My heart tugged. Why did he have this effect on me? Why did I let him have this effect on me?

I shook my head and focused on Morgan's joke. "No, thanks."

We kept our march weaving through thick trees and bushes, and Morgan kept complaining, though he had stopped tugging on his shirt. His hand rested over a side pocket on his belt. Every few seconds his fingers would tighten around whatever was there, as if he was making sure it hadn't gone anywhere.

It was odd, but before I could mull over it the trees opened to a stone path, which lead to a clearing. Everyone stopped and gawked.

Ceris smiled. "Behold, the Antar Pylon."

The pylon, a stone column over two hundred feet tall with a square base that thinned to a pointy tip, sat in the middle of the large clearing, illuminating everything around us with its eerie white glow. The stone path continued, adorned by bushes of orange and yellow flowers, until it met other paths that came from all directions, forming a square area around the pylon.

"Do you feel anything?" Victor asked. When Ceris shook her head, he turned to the others. "Mitrus? Morgan?"

Ceris laughed, sounding annoyed. "If I don't feel it, you think they will?"

Victor shrugged. "Just making sure."

I pushed past them, pointing to the pylon. "Can anyone see that?"

Keisha rolled her eyes. "Duh. I think everyone sees the pylon."

"No," I said. "Not the pylon. The silver symbol flashing over the biggest stone in its base."

Ceris turned big eyes at me. "You can see it?"

"Yes."

Morgan walked to us and squinted at the base of the pylon. "I can't see it."

"I don't think any of us can see it," Victor said.

"Only Nadine," Micah said, sounding rather proud. Proud of what?

"And me," Ceris said, her tone indicating she was the queen of this parade.

Ignoring her condescending remark, I asked, "What does it mean?"

The silver symbol was almost imperceptible in the pylon's white glow. Wavy lines formed small drop-like shapes, contained in a circle.

She walked toward it. "It's Izaera's symbol."

"Izaera?"

"The goddess of nature and seasons," Victor said, staring at the pylon.

Morgan stopped at the edge of the path and turned to us. "How can she see it and we can't?"

Ceris eyed me, her look appraising. "I don't know. However, Izaera should be near."

"Near as in here?" I asked, and Ceris nodded. "But no sign of the scepters?" This time she shook her head.

We approached the center of the clearing. A step from the center square, a strong wind blew us back, and a flash of light blinded us. I reached for my sword but froze when the light faded.

An ancient-looking man wearing brown pants and a tunic while holding a branch-like staff stood before the pylon. His brittle, long white hair and beard looked like they were going to fall out at any moment because he had to be over a hundred years old.

Looking at Ceris, the man bowed. "My Lady," he said, surprising me with his strong voice. "I wasn't expecting you." His canny eyes scanned us, taking us in one by one. "Or your friends."

Ceris put her hand out, pointing at our swords. Victor and Micah were the first to put them away. I hesitated but followed their lead.

"Zelen." Ceris took a few steps in his direction. "I'm glad to see you are well."

"As well as one can be in such times," Zelen said. "My Lady, a long time ago I would have called my nymphs and prepared a banquet for your visit. But times have changed. As much as I respect and admire you, I need to ask you to leave."

"I know my presence brings danger to your forest, but I need to talk to you. It'll take just a minute."

He didn't look satisfied, but nodded. "You have one minute."

"You don't remember them as they are now, but here are Levi and Mitrus." She gestured to Victor and Micah.

Zelen's brown eyes bugged. "It can't be."

"It can," Victor spoke up. "Mitrus and I are trapped in human bodies due to the evil machinations of Imha and Omi. We plan on fighting against them, and we need all the help we can get."

Zelen looked Victor and Micah up and down. "You can't fight them in human bodies."

"We're working on that," Micah said.

The forest protector shook his head. "I don't understand."

"That doesn't matter right now," Ceris said. "I have seen you fight against Imha's powers and her demons. I know you want her chaos gone, as we do."

"All the help you can get, huh?" His gaze shifted from Morgan, to Keisha, to me. "A priest and hm, a hero, right? But I don't know who the third one is."

Ceris waved me off, as usual. "She isn't important."

Really? Ha. I so wanted to walk out on them now. I would love to see her come to me and beg for my help when Victor was in pain.

"But she is," Zelen said, his eyes still on me. "Her aura is different and powerful."

It wasn't the first time I had heard that, and I got the impression it wouldn't be the last. I just wanted to know what it meant. I made a mental note to ask about it later.

"She was blessed with the Destiny Gift a while back," Micah explained. "It's gone now, but she *is* important." He glared at Ceris, and she only shrugged.

"Interesting," Zelen muttered. Behind him, the symbol shone brighter for a few seconds. Zelen followed my gaze before returning his eyes to mine. "You can see it." I nodded. "Very interesting."

Ceris stepped in front of me, cutting the forest protector from my line of sight. "Zelen, can we count on you?"

The old man sighed. "My Lady, an open war isn't my style. I would rather fight my own battles alone with my nymphs."

"But Imha will destroy your forest."

Defiance flashed in Zelen's eyes. "Let her come, and we shall see about that."

A tingle ran down my arms, and I turned to my right. Something reddish flashed between the trees. I opened my mouth to say something, but Rok sprung from between the branches on my left, cawing as if his lungs would explode.

Beside me, Micah tensed. "Demons."

20

Swords drawn, we formed a small circle beside the pylon facing the trees.

Between Ceris and Keisha, Zelen's tiny figure grew a few inches, his brown eyes becoming golden with pure rage.

"It's your fault!" he shouted.

"We weren't followed," Ceris assured him. "You have my word."

He narrowed his eyes at her but didn't say anything. He tapped the end of his staff on the grass three times. A second later, a dozen nymphs sprouted from the ground around us. Like the ones I had seen before in a vision, they were beautiful, delicate, with skimpy dresses covering little of their pale skin, and long colorful hair adorned by flowers.

They positioned themselves between the trees and us.

"The demons are close," Morgan whispered on my left.

Micah was on my right, one sword in each hand. He looked badass, except for the quick glances he stole at me. His black eyes shone with worry.

"I'll be fine," I said in a low tone.

His jaw flexed. "I'll believe it once we're out of here."

Morgan's movement caught my attention. He switched his sword to his right hand, and he delved his left hand in the side pocket of his belt. When he pulled the Crimson Dagger from there, I gasped.

"You still have that thing?" I asked, not hiding the incredulity from my voice.

Instead of answering me, he said, "They are here."

Turning to face us, half of the nymphs wiggled their bodies in odd ways. Their skin shifted from whitish to grayish, their hair lost its volume and color, becoming dull and black. Their nails and teeth elongated, looking like razors.

"By the Everlast," Zelen whispered.

They lunged at us.

The other six nymphs stood frozen in their places, apparently shocked to see their sisters becoming demons right in front of their eyes.

One of the nymphs-turned-demon had its claws aimed at me. Swallowing the memory that it had been a nymph a few seconds ago, I raised my sword, ready to strike. However, Micah stepped in front of me and slashed its chest. It jerked a little, trying to hit him, but he ducked and swung his sword across its ankles. It fell back and thrashed for a few seconds, then stopped, its once bright eyes becoming a sickening glossed white.

"What the hell was that?" I asked, spitting my words with frustration.

"A demon," Micah said, knowing too well that wasn't what I meant.

I gripped the hilt of my sword tight. "I can take care of myself."

He loomed over me, the heat of his body brushing against me. "I know that."

"Do you?"

"Hey, you two." Keisha bumped into me before piercing her sword through a nymph-demon's chest. She pulled her sword out, and the body dropped to the ground. She turned to us, one hand on her hips. "This isn't the time to bicker like an old married couple."

"Excuse me?" I asked at the same time Micah said, "What?"

With Victor and Zelen, Ceris approached us. "We need to go."

I looked around. Everyone seemed okay. Victor cleaned his sword on his pants, Morgan put the Crimson Dagger back into his pocket—I made a mental note to talk to him later—Keisha seemed to be still ready for battle, Micah stood beside me, his tension making me tense. Zelen watched his dead nymph-demons with such desolation in his eyes. The other nymphs had gotten together in a circle, hand in hand, chanting in a language I didn't understand.

Without a word Zelen approached them, breaking their circle, and headed toward the body of a non-demon nymph lying on the grass.

"One of them jumped onto her first," Keisha said. "I killed the demon, but I was too late."

I put a hand on her arm. "You did what you could."

Morgan stiffened, Micah sprung in front of me, and Ceris cursed.

"What?" Victor asked.

"More are coming," Zelen said, his tone dejected.

Near the trees the grass became a dark green, then brown, and finally black. Next, the bordering trees were affected, their trunks shrinking, the leaves turning brown and falling. Slowly, the poison spread toward the center. It had advanced three feet when demons appeared among the trees. Many demons—Ornek and Arak—stared at us as if we were the banquet they were promised after a week of starvation.

We huddled in a circle, weapons in hand. Zelen looked pained, as if the death of his forest physically hurt him. Maybe it did.

As slowly as the poison that was killing the grass and the beautiful bushes along the paths, the demons stepped into the clearing.

"We need to get out of here," Ceris said in a low voice. "We need to get to the edge of the shield. Unless you can drop it right now."

"I can't," Zelen answered. I didn't dare glance back at them with all these demons advancing on us. "I would need spell ingredients I don't carry with me."

"All right," Ceris said. "Once they attack, we advance through the forest. Please, stick together."

The poison reached halfway, and the demons were two feet behind it. My grip tightened on the hilt of my sword.

Suddenly green vines surged from the ground, tall and thick, twisting around the demons, trapping their arms and legs, immobilizing them.

"It won't hold them for long," a serene voice said from behind me.

We all turned and in the center of our circle a woman, wearing a white dress similar to Ceris, stood tall. Her skin was almost as dark as Keisha's was, her hair was reddish brown like the ground, and her eyes were a deep green like leaves. In her right hand, she held a scepter topped by a green orb.

"Izaera," Ceris whispered.

She stepped forward, and both women embraced in a brief but tight hug.

Izaera rested her hand on Ceris's cheek. "It's good to see you, my sister. But you and your friends need to go. My magic won't hold them for long."

Ceris grabbed her hand, enclosing it between hers. "Come with us." Izaera looked divided. "Please, sister. It hurts me to say it, but this place is no more. Come with us."

She nodded, and then turned her back to us. She approached the pylon and the silver symbol on the stone with the orb of her scepter. Green light shone from it and seeped into the orb causing it to shine even brighter. Something silver swirled inside it, and I leaned forward, trying to get a better look.

"We gotta go," Victor said, watching the demons as they fought against the vines. Some had broken half-free already.

Izaera pulled the scepter away from the pylon, and its glow faded, leaving only dull white stones behind. We turned on our flashlights.

"Done." She turned to the trees pointing her scepter to the demons in front of her. Instantly the vines pulled them to the side, and more vines appeared, creating a wall that flanked the path she had just opened. "Hurry," she said, gesturing to the path.

Morgan was the first to run through, followed by Keisha, Ceris, and Victor. Micah and I were next, with Zelen and Izaera right behind us, then the nymphs. Halfway down the path, the growl of demons and the snapping of vines told me we needed to rush.

A claw broke through the wall of vines and scratched my upper arm.

"Ow," I muttered. I raised my sword, but Micah was faster. His blade sliced through the air, taking the demon's arm with the cut—déjà vu. The limb landed on the ground with a pool of blood.

He grabbed my hand and pulled me forward. "How bad is it?" He stole a quick glance at the wound.

"Not too bad," I said, peeking at it. Three red lines with a little blood trickling from it. "Just scratches."

We reached the trees and increased our speed. The demons were breaking free.

Weaving through the dying trees, I tripped and stumbled, my steps stalled by grabbing roots and my legs snagged on branches.

Fifteen minutes of running—my heart pounded in my chest—and growls echoed from directly behind us.

"We're almost there!" Ceris cried from the front of the group.

Almost there was relative. It could be ten steps; it could be another ten minutes. Honestly, I didn't think we had that long before they caught up with us.

The trees and shrubbery thinned out as we approached the edge of the protective shield, making it easier to maneuver through the woods. My footfalls fell deftly now.

A growl of a demon sounded to my left. Micah, still holding my hand, yanked me out of the way, and then kicked the demon. He was about to swing his sword at it, but Izaera used her powers. Vines twined around the demon's arms, legs, and torso, and tugged it high into a tree, where it dangled like a wild beast caught in a hunter's trap.

"There's no time," Izaera whispered.

"What?" I asked, confused.

I glanced back. She stopped and pointed her scepter at

the demons charging her. More walls of vines surged, blocking their way, but it was easy to see that it wouldn't hold them for long.

She moved again but not as fast as before. What was she doing?

Micah's grip tightened around my hand. "By the Everlast." He cursed under his breath.

I looked at him. "What?"

"Omi," he said, glancing back.

Ceris and Morgan had already slowed their steps and were watching behind us.

Big trees fell to the side as if they weighed as much as each of their leaves, opening a path covered in fire.

Omi sauntered over it with a big smile on his drunken face. "By the Everlast, look what we've got here."

Micah pushed me behind him, and Victor came to stand beside him. I was towered by giants, but most of all, I felt cheated. Why did they feel the need to protect me? I could take care of myself.

Ceris extended her hand, and her scepter appeared on her palm. She stood beside Izaera and Zelen, with Keisha behind them. Morgan seemed undecided if he should stay by Keisha or by Micah and Victor.

"You destroyed my forest, Omi," Izaera said, her voice much more confident than before.

He scoffed. "Who cares about a forest? Not interesting. Now, interesting are those two men in front of Nadine. Their auras are quite interesting." I watched him through the small space between Victor's and Micah's arms. His gaze found mine, and I gasped as goose bumps crawled up my arms. His eerie smile widened. "Hello there, Nadine. I missed you. Oh, and I miss your family too."

Rage bubbled in the pit of my stomach, surging up like a volcano and transforming my rage into stamina. I pushed Micah and Victor aside and marched forward with every intention of slashing Omi's throat with my sword. Big hands clasped around my arms and held me back.

"Let me go!" I hissed.

"That's what he wants," Micah whispered, holding my left arm. "To provoke you and have you go to him."

I jerked against his hold. "It's working."

"Don't let it work," Victor said, his grip firm around my right arm.

Omi chuckled. "Oh, Nadine, won't you introduce me to your friends?"

In his dreams. Even then, he would have a hard time getting any answers from me.

"You're wasting your time, Omi," Ceris spoke.

His eyes turned to Ceris, a wicked shine in them. "Ceris, my dear sister. I enjoyed our cat and mouse game. It has been fun, really, but everything has a limit. Time to surrender."

Ceris let out one of her witch-like laughs. "Do you really know me so little?"

Narrowing his eyes, Omi tilted his head. "Not really."

He raised his hands to the sky, and Akuma flew down, at the same time more Arak and Ornek popped out from behind trees.

"Run!" Ceris said. Her scepter was in her hand, and she produced a shield between Omi and us. Then she turned and darted with us. "Only a few more yards. Go!"

The shield detained Omi and the demons for a couple of minutes.

I looked up in time to see one of the winged demons descending with eyes and claws trained on me. I waited until it was closer, then jumped to the side, and slashed its wing with my sword. The demon let out an agonizing shriek, then turned to me, its claws ready once more. It swiped, and I parried it drawing its gooey blood. It came at me again, and I ducked stepping around it and slashing its side. The creature cried, spitting rage. I emerged behind it, and before it realized where I was, I buried my sword in its chest.

It cried and thrashed. When I pulled my sword out, it collapsed face-first to the ground.

Micah was right by my side, fighting two demons; Victor was by Micah's side, fighting another two. Keisha was a few feet farther, and she had three demons sweating. Morgan had the Crimson Dagger, and it was all he could do to defend himself. Zelen fought one demon with his staff. For an old man, he was quite agile. Izaera conjured more vines while throwing green bolts that rendered demons immobile. Ceris created shields to detain the demons and threw pink energy balls at them.

A guttural growl sounded from behind me. I sidestepped as the dumb creature rushed me, catching it with my blade across the abdomen. It fell on its knees before slumping to the side—dead in the withering grass. My heart thundered in my chest, and I couldn't think about what my fate would have been had I not heard its growl.

Another Ornek announced its arrival, its growl raised the hair on my neck. It swung its claw at my face, and I jumped back in time, feeling the swoosh of its talons against my cheeks. My heart pounded, and I stepped into it feigning right. The creature fell for it, and I let my sword drop on its side. It shrieked, trying to claw me as it collapsed on its knees. With a growl of my own, I raised my sword and pierced its back.

I pulled my sword back, nausea swirling in my stomach. I wasn't one to feel sick easily, but I was deliberately killing—demons, yes, but killing nonetheless.

I put a hand over my stomach but had to focus back on the fight when an Arak and an Ornek charged me.

Coordinating their attacks, the Arak parried my blow, and the Ornek caught my wrist. It twisted my arm in hopes I would let go of my sword. I groaned with the pain. The Arak clawed my shoulder, and it was about to do it again when I decided to make it or break it. I bent my knees and let my whole weight pull me down, bringing the demon with me. Holding the demon's arm, I fell on my back and pushed it over me with my legs. It toppled over the Arak, and both tangled to the ground. Ignoring the pains and aches, I jumped up and pierced my sword through both demons. The sounds of cutting flesh and the nasty smell of their gooey blood made me sick, but I pushed all I could, making sure both were dead.

"Wow, darling, that was impressive," Micah said. I pulled my sword from the corpses and looked up. He winked before slashing the throat of the demon he fought. Then he turned to me with one of his cocky smiles. "And hot too."

I rolled my eyes. Great timing.

The ground shook as a loud boom echoed through the forest. Micah gripped my elbow, and we used each other to stay upright.

I looked around.

Ceris produced a large shield around us, and Omi cast a huge, heavy bolt. He threw it at the shield. It hit and broke the barrier, causing a similar boom that vibrated through the air and the ground.

"Keep moving," Victor said, pushing through the bodies on the ground, toward the border of Zelen's shield.

We moved, fighting the few demons that reached us around the shield. A new boom resonated through the air every few seconds, almost sending us to the ground.

"Here," Zelen said. He was a few feet in front of us. "The shield ends here."

Micah grabbed my hand again and pulled me forward, killing demons that stepped in our way as if he were a machine. Victor had an arm around Morgan's waist, hauling the priest to Zelen.

Izaera was right behind us. "Ceris!" she yelled. "Come, sister." She raised her scepter and vines shot out from the dying grass and wrapped around Omi. "Now!"

Ceris raised one last shield, and then made a mad dash. Her steps dragged as if she were running in slow motion. At the barrier, Victor waited for her, his hand extended.

"Come on," he said. I could hear the urgent tone in his voice, and it tugged at my heart, almost like a jealous pang. He still loved her. "Come on."

We waited with him, hands already clasped.

"Izaera," Zelen said. "You can take them out of here."

She shook her head. "I don't know where to and only the Fates know how long it would take to find her again."

Zelen opened his mouth, but he was interrupted.

"Aaaahhhh!" Omi broke free. Without wasting a second, he destroyed the shield with one of his bolts. The fire was back, stronger and bigger, and more demons made their way out of the trees.

Keeping one foot on the other side of the barrier, Victor reached for Ceris. When her fingers brushed his, he clasped his hand around her wrist and pulled her to him. She bumped into him, knocking them back, just outside the barrier. His arms tightened around her.

Behind them, a sea of red bolts flew toward us.

"Oh, God," I whispered.

"Ceris, now!" Izaera shouted.

Ceris closed her hands over ours and transported us to safety.

21

WINCING, I OPENED ONE OF THE CABINETS AND GRABBED A bottle of Tylenol. I ached all over. Thankfully I had only a few scratches and exhaustion, which was better than Morgan and the open gash across his stomach. After cleaning the wound as best as he could, Victor stitched the cut. One of the perks of being a former medical resident.

Victor also checked on Keisha, but like me, she only had scratches. He tried looking me over, but I knew enough about cleaning scratches to do it on my own. Now, I needed painkillers. Lots of them.

I closed the cabinet, and the mirror on it showed Ceris behind me standing under the doorframe of one of the partitions in the infirmary, her hair tangled, her dress stained with blood and dirt, her expression tired.

I unscrewed the cap, took out three pills, put them in my mouth, and swallowed them.

Sighing, I turned and leaned against the counter, crossing my arms. "How are the others?"

"Morgan will be fine," she said. "It'll take him a while to

heal, but he'll survive. Keisha is camping in his bedroom tonight, to keep an eye on him."

"What about Izaera and Zelen?"

"They are in shock, to say the least. They lost their forest and were forced into hiding. However, Zelen seems worse since he had no idea his nymphs had been corrupted."

I still wondered about how that happened. "That was a shock to all of us."

"It was."

I hated seeing this side of her. Caring, compassionate, a true mother and guide to her herd. It made the rage I felt over all she had done to me seem unreal, misdirected. She had been evil, hadn't she?

"Is there anything I can help you with?"

Her brows slammed down. "Not really."

"I should get some rest then," I said, walking toward the door.

She stepped to the side, allowing me to pass. "Yes, you should. Everyone is in need of rest right now."

I walked out, then one of my mental notes prickled in my mind and I couldn't ignore it.

I stopped and turned, staring into her eyes. "Earlier today, Zelen mentioned I was different, that my aura is powerful but not strong." How could something be powerful but not strong? "Imha said the same thing when I was with her, and the Fates said it too before. What does that mean?"

She held my gaze, and I wondered if she would lie to me. "I don't know." Even though I wanted to believe she was lying, I could see in her eyes that she wasn't. "I honestly don't know. Yes, you're different. I can feel it too, but I don't know what you are."

"But I am something?"

"I don't know."

Great. More doubts and worries for me. I nodded and resumed my walk, thinking of what I could be. Apparently, not a hero, not a priest, not the vision girl.

"Nadine." Once more, I turned and looked at her. "I'm sorry. For your family. I'm really sorry about that."

My family. I tried not to think of them much. I tried to keep those feelings and memories bottled in a dark corner of my mind, where I wouldn't stumble on them. However, when someone mentioned my family, the memories came rushing back to me.

Tears burned my eyes, and I blinked so I wouldn't cry in front of her. "Me too," I whispered.

***

SINCE OUR RETURN FROM THE FOREST, ONE THOUGHT HAD clouded my mind. So, after grabbing the Tylenol and bumping into Ceris, I went looking for Micah.

His bedroom door was closed. I knocked, hoping he was here so I wouldn't have to search for him all over the shelter.

I raised my hand to knock again and the door opened.

Micah stood beside the half-open door, his hair unruly, his dark eyes curious, and his chest naked.

My throat felt dry, and my heart skipped a beat.

My gaze rummaged his fine torso. God, he was more than fine. The urge to graze my nails over the hard muscles of his chest and abdomen rushed through me, bringing a heat wave with it.

His muscles weren't everything though. His tattoos drew me in too. He had a coiled snake on his left shoulder, four lines of Hebrew writing over his chest, and tribal drawings to the side of his abdomen, which spread onto his back.

To complete the package, he wore his mother's necklace, which showed me that, even after finding out he was a god and his human parents had been nothing but vessels, he cared. It was much harder to stay immune to him and his charm when I knew he cared.

"Darling," he said, breaking my daze. The heat in my body shifted to my cheeks when I forced my eyes to meet his. He offered me one of his devilish grins. "To what do I owe such a visit?"

"Uh," I muttered, because I had completely forgotten what I had come here for. That was what I got for seeing him only in his dark jeans.

He chuckled and the heat on my cheeks became molten lava. "Cat got your tongue, darling? Or was it something else?" He raised one of eyebrows.

I could smack that cocky expression from his face. Focusing on that, I took a deep breath and finally spoke up. "I want to ask you a question about the Soul Oath."

His expression hardened. After glancing to the sides of the corridor, he stepped aside. "Come in."

I entered his room and was a little disappointed to find it was exactly like mine, exactly like all the rooms here. For some reason, I expected Micah to have a nice place, with a big bed, a comfy couch, fluffy rugs, and posters of Harleys and sport cars and naked women on the walls.

Crossing his arms, he leaned against the closed door. I almost drooled again because, hmm, that only made the muscles on his chest and arms and shoulders tauter.

"What is it?" he asked.

I shook my head, trying to clear my thoughts. "While we

were fighting in the forest, I worried about dying. I mean, what if I die before you and I can honor the Soul Oath? What if I'm killed during one of our battles during the war? What will happen then? I'll just die, and my family will stay in the underworld?"

"Your soul is mine regardless of how and when you die. If you die tomorrow ..." He paused, his expression pained. "The Soul Oath will be honored even if you die tomorrow. Your soul will be mine, and I'll bring back your family once the war is over."

Relief filled me. "Thank God. That was all I needed to know." I stepped toward the door, toward him, but he didn't move. His eyes were hard on me, and I felt my cheeks warming again. "I'll leave you be now," I said. He didn't move though, and he didn't stop staring at me. The heat spread from my cheeks to my body, even though I couldn't tell if he was staring at me because he was mad or because of some other reason. "Micah, let me open the door, please."

I counted the seconds, until he finally moved aside and opened the door for me. "Good night, Nadine," he said, his voice devoid of emotion.

"Good night," I whispered as I walked past him, feeling the weight of his gaze on me.

As soon as I stepped out, he closed the door, and I hurried back to my bedroom.

THE NIGHT WAS HORRIBLE.

The same nightmare with my family populated my mind, and when I tried to focus on something else and fall back asleep, I would remember what happened in the forest. The nymphs turning into demons, more demons surrounding us, Omi provoking me, the fight, the claws, the blood, the gore. I didn't know how I went through all that without breaking down because right now all I wanted to do was hold Pinky and hide under my pillow.

To calm my mind, I hummed a lullaby. It did relax me, but it also brought tears to my eyes. My pillow had a wet blotch when I finally drifted to sleep again.

"Hey, Nad." Someone shook my shoulder, the one with the bandage.

"Ow," I complained, recoiling farther into the bed. Yawning, I opened my eyes. "Hey, Keisha."

"Morning, sleeping beauty. Lady Ceris is calling everyone for a meeting."

"Now?"

She smiled. "It's almost noon!"

Really? Well, at least I did get some sleep. After too many nights dealing with nightmares, sleeping in late was a nice change.

I sat up. "Okay, okay. I'll be there in about ... thirty minutes."

"Lady Ceris said now."

"I need a shower, clean clothes, and food. Only then will I be able to sit through a meeting."

"Suit yourself." Keisha marched to the door. She paused, her hand over the knob. "You did well yesterday, you know." I raised my eyebrows. Was she talking to me? "I mean it. You fought well, and you didn't give in when Omi tried to bait you."

The memory of Omi provoking me came back to my mind, bringing rage and hatred with it.

"Oh, I wanted to smack that smirk from his face."

"I know you did. But you didn't." She tilted her head. "I confess I was a little skeptical when we began training because you were a novice, but now I'm happy you asked me."

"Me too," I whispered.

She nodded and left my room. I reluctantly jumped out of bed and got ready for said meeting. Shower; put on jeans, red sweater, black boots; stop by the cafeteria; make a sandwich and black coffee; eat and drink while walking to the conference room.

Twenty-seven minutes later, I entered the conference room holding half a sandwich and a coffee mug.

Keisha, Victor, and Micah sat in the same places as last time, and Zelen took the seat Morgan had taken before.

I sat on my chair. "Where are Ceris and Izaera?"

Victor rested his elbows on the table and clasped his hands together. "They were here until a few minutes ago. They wanted to discuss something in private."

Silence reigned for a couple of minutes. Meanwhile, I finished my sandwich. But not my coffee.

I sipped from my mug and noticed Micah staring at me. I held his dark gaze long enough to spread heat through my cheeks, and then focused on my mug.

I didn't understand him. Not at all. Was it just me, or was he sending me mixed signals all the time?

As much as I tried fighting it, I couldn't help but feel something for him. Irritation? Curiosity? I didn't know. When he looked at me like that, all I wanted was to ... do what? Slap him. Kiss him. Maybe both. Then kiss him some more, until the air around us went up fifty degrees.

I shook my head, ashamed of thinking such things. We were at war, I needed to focus on that only. Finding the scepters and winning the war. No room for hate and love drama.

The door opened, and Izaera and Ceris, carrying what looked like a long scroll, stepped into the room. Izaera sat beside Micah, and Ceris took the seat beside her and Victor.

"I see we are all here," Ceris said, pinning me with her annoyed gaze. I offered her an equally annoyed smile. "As we suspected, the forest is gone. Somehow, Omi was able to lure some nymphs and enchant them to turn into demons prior to our arrival. When the right time came, they struck."

I tried to hold my tongue because I knew Keisha and me —and Morgan, when he could come—were more like guests in these meetings than anything else, but I couldn't stay quiet. "And the other nymphs?"

"A great number of my dear nymphs died during our fight, but some were smart and took advantage of the distraction to escape," Zelen said. "Where they are hiding, I don't know." He stared at Ceris. "I owe you my life and that of my nymphs. With my forest gone I'm weaker, but you can count on me. I'll do whatever I can to help you win this war."

A relieved smile appeared on Ceris's beautiful face. "That's good to hear."

"Me too," Izaera mumbled. All eyes turned to her. She sighed. "I mean, I'm weak too. With almost all green gone, almost all clean water gone, no blue sky, and polluted air, my powers are weakening. I can feel my energy draining out of me ... into oblivion."

Ceris rested her hand over Izaera's. "You're strong, sister. No matter what. Hang on. We will win this war, and the green will come back."

Lowering her gaze, Izaera patted Ceris's hand.

"One thing is bothering me," Micah said, drawing the

room's attention to him. "How Omi knew we were going to be there?"

"I was wondering the same thing," Ceris said.

"It could be a coincidence," Victor said. "Being one of the only green spots on Earth, Omi and Imha must have had their eyes on the forest for a while."

Ceris tapped her chin. "It could be, but it's hard to believe."

"Are you suggesting someone here told Omi and Imha of our plans?" I asked. All gazes fell on me. "If we have a mole, how did this person communicated with Omi? We could check everyone's phones, but I doubt you'll find anything. And nobody left the bunker. Except you, Ceris."

She narrowed her eyes at me. "Are you suggesting I told them?"

I raised my hands in a peace offering. "Of course not. I'm just saying it doesn't make sense."

"It could be a coincidence," Zelen repeated Victor's words. "I know demons were close to us. They had an eye on us for a while, probably getting ready to attack."

"True," Izaera said. "Demons were getting closer and closer to us."

"That's an unfortunate coincidence then," Victor said.

Micah yawned loudly, raising his hands above his head and lifting his shirt a tiny bit—enough to show half an inch of his glorious six-pack. Everyone stopped and watched him. Ceris and Victor gave him an annoyed look, Zelen and Izaera shook their heads, and after gawking for a few seconds, Keisha lowered her gaze.

Unaffected, Micah knotted his hands behind his head. "So. What's the next step?"

"Finding the scepters?" I said, sounding a little too righteous. Oops.

Victor unclasped his hands and folded his arms over the table. "Well, that isn't going too well, is it?"

"But it should be priority."

"It should," Ceris said. "Unfortunately, as Levi pointed out, it isn't going well. So, I propose we try to find another one of the creed gods."

Unbelievable.

Micah cleared his throat. "Izaera, during all these years, you never had any contact with Sol, Lua, Ronen, or Maho?"

For sake of the discussion, I assumed those were the names of the other gods and goddesses.

"No," Izaera said. "Never. All I know is they went into hiding, like I did, and I never heard from them again."

"You were hiding where your powers were strongest," Victor said. "So probably they are too."

"That's a good point," Ceris said, her gaze distant. "We should try to find them. Having all of us together against Imha and Omi will make a huge difference. The odds might change in our favor then."

Leaning back in his chair, Micah crossed his arms. "But once again, we'll search for them with only a vague idea of where they are, just like the scepters. We'll waste time."

"What do you suggest we do?" Ceris sounded annoyed again. "Sit here and wait for a miracle?"

Micah stared at her, his eyes with a resolute shine. "You know what I suggest."

Ceris tsked. "You also don't know where they are."

"But it's easier to find them," Micah said. Were they talking about the Death Lords again? "Find dead people, and you'll find one of them. Talk to him, pass the word of a meeting, and done. We'll get them all together, and we'll have them on board."

"What makes you so sure they will be willing to help?" Victor asked.

"What made you so sure Zelen would help?" Micah retorted. "What makes you so sure anyone you want to go after will help?"

"He's got a point," Zelen said.

Micah continued, "Well, I can tell you that besides what the Death Lords and I did, what they still do, we were a team. I knew I could count on them for anything, and I know that hasn't changed. If they find out I'm alive, if we tell them of our quests, I'm sure they will join us."

Ceris sighed. "I don't know."

Izaera squeezed Ceris's hand. "You took a chance with Zelen, and you would have taken chances with other deities. I know you have issues with Mitrus, we all do"—she glanced at Micah, making her point. He shrugged—"but I believe he's on your side, our side, this time. Give him a chance."

A long minute passed. Ceris seemed to mull the options over in her mind. To me, there was no question. Come on, she was willing to go after anyone, why not Micah's guys? It was only fair.

Her gaze met Victor's. He nodded at her, assuring her it was the right thing.

"All right," she said, sounding defeated. "I'll find them and set up a meeting."

22

———

Ceris left right after our meeting, and Keisha called me to train. Since I had nothing better to do, I accepted.

I changed into yoga pants and a tank top, pulled my hair into a ponytail, and met her in the gym. She wasn't there yet, but Micah and Victor were. They talked in hushed tones.

"Hmm, sorry," I said, whirling around to leave the room.

"No," Victor said. "It's okay. We didn't know you were going to train right now."

"I can come back later," I said, pointing to the door behind me.

"No, it's okay," Micah said. "We're done here."

He started for the door. I stepped to the side but couldn't help watching him as he walked by me. To my surprise, he watched me too. Our eyes locked, and I inhaled a sharp breath, my heart speeding in my chest. Was it really a surprise? Maybe it wasn't.

He walked out, and I watched as his gorgeous frame retreated down the hall.

"Sorry about that," Victor said, drawing my attention.

"You don't have to apologize for anything." I walked farther into the room. I wanted to start stretching, but I didn't feel okay doing it with Victor watching.

He took three steps to the exit, but stopped. "How are you doing?"

The question caught me by surprise. It took me a minute to find an appropriate answer. "I'm fine. I'll be fine."

"Good." He stared at me, and his sea-green eyes seemed vulnerable. "I want you to know I'm here for you. You know, if you need to talk. I know you must still resent Ceris for what she did and—"

"And you don't?"

He sighed. "I do, but it's more complicated than that."

I crossed my arms. "Really?"

"We've been together for thousands and thousands of years. People change. People make mistakes."

"How about gods?"

"Gods make mistakes too." He ran a hand through his golden hair. "I'm not saying I forgave her; I'm not saying everything is all right. It isn't all right. I still haven't forgiven her. Nevertheless, I know I can live around her and count on her when I need her. In spite of her mistakes, she'll always be there for me, and I'll always be there for her."

"You know, from what I read, you two shared one of the most beautiful love stories."

"A couple of months ago I would have scoffed at that, but the truth is Ceris means a lot to me, and I hope I can forgive her."

Jealousy ran in my veins. Not because Ceris had Victor, but because I would never have what they had, what they would have over and over again.

"You will," I said.

He nodded.

Keisha walked in the room a few seconds later. Her gaze shifted between Victor and me. She settled for Victor. "My Lord." She bowed briefly. "Am I interrupting something?"

"No," Victor said. "I was just leaving. Have a nice ... training."

He walked out of the room, and Keisha widened her eyes at me. "What was that?"

I shrugged. "Nothing."

"You know, I'm not just a warrior, I can be a friend too. You can talk to me."

I glanced at her. A girlfriend to bitch about the boys and my hatred for Ceris's actions. If she wasn't such a fan of them, that would have been perfect.

HOURS LATER, KEISHA LANDED A BLOW WITH THE WOODEN sword to my stomach. The force of the impact sent me sprawling backward, and I fell gasping for air.

"Holy shit," I wheezed.

"Crap." Keisha crouched beside me. "Are you okay?"

Blinking back tears, I nodded. I pressed my hand over my stomach, hoping it would take away the pain, as if my magic —or whatever that was—worked on me too.

When I caught my breath and the pain subsided, Keisha helped me up. "It's past eight. I guess we should call it a night."

"My hungry and hurt tummy agrees," I mumbled, still sounding like a hoarse chicken.

Keisha laughed.

We walked into the hallway, heading toward our

bedrooms. She glanced at me. "I know Lady Ceris deceived you and Lord Levi a few months ago, but I don't know exactly what happened. It's hard not being a little curious about it, especially when I run into you and Lord Levi like that earlier. And I know you omit things, which makes me more curious."

I sighed. What happened wasn't a secret, but I didn't want to tell the world how stupid I had been. The only other person who knew about it was Morgan, but he was my friend. Well, Keisha could be too. She said she wanted to be.

"Ceris gave me the Destiny Gift from the Fates so I would have visions of Victor." I refused calling him and Micah by their true names. It didn't feel right. "She wanted me to fall in love with him, and she succeeded. I had the hugest crush on him. Victor and I spent a lot of time together, and I think he felt something for me too. Well, I know he did, but I also know he was confused and alone. He didn't want to get close to anyone and ended up getting close to me. Then Ceris came into the game, and we found out who he is and what she had done, shattering my heart. The end."

The thing was, my heart hadn't shattered. Not really. Whatever I had felt for Victor hadn't been real. There was nothing there to be shattered. Yes, I still thought he was too good-looking, even for a god, but other than physical attraction, there wasn't much left. I didn't feel like we had a connection anymore. I had been confused and hurt after Ceris took him from Cathedral Rock, but those emotions subsided and I realized perhaps I wasn't as hurt as I first thought.

"That's ... wow."

"Yeah."

"Did you love him?"

"I don't know. Maybe, yes. But if the feelings were created, then did I really?"

"That's one messed up love story," she said before narrowing her eyes at me. "What about Lord Mitrus?"

My heart skipped a beat. Was I that easy to read? "What about him?"

"He was there during it all, wasn't he?"

"He was."

"And nothing happened with him?"

"No ... why are you asking?"

"Because of the way he looks at you, as if he owns you."

Oh, she had no idea how true that statement was. However, he didn't own me; he owned my life and my soul, the one he would send to the underworld one of these days. Nothing more. I took a deep breath. No need to get cold feet about it now. It wasn't happening soon. Besides, it had been my idea. An idea that would bring my family back to this world. I was more than happy to die for them. In fact, I couldn't wait for that to happen.

Still a painful pang spread through my chest. Why? It was probably because they would go on, yet I wouldn't see it, I wouldn't be with them. Or could it be because of something else too?

"You're misreading things."

"I'm not. I know what I see, and I can tell the others see it too."

Really? Was it obvious? I wondered how I hadn't noticed it. I mean, I noticed him looking at me, but that was the normal Micah—always a charmer.

We reached her bedroom.

"I'll wake you up earlier tomorrow so we can train. Goodnight."

"Goodnight."

She disappeared into her room, and I turned to mine.

After a warm shower, I roamed the cafeteria, and was glad someone had cooked a big bowl of pasta and meat sauce. I was dying for real food.

When I was done, I didn't know what to do. I thought about going back to my bedroom, but that didn't sound appealing, even though it was getting late and I was tired.

I turned to the hallway leading to Morgan's room. It was late, but I wanted to see how he was doing.

His bedroom door was closed, but I didn't knock before opening it, in case he was sleeping. I didn't want to wake him up.

"Hello there," he said when I stepped in. He was in bed, propped up by pillows, a book in his hands. The only light on in the room came from a table lamp beside his bed.

"Oh, good, you're not sleeping."

"I think I already slept enough for a week. I'm done with sleep. At least for a couple more hours."

I approached his bed. "How are you?"

He set the book down. "Ah, I'm fine. It still hurts whenever I try to move, but Lord Levi did a good job. The stitches are holding up well."

"Good." I didn't know what else to say. I scanned the room, in search of a topic. My eyes fell over the book in his hands. "What are you reading?"

"Rereading. *The Art of War* by Sun Tzu," he said. "It's an old book but good."

"Hmm, I think I heard about it in one of my literature classes."

"I bet you did." He put the book on the nightstand, wincing in pain, and then watched me. "What is it, Nadine? I can see you have something you want to say."

"Well ..."

"Come on, Nad. I'm your friend. Talk to me."

"All right. Well, I'm concerned. I saw you with the Crimson Dagger while we were in the forest." He lowered his gaze. "Why do you still have it? That dagger is dangerous. You told me that. You said whoever possessed made a deal with Omi. Have you made a deal with Omi?"

He stared at me, appalled. "Of course not!"

"Then why do you still have it?"

"I don't know. I mean, we got it from Brock, and then Brock was gone and the dagger was just there. It's beautiful, powerful, and sharp. I decided to keep it in the temple's vault with the other precious books and things like that. But once I was called to come here, I knew we would be fighting and I thought it would make a nice weapon."

"Doesn't it affect you? Keeping it like that?"

"I wasn't the one that struck the deal with Omi. The deal probably fell through once Brock was killed, and the dagger became simply that. A beautiful dagger, no powers or deals attached."

"Are you sure?"

"I am sure." He offered me a tired grin. "Do you really think I would do anything that might bring harm to the creed?"

The memory of him rushing out of the hotel in Wichita to keep the demons off Victor and Micah came to mind. And after being attacked and almost killed, he had come to us, even knowing there were more demons with us.

I smiled, feeling silly. "You wouldn't."

He smiled back. "See, you know me, but I appreciate the concern. I would probably have worried about it, if you were the one with it."

"I know. Sorry about that." I patted his hand. "Well, I'm going to let you rest."

"As if I needed more rest." He shifted his weight, trying to adjust his pillows, and ended up cringing in pain again. "Perhaps I do."

I chuckled. "Good night, Morgan."

"Night, Nad."

I exited his bedroom, closed the door, and leaned against it. I truly felt silly. How could I have worried about Morgan? He was on our side. I knew he was, and he would always be.

23

Next morning Keisha woke me early as promised, and we trained all day.

"Like that," Keisha said, approving of my stance. She threw herself at me, raising her wooden sword over my head, but I whirled around, almost as fast as she moved, and struck my wooden sword on her back. She groaned and laughed. "Nice!"

She reached behind her back and made a face.

"Was it too strong?"

"No, no. It was great." She stretched her arms over her head, shook her shoulders, and took her stance. "Again."

"Wait. It's past four in the afternoon. How about a break?" We hadn't eaten anything since lunch and even that had been a light snack. I was starving.

"One more time, then a break."

"Fine," I muttered. I was tired and hungry. My tummy would appreciate a snack right now. However, Miss Keisha wanted one more fight. Fine. I would give it to her.

This time I didn't spin around her, but I ducked under her

sword striking it with my own, hard and fast, making her lose her grip, and as her sword fell on the floor, mine leveled at her throat.

"Wow, you're getting good at this."

I smiled, proud of myself.

"Indeed."

Losing the smile, I turned to the door. Micah was there, impeccable and handsome as always, watching us. Oddly, he was wearing sweatpants almost as tight as his jeans, a thermal shirt, and sneakers—clothes I never thought I would see him wearing, even if they were all black, of course. His eyes were intent on me, and that alone disconcerted me.

"How long have you been there?"

"For a while," he said, stepping into the room.

Keisha bowed to him. "My Lord."

"Keisha, why don't you take a break?" Micah picked up the wooden sword from the floor. "I can practice with Nadine for a while."

"I'm okay with Keisha," I said.

He turned to me. "You're used to her moves, darling. You need to practice with someone you never fought before."

Without a word, Keisha bowed and left the room as if it was on fire. Traitor.

I scrunched my nose. "You know what? I need a break too."

"After we go a round," he said, pinning me with his eyes.

Micah took off his shirt.

I was about to argue some more, but that was lost the moment his shirt fell on the floor. I tried not to stare, but it was hard. Too hard. A heat wave washed over me, and I was sure my cheeks were red. "What are you doing?"

His abs and his chest were sculpted perfectly. Just like a

god should be. His tattoos seemed strategically placed, to emphasize his flawless body. Damn, he couldn't be more gorgeous or more perfect if he tried. It was unfair really. The other creatures of this Earth, the other lesser gods, the other humans had nothing on him. I could only do so much not to drool over him.

"The shirt will restrict my movements," he said, quickly touching the pendant of his necklace.

Pushing back the feelings flooding my senses, I put on a blank mask and glanced at his legs. "And the pants won't?"

I smacked my hand over my mouth. Smooth, Nadine. The pants had nothing to do with it. Besides he was wearing sweatpants, and they wouldn't restrict any of his moments. Though they were a little on the tight side ...

He put his hands over the waist of his pants, flashing me a teasing grin. "If you want me to take them off too, all you need to do is ask."

I swallowed. "That's not what I meant."

He leaned into me and whispered in my ear. "Relax, darling."

Easy for him to say. How could I relax if I was to fight a god? A half-naked god?

He positioned himself five feet from me and raised his wooden sword. Ready to fight.

Focusing on a dark stain on the floor because really, if I looked at him for too long, I was done for. My heart would be done for.

I exhaled and lifted my sword.

We engaged.

Fighting Micah was a surprise. He was fast and elegant, and several times I had the urge to step back and watch him —which was when he caught me off guard—but he was also focused and competent. He showed me where I should move faster, when to raise or lower my arm, what to expect. His fighting was different from Keisha, and I admitted—to myself —that he had been right. Fighting him was actually a good thing.

After a couple of rounds, I was starting to lag.

"Come on, darling."

Micah raised the sword over my head, and I barely had time to move out of its path.

"I'm tired. Keisha and I trained for four hours this morning and another four this afternoon."

"You can't pause a real battle."

"This isn't a real battle."

"But we're training for one. You have to believe it is."

Groaning, I turned my back to him, with every intention of walking away, but he stepped in front of me, swinging his sword at my head. I jumped back and parried the blow.

"Hey!"

He advanced on me. "Come on!"

"I want to stop."

"Not yet."

I blocked another one of his moves and retreated two steps. I was already winning some rounds when fighting against Keisha, but I hadn't won even half a round against Micah yet. He was not only good, but his fighting style was unknown to me. I had no idea how to end this fight without letting him win.

He swung his sword toward me. I threw up my sword to block his blow, but the force of his strike sent my weapon flying across the room. I gasped and held my breath. The tip of his sword lingered above my heart.

"You didn't even try."

I glared at him. "I told you I'm tired."

He dropped his sword and swung *his arm* at me.

I ducked. "What the hell?"

"Fight!"

He did a perfect roundhouse kick, and I stepped back, but tripped over one of the swords and went down. Before I did, though, I grabbed his wrist, in order to regain my balance. Instead, he fell over me.

His hand cradled my head before we hit the ground, and the only place that really hurt was the middle of my back, where the wooden sword was. However, Micah's weight over me took the air out of my lungs.

A new wave of heat traveled low, very low, and my heart hammered against my ribs. He was heavy, but God, this didn't feel bad. Not bad at all.

"That wasn't exactly what I had in mind."

I scoffed. "Yeah, right."

He pushed up on his elbows but stayed close. The pendant of his necklace nestled right on my cleavage, the cool metal chilling my hot skin.

Micah looked at it and smiled. "Oh, lucky necklace."

I groaned. "Get off."

Losing the smile, he turned his eyes to me. "Are you all right? Did you hurt yourself?"

I stared into his eyes. Those endless black eyes. They were on me with urgency and concern. Whenever Micah was like that, I was caught off guard.

"I'll be better when you get off me."

He smiled, making my heart skip a few beats. "I know you love me and my body, darling. You don't mean that."

I put my hands on his shoulders and pushed him back. "Get off."

He didn't budge. In fact, he adjusted himself so his body covered every inch of mine. I gasped. His mouth hovered an inch from mine, and his intense gaze was doing wicked things to my self-control.

"Say it like you mean it." His voice was low. Dangerous.

I opened my mouth to tell him to go, but nothing came out. Instead I inhaled and his sandalwood scent washed over me, clouding my senses. My gaze shifted to his mouth. He groaned before diving in.

His lips touched mine for a second, and then he hesitated. But I didn't. My arms wound around his neck and pulled him back over me, my mouth closing over his. That was all the incentive he needed. His mouth opened with hunger and need, making me shiver.

I had no idea what came over me; I just knew that, at this moment, I needed this. I needed to feel this. I wanted to feel needed. I wanted to be kissed. I wanted to be loved, even if for a moment. I was alone in this world, and I missed being someone to someone. I missed having people who actually cared for me, not just greedy deities who only wanted me around because of my healing touch.

One of his hands clutched my waist, pressing me against him as if my body wasn't flush to his already. I ran my nails over his bare, muscled back, glad he had taken his shirt off after all. The hand on my waist traveled up, under my tee, and I shivered again, arching into his touch. He slowed the kiss, going deeper, if that was possible, entangling his tongue with mine, and dragging moans out of me.

His lips left mine, and I was about to protest when his mouth trailed a searing path to my neck, extinguishing any coherent thought from my mind. He bit gently on the soft spot between my neck and shoulder, and I cried.

"By the Everlast," he whispered, before returning his mouth to mine.

All I could feel was his hard body pressed over me, his sweet lips on mine, and his hands on my skin. I wanted it all. I wanted him. I wiggled under him, so my hips were perfectly aligned with his, and pressed over the large bulge down there. He inhaled sharply, but he didn't stop. Instead he thrust into me, making me gasp.

Without breaking the kiss, I reached down to his pants.

He froze, and in the next second, he was up, his eyes wide in shock. Or terror? Or what?

I propped myself on my elbows and stared at him. The heat of embarrassment crept up my face, while my body felt incredibly cold without his.

A knot formed between his brows, and he looked down at his shirt on the floor. He opened his mouth and then closed it. His jaw flexed, his fists clenched.

"I shouldn't ... I can't," he muttered. He shook his head once, picked up his shirt from the floor, and walked away.

What the hell was that?

AFTER MICAH LEFT THE GYM, I STAYED ON THE FLOOR FOR several minutes, replaying everything in my head. What had I done wrong? I mean, it was Micah. The cocky guy who seemed to flock all the chicks under his wings, but now he didn't want anything to do with me.

And why the hell had I let him get to me like that? I had looked like a desperate, needy girl, and I hated that. One of the reasons I was training and fighting was not to look weak and needy. Then I throw myself at a guy. No. Not just a guy. A god!

Again ... oh my God.

I needed to get a grip, to hide in the deepest hole on Earth, or something.

Instead I went to my bedroom, curled up with my pillow and Pinky, and cried. I thought of my family, how I missed them, how I wished I could change things faster. I thought of the Soul Oath, about my family being alive again, about my death. I wondered if Micah would kill me himself, if he would make it painless and quick, or if he would enjoy making me suffer. Well, he wasn't that heartless, was he? Since I first met him, he had shown me signs of not being a total bad boy. He was good, I knew he was, and he would honor the oath. He would kill me quickly and painless, and he would make sure my family was okay.

Then I thought of how pathetic I must have looked after that kiss. I would never admit it out loud, but I still believed all those feelings were in me. The lust, the need to feel loved, the there's-more-to-this-guy feeling. However, I had no idea how to go about it. Actually, I was starting to think I shouldn't do anything about it.

Finally, I drifted off to sleep. Until the nightmares shook me awake.

I jumped out of bed, starting to believe that the bed was the one that didn't allow me to forget how horribly my family had died and how I couldn't do anything to save them.

I put on sweatpants over my shorts and a coat over my tee, and marched out of the room.

I wandered aimlessly, counting each stain or crack on the walls, how many tiles composed the hallway, how many lamps hung from the ceiling, all to keep my mind busy.

"Damn it," Keisha's voice came from behind the gym's closed door.

I opened it and looked inside. Dressed in workout clothes, she hit a punching dummy at three in the morning.

"Hey," I said, stepping in.

She whirled to the door. "Oh, hey. Did I wake you up?"

"No, no." I hugged my coat tighter around me. "I just couldn't sleep. You?"

She reached for the towel on the floor and wiped the sweat from her face. "I haven't slept much. I've talked to Lady Ceris, and she thinks it's because of my hero's metabolism. More stamina, more energy, and those things."

"Oh." I started wondering if anyone slept in this compound.

She sat down on the mat, her legs extended in front of her. With a groan, she bent at the waist and stretched her torso over her legs. "I might be a good warrior, but I have no flexibility."

I sat down a good eight feet from her. "That's not true. Compared to me, you're very flexible."

"Nu-uh. I've seen you stretching, remember? You're like rubber compared to me." She straightened her back again and looked at me. For some reason, I felt like I was under a microscope.

"Hmm, sorry." I stood up. "I barged in here and made myself comfortable. I didn't mean to interrupt your training."

"Don't be ridiculous." Keisha gestured for me to sit back down. "I could use a break. And girl talk." She smiled. With a smile of my own, I dropped back on the mat. She pulled her legs to her chest and hugged her knees. "So, what's bothering you?"

"Nothing," I said too quickly.

She tilted her head. "Really? I spend a lot of time with you. I know when something is bothering you."

I scrunched my nose. "Am I that easy to read?"

"Sometimes." She scooted until she reached the water bottle on the edge of the mat. "Am I going to have to beg, or you will spare me the humiliation?"

I picked some lint from my sweatpants, wondering what to do. I could not tell her anything. She wouldn't become more than those people we called friends but didn't really know. More like acquaintances. Or, in our case, allies working together for a common goal.

However, I could open up for once in my life. I never told Raisa anything because I was afraid of what she would think of my visions, and if I told her I knew Victor from my visions, or that I could heal him and Micah, she would have freaked out on me. Or not. I would never know. However, Keisha was here. She knew everything, including a bit of our messy past. She knew about the gods and the creed, the powers, the healing—everything. What did I have to lose?

Nothing. I might even gain something. A real friend.

"Micah kissed me this evening," I blurted out before I lost my nerve. She choked on her water. "Oh, God." I scooted to her ready to slap her back, but she raised her arm and took a deep breath.

"I'm fine," she said, her voice raspy. She took one more sip of her water before turning her wide eyes back to me. "By the Everlast, that's ... wow. He's a god. You kissed a god."

I groaned. "Thanks for the reminder."

"What? Was it that bad?"

"Oh no. Not at all." Heat surged in my body just remembering how good it had been. "But he stopped it. He retreated from me and left the room as if I had leprosy."

She frowned. "But I had the impression he liked you. *Liked* liked you, you know."

So I hadn't been the only one to see those mixed signals? Because I had seen them. I knew I had. And the fact that he had kissed me at all was proof.

"Well, I don't know. I don't understand. One second he's all hot and coming at me strong, and I'm fighting like hell to stay away, but then the next second, he melts my walls and he's the one who backs away."

"Perhaps you two have a Romeo and Juliet thing going on."

"What do you mean?"

"Instead of the enemy families, think about what he is. A god. Immortal. He shouldn't fall for a human, but he can't really help himself."

I snorted. "Micah falling for *one* girl, for real? Nah, not happening."

"What makes you say that? Have you seen him with a lot of girls?"

I thought about it. The truth was, I had never seen Micah with any girl. He had always been around me—except for the three months they all disappeared. Nevertheless, since I met Micah, he hadn't been with any girls. None that I knew of.

"I've never seen him with any girl," I confessed, feeling silly for assuming he was a Casanova. Just because he acted like one, didn't mean he was. I shook my head.

"See? I must be right. He knows he shouldn't fall for you, but it's stronger than him."

That sounded epic. "How many romance books have you read?"

"I preferred fantasy, actually. You know, with sword fights and sorcery." She winked.

I laughed. "Oh God, how didn't I see that coming?" She laughed with me. "How about you?" I asked once we calmed down. "Did you leave a boyfriend behind?"

"Nope. That is an odd thing, you know. I used to be flirty. I didn't hook up with many guys, but I liked looking at them, flirting with them. But once I came here, I don't know. I don't think about guys that much anymore. I mean, I still do some, but my main focus is this." She gestured to the room. "To be the best warrior I can. To train myself, to train you, to fight the battles for my gods, and help them win this war."

This hero stuff sounded like a major brainwash. "Wow."

"I know this new drive came from being a hero, but I'm not complaining. I love it, actually. I feel fortunate the Fates chose me."

I didn't know if it was hero magic working, but she sounded sincere and she did look comfortable in her warrior skin.

"I'm glad you're happy with it," I said, really meaning it.

We talked some more about life in Chicago and New York, what we did before everything changed, about our friends, our families. For once, it didn't hurt as much to talk about my family. Tears brimmed in my eyes, but I didn't feel like curling up and bawling.

However, what Keisha said about Micah stayed in the back of my mind. In the end, I pushed those thoughts completely away. She couldn't be right about it. And even if she was right, I had a timer on my life—a timer I had put there. Hoping about impossible things would make everything worse.

24

THE NEXT MORNING, KEISHA AND I GOT IN TWO HOURS OF training before Ceris interrupted. Apparently she had located one of the Death Lords, and had set up a meeting for later that evening.

As expected, the entire compound thrummed with tense air.

One hour before the appointed time, Keisha and I walked into the conference room, wearing our armor and with our swords hanging from our belts.

Micah's eyes bugged when he saw us. "What the hell?"

He and Victor were dressed like us. The only one at odds was Ceris, who still wore her goddess-like white dress.

"What?" I asked, infusing my voice with confidence.

I fought the urge to recoil from his powerful stance. Stupid, that was how I felt. Stupid for thinking I had feelings for him, and that he might actually have feelings for me. Micah was the person who got all the girls at the party and never settled for one. Ugh, he was the god who actually had an on-and-off affair with a goddess. Even if she was the source of evil and everything that was wrong in this world, she was a goddess. I could never compete with that.

Who said I wanted to? I didn't. I was caught up in the moment, in the feeling of solitude, in my misery. He had been there, free and loving, offering me attention, which was all I wanted at that moment. I had been naive and stupid. Plain stupid.

"Where do you think you're going?" Micah demanded.

"The same place you're going."

"Hell no."

Seriously? Of all the things we could discuss and be mad about, he chose to yell at me about helping them?

I thrust my hands on my hips and glared at him. "Why not?"

"Because it's dangerous."

I scoffed. "First, you're the one who said we can trust them. Second, you know I can take care of myself."

"Like you just said, we can trust them. No need for the two of you to come with us."

I pointed to his belt. "Then why are you taking a sword and two daggers?"

"Precaution."

"Well, take us as precaution too."

"By the Everlast, can you two stop?" Ceris interrupted. "You two act like an old married couple, bickering all the time."

Micah's jaw popped. "I don't want them to come."

"Unfortunately, I agree with Nadine, Mitrus," Ceris said. What the hell? My head snapped to her and watched her with wary eyes. It was a trick. She *never* agreed with me. "I can take one or ten people using the same amount of power. I don't see why we can't take them with us. As precaution."

Apparently, it wasn't a trick, and hell was probably freezing over.

"I don't like it," he snapped.

I leaned closer to him and whispered, "Nobody said you needed to like it."

"Now that that has been settled." Victor stood, his voice carrying an annoyed tone. "Can we get this over with?"

After checking weapons and lanterns and water, and Micah slipping a dagger inside one of my boots—what was his deal?—we put on winter coats, gloves, and beanies, and walked out of the bunker.

It was incredibly cold here, and according to Ceris, if we stayed out like this for more than ten minutes without appropriate clothing, we would end up with hypothermia. I didn't want to test her theory. I rushed my steps and crossed the invisible barrier of where Ceris had cast the shield.

She held our hands and transported us out.

This time, we visited only three places—and took our winter stuff off at the second one—before showing up at the right place.

This morning, Ceris told us she talked to one of the Death Lords, and he agreed to meet them on an abandoned beach in South Africa.

Ceris dropped us exactly on the sand, which looked more like dirt than sand. To our right, high waves crashed onshore, looking like they could swallow us whole if we got too close and drag us to the depths of the black ocean.

"I can feel something," Ceris said. "This way."

We marched south, with the ocean to our left. Victor and Ceris walked in the front, Keisha behind them, and Micah with me several steps back.

"Do you like defying me?"

I gaped. "Excuse me?"

"I'm a god. You do know that, don't you? Then why do you insist on defying me?"

"Because I'm not your slave, or your doll, or your blind follower. And jeez, that ego of yours." I kicked a broken shell on the sand. "Why do you do this?"

"This being ...?"

"I don't know—this." I gestured between him and me. "One minute, we're fine, you're behaving, we can even pretend to be friends—"

"Or more," he added.

I swallowed, certain my cheeks were red. "Then the next minute, you're acting like you hate me and I disgust you and you wish me dead already." He stepped in my path, and I bumped into him. "Hey!"

He leaned into me, his eyes hard, hurt. "Do you really think I want you dead?"

I held my chin high. "That's the thing, I don't know. And I don't care."

The last part was a total lie, but I would never admit it. Because I couldn't even admit it to myself. I had agreed to die; it didn't matter who wanted me dead or not.

I started walking around him, but he grabbed my arm. "I do—"

"I see light ahead," Ceris called out from the front.

My heart pumped furiously in my chest, but I forced myself to concentrate on the task at hand. I jerked my arm free and marched to where the others stood.

Twenty feet down a dune, five attractive men dressed in black—what a shocker—stood side by side. A dozen beach torches created a wide semi-circle behind them.

Five? I thought there were eight.

With furrowed brows, Micah came to a halt by my side.

"Well, Lady Ceris, you said you had something important to discuss," the one in the middle said.

"Yes, Dane." She took a step forward, her gaze searching the area. "Where are the others?"

"I won't answer your question until you answer mine," Dane said. "What is it that you need to discuss?"

Ceris glared at Micah, but he only nodded at her.

She cleared her throat. "This may sound insane, but Mitrus isn't dead." She gestured to Micah, and the heavy gaze of the men fell on him.

Micah opened his mouth, but Dane cut him off. "Is this some kind of trick?"

"No," Micah said. "It's me. Dane, Amiel, Jed, Riel, Keon. It's really me. When Levi"—he gestured to Victor—"killed me, we were reborn as humans."

"Humans?" Dane watched them. "How is that possible?"

"The same way it was impossible to kill a god," Victor said. "Yet, it happened."

Dane's eyes became two thin slits. "Can you prove this isn't a trick?"

Ceris scoffed. "Can't you feel his aura?"

"Yes." Dane pondered. "It's the same feel, but not the same intensity."

"That's because I'm trapped inside a human body." Micah advanced another step. "Where are the others? Deven, Eklan, and Chael?"

Dane shook his head once. "After you died, we were lost. Deven, Eklan, and Chael didn't want to go on with their duties. For the first time in their long lives, they were free to decide. They became their own Lords and disappeared. We never heard from them again."

Micah gestured to the five of them. "And you stayed."

"We stayed," he said, his voice proud, his chin high.

"Dane," Ceris interrupted. "We aren't here for a social visit or for you to acknowledge your master is back. We are here because we want your help."

"With what?"

"Defeating Imha and Omi," she said.

He frowned. "You want to kill them?"

"Unfortunately, we can't. We plan on neutralizing them and hope they go back to their old selves while we clean up their mess."

"And what's in it for us?"

"Excuse me?"

"The thing is," Dane said, walking toward us. "I'm the leader of my own pack now. I'm their master." He gestured to the other four. "What makes you think I want to help you and end up working under Lord Mitrus again?"

"I can't believe this," Micah muttered, his hands closed in tight fists.

I reached for him and caressed his lower arm with the back of my hand. I didn't exactly know why. He jerked his arm away and marched down the dune.

"I am your master," Micah said. "But before that, you were my friend. All of you. What happened to that?"

"Friends?" Dane snorted. "Your friends? We only pretended to be your friends because of the power. We never liked you. You're a dick. An egocentric dick. Nobody is your friend."

One of the others stepped forth and spat at Micah's feet. "We would rather die fighting against Imha on our own than to work for you again."

Hurt flashed in Micah's face, so fast, I thought I had imagined it.

Then he was all rage. "You traitor!" Micah pulled his sword from his waist.

Dane laughed. "Swords, really?" He sneered. "I don't need swords. I have my power." He flung not one but three black bolts toward Micah, one right after the other.

The first bolt exploded on Micah's chest, the second on his right thigh, and the third on his left hip, pushing him to the ground.

Then the chaos started.

In a flash, Keisha was in front of Micah, swinging her sword toward Dane. Ceris cast a shield around him, to give him time to recover, while she attacked two other Lords, and Victor joined Keisha in the fight. I rushed to Micah.

Breathing deeply, he pushed up on his elbows and groaned. "Son of a bitch."

The center of his chest armor had melted, the shirt under it was in rags, and his skin was marked.

"Can you stand?" I asked, grabbing his arm.

Micah helped me more than he should, and he was straightening his back when the shield broke.

Dane twisted away from Keisha and came at us, a sick shine in his black eyes.

"Are they immortal?" I asked, dragging Micah back.

"They are ageless, not immortal," he said, wheezing.

After a few steps, I dropped him. "Good."

I stepped in front of Micah and raised my sword.

Dane threw an energy ball at me, but I jumped to the side. He threw another, and I moved away from its path. My movements brought me closer and closer to him, and I didn't think he was even aware of it.

"What are you, his new toy?" Dane asked with a naughty smile. He was trying to get to me. I wouldn't let him. "Because, you know, he used to have many toys. I bet he still does."

I felt the bolt zoom past my arm when I moved to the side, its heat scorching my skin. I could have cried in pain, but I wouldn't give Dane that satisfaction.

Instead I whirled around and ran toward him.

"You want to do this the old-fashioned way, fine." Black smoke poured from Dane's hand, spreading wide above his palm. A few seconds later, it became a beautiful black sword. What was it with these guys and black? "Come and get me."

He parried my first blow, deflected my second blow, and he blocked my third blow. He dodged my fourth blow, and pushed me back a couple of steps after the fifth blow.

God, this idea was stupid. Who had suggested it again? Ugh.

No time to change that. I engaged him again.

A terrible scream filled the night, and my heart skipped a beat. I scanned around. Ceris and Victor fought three opponents with magic and swords. It was hard to admit, but they made a great team. They really did.

A second scream ripped through the air. My eyes moved. Farther back, Keisha was on the sand, a hole bigger than Micah's in her armor, on her right shoulder. In front of her, a Death Lord was ready to strike her again, but Ceris knocked him to the side with a bolt. When he returned to his feet, he lunged at the goddess.

Taking advantage of my distraction, Dane punched me in the jaw, and I staggered to the side. Stars blinded me and pain exploded on my face. Son of a bitch, that hurt!

"Ah!" I yelled when he grabbed my hair and pulled me back, causing me to fall on my knees.

"Beg for your life, princess," he said, his mouth near my ear. "Beg for your petty life."

If only he knew I didn't mind dying.

A black bolt appeared in Dane's palm.

"No!" Micah yelled from somewhere behind us, his voice rough.

Dane laughed. "How pathetic."

I lowered my lashes, wishing not to feel much pain before dying, just as new cries echoed around us, making my eyes pop open.

They were battle cries coming from three men who emerged from the shadows. Three other Death Lords. Deven, Eklan, and Chael.

One of them rushed to Micah and despair made me sick. Oh, God, he would kill Micah. To my surprise, the man helped Micah to his feet, while the other two helped Ceris and Victor against Amiel, Jed, Riel, and Keon.

"No, no, no," Dane muttered. Still gripping my hair, he hoisted me up. "Come."

Dane dragged me closer to the shadows. I opened my mouth to scream for help, but he cast a rope of energy around my face and over my mouth. I tripped and Dane yanked harder. Hurtful tears sprung to my eyes.

The distance between the others and us grew. The guy who had been with Micah seconds ago was now with Keisha, and Micah was gone. Victor and Ceris still fought the other four, but now, with help, they were equally matched.

Dane stopped, and I bumped into him. I elbowed his ribs, then spun around and kneed him in the groin. Groaning, he doubled over, and I made a run for it. He caught me by the waist and pulled me back to him, a tight hand over my neck, and the other around my joined wrists.

"Bitch," he whispered, his mouth on my cheek. I wanted to hurl.

He dragged me farther from the light of the torches. I didn't know why, but I was sure that once he reached complete darkness I was done for. I jerked harder. He lost the grip on my arms, and that was enough for me to elbow him again. He didn't let go this time, but his hand loosened its hold enough that I was able to pry it from my neck. I didn't whirl around and try to fight him. I ran, not because I was afraid of dying, but because I wanted more time to help Micah and Victor get their scepters. I glanced over my shoulder. Still in the same spot, Dane smiled at me.

My eyebrows knotted. Then I bumped into something hard and fell on my back. A black wall, much like the shields Ceris cast, stood between the torchlight and me.

I shook the sand from my hair, and I scurried to my feet.

Dane was right by my side. He conjured black cuffs around my wrist. "Stop running, bitch. I'm gonna take you with me, and you'll wish I had killed you here on this beach."

A sick feeling settled in my stomach, and the reminiscent images of my time with Imha and Omi invaded my mind. I wouldn't be anyone's bait anymore. I wouldn't be tortured again. I wouldn't be a demon's piñata. I wouldn't have anyone captured and killed because of me. Oh no.

I glanced around. My sword was lost somewhere, but I had a dagger inside my boot.

Dane beckoned his hand, and a tug on the cuffs made me follow him. "I'll enjoy playing with you."

Oh, God.

It was now or never.

I tripped on purpose, bending my head over more than necessary, causing my hair to fall like a curtain, obscuring my movements. I reached for the dagger and when Dane used his magic to pull me to my feet, I held the dagger tight.

All right. This would hurt, but I couldn't chicken out. One fluid stab and it would be over. If I allowed my nerves to overwhelm me, I wouldn't reach my heart and that would be just like torture.

I took a deep breath.

Three.

Two.

One.

In a flash, Micah was in front of me. He took the dagger from my hands, spun around, and threw it at Dane. Dane's eyes widened as he looked down at the dagger embedded in his heart.

"I can't believe you did this," Dane said.

"Me neither," Micah whispered.

Dane's body fell back, but before he could hit the sand, his body flickered, becoming black smoke. A strong wind blew it away.

As if they felt what happened, the other four Death Lords stopped and gaped at us. At the same time, they conjured black bolts and threw them at the ground.

"Grab them!" Micah shouted, but it was too late.

Black smoke lifted from where the bolts had hit, surrounding them. The black tendrils spun and looped toward the sky, until the dark wisps bled into the blackness of the sky, taking the Death Lords away.

Ceris, Victor, and the other two helping them stepped back, away from the smoke.

Micah turned to me, rage in his features. "What the hell was that?"

The cuffs gone, I massaged my wrists and held my chin high, unafraid of him or his rage fits, but I didn't say anything. There was nothing to say.

He halted before me. "I'm talking to you. What do you think you were doing?"

"Not now, Micah, please." A lonely feeling burst in my chest and, surprising even me, I stepped into him and wound my arms around his waist, resting my head on his chest. He buried his face in my hair, his arms tight on my back. I listened to his steady heart and felt safe. When I pressed closer, Micah winced.

I jumped away from him. "Oh, God."

He put a hand over the wound on his chest. "It isn't as bad as it looks," he said, through gritted teeth.

"You don't need to be tough all the time, you know."

Through the pain, he showed a brief grin. "Of course I do."

Shaking my head, I grabbed his arm and put it over my shoulder, then passed my arm around his waist.

As we took the first step toward the others, Victor rushed to us. "Everything all right? What happened?"

"We're fine," I said, not in the mood to retell everything.

Victor took Micah from me, and we walked back to the others.

Ceris was beside Keisha, who was lying on the sand, looking too pale. Blood trickled from the wound on her shoulder. It covered the area, obscuring the severity, but by the way she squirmed in pain and how her eyes rolled back every few seconds, it wasn't good.

Ceris looked up. "We need to take her to our place. Now."

Victor gestured to who I thought were Deven, Eklan, and Chael. "What about them?"

She cursed.

The one in the middle looked at Ceris. "We just wanted to help, my Lady."

"I want to believe you, Eklan, but after what your brothers did, it's hard to trust anyone."

Eklan nodded. "After our Lord's death, Dane simply decided he was in charge. At first, we accepted because we needed someone in charge. Then Dane went crazy. At one point, I thought he was working with Imha, spreading chaos, but when she came and made an offer, we saw that Dane was on his own and taking us with him. We didn't accept that, so we left."

Micah tsked. "The Death Lords are divided into two groups?"

"Sort of," Eklan continued. "We've been trying to do our work, but it's too much for only the three of us."

"I know," Micah muttered, his fists clenched. "Thousands of souls are probably trapped within this world."

Eklan frowned. "You know?"

Micah nodded. "I know this will sound insane, but it's me, Eklan. I'm Mitrus."

Eklan and the others gaped. "But that's—"

"Impossible," Ceris finished for him. "But it isn't. This conversation is important, but so is taking Keisha to safety. We need to go." Ceris looked at Micah. "What do you want to do?"

Surprise flashed briefly in Micah's eyes before returning to his normal commanding, superior shine. He turned to the Death Lords. "Come with us. We'll explain everything."

25

———————

I leaned against the door and watched Victor give instructions to Micah.

"Drink lots of water and rest. I mean it."

"Shut the fuck up, doc," Micah teased, with a chuckle that ended in a wince. "By the Everlast, this hurts."

"You're lucky Ceris spelled your armor; otherwise, the wound on your chest would have gone through your lungs."

Micah wrinkled his nose. "What a pretty picture."

Victor shook his head. "All right. Time to rest. I'll check on you later."

He turned and paused upon seeing me there.

"How is he?" I asked in a low voice.

Victor approached me at the door. "He'll be okay. But I mean it. If Ceris hadn't enchanted our armor, his human body would have died and his soul would have been lost." He sighed. "He's a little groggy because of the strong painkillers I gave him."

"And Keisha?"

"I've been coming and going from her room. She's okay,

for now." He glanced at the door behind us, and then continued in a lower voice, "Her armor wasn't enchanted. Ceris swore to me she enchanted all of our armor, but Keisha's wasn't. The bolt ripped right through it, through her skin, and burnt a hole just above her heart. She lost a lot of blood, not to mention the third degree burns surrounding the open wound. If it wasn't for her hero's healing, she would've died by now."

Even with my problems with Ceris, I couldn't believe she would miss Keisha's armor on purpose. Putting Keisha at risk meant she was putting Victor at risk too, and the goddess would never do that. She needed everyone strong to protect Victor and the creed. Yet, Keisha's armor had somehow been missed.

"You should get some rest too," Victor said, cutting through my thoughts.

I nodded. "I'll try after I sit with Micah for a while. If that is okay. I mean, he could be in bad shape."

The corner of his lips tugged in a small smile. "He's fine. Just don't take too long. He does need to rest, and you do too."

I nodded again, Victor walked out, and I stepped inside.

Micah looked pale and weak in the infirmary bed with an IV in his right arm. I approached him from the left.

He noticed me and smiled. "Hey, darling."

I rested my hand on his arm. "You scared me back there, you know."

He stared at me, all the grogginess gone. "I scared you? You scared me! What the hell were you trying to—?"

"All right, all right." I patted his arm. "We can argue about this some other time. Right now you need to rest." Honestly, I didn't want to argue about what I almost did at the beach. Not now, not ever.

"You're going to get an earful later." He closed his eyes. "Where are Deven, Eklan, and Chael?"

"They were talking to Ceris a few minutes ago. She was explaining everything to them."

"And their reaction?"

"They seemed surprised."

"Good or bad surprised?"

"Good surprised. They seemed relieved you're alive, even if you're human. She explained about your scepter, and I think they will stay and help us."

A small smile adorned his battered face. "That's good. Very good."

"It is."

He sighed. "I hate to say this, but Ceris was right. We shouldn't have gone. It wasn't worth it."

When weighing the good and bad, I guessed he was right, butI couldn't tell him that.

"We have three more allies. That counts for something, doesn't it?"

His eyes fluttered open, and his jaw tensed. "You heard Dane. They were never my friends. They never cared for me as I cared for them. They hate me."

I ran my fingertips on his lower arm. "Hey, don't say that. My guess is Dane lied to you to get under your skin."

"It worked." His gaze flickered to my hand on his arm.

I pulled my hand away. "Don't do that to yourself. Chael, Deven, and Eklan are here, aren't they? I don't think they would have come if they hated you. In fact, I think they would have killed you back at the beach when you told them who you are if they hated you, if they didn't want their master back."

He scoffed. "Master ... I hate that word." He slid his hand

in mine and squeezed. "Nadine, about the other thing Dane said. About ... toys. My toys. I—"

"How about we also continue this conversation another time?" I cut him off, not ready to hear whatever he wanted to tell me. "You should relax and rest now."

I started pulling my hand away, but he held it tight. "Wait, Nadine. You promised me you wouldn't try to take your life like before. You broke your promise."

I averted my eyes. This wasn't the time to talk about this. Using my hand that he still held, he pulled me closer. "Your soul is mine," he said in a low, dangerous tone. "You don't have the right to kill yourself anymore."

I pressed my lips together, willing the tears away. "I won't be tortured again. I will take my own life before I let that happen."

The rage slipped away from his face, replaced by worry. He reached with his other hand and pushed a strand of my hair behind my ear, stroking my skin gently. "I won't let that happen. Never again. Now promise me you won't try to take your life again."

I averted my eyes and shifted my weight. I couldn't promise that. If someone captured me or if I was tortured, I would kill myself if given the chance. I wouldn't let my captor use anyone else to get to me. I wouldn't let anyone else die because of me.

"Nadine, pr—"

I kissed his cheek. "You need to rest. I'll see you later." I hurried out of the room as Micah called my name again.

I turned a corner in the hallway and bumped into Deven.

"Oh, sorry," I said, stepping back.

He offered me a grin, much like Micah's when he was in a good mood. "No worries. You're Nadine, right?" I nodded.

"I'm Deven. This is Chael"—he gestured to a guy with a military buzz haircut and hazel eyes—"and Eklan." A guy with smooth black skin, black eyes, and dreadlocks waved at me.

"Hi. Nice to meet you all."

"I hear you can heal Lord Levi and Lord Mitrus," Chael said. "That's cool."

"Is it true you don't know what you are?" Eklan asked.

Heat flooded my cheeks. I hated being in the spotlight. "Nobody knows what I am."

"That must be odd," Deven said.

I cleared my throat. "It has been a long day. If you'll excuse me, I need to rest."

Deven stepped out of the way. "Of course. But first, can you tell us which room is Lord Mitrus's?"

I pointed over my shoulder. "Third door on your right."

"Great. Thanks."

I nodded and walked past them. An urge to glance back assaulted me, but I held on. Something about them bugged me, but it was probably because they looked as confident and cocky as Micah, and I had already had enough of that.

SLEEP DIDN'T COME EASY, AND WHEN IT CAME, NIGHTMARES crowded it.

Because of that, I was up too early.

I slipped on yoga pants, a tank top, my sneakers, and crept into the kitchen where I whipped up a black coffee and a few pancakes. I left some on a plate for whoever came in first and felt like eating them. I refilled my coffee mug and headed to the gym.

After almost forty minutes of kicking, punching, and sweating, Ceris walked in the gym.

I missed my blow, tripped, and almost fell, my mouth hanging open.

She was wearing sweatpants and a tee, and had tied her hair into a long braid on her back. At that moment, she looked like a mix of Ceris and Cheryl.

A longing pang ran through my chest.

I put my gloved hands over my waist. "What are you doing?"

"Keisha and Micah are hurt, so I thought you could use a hand with training."

I scoffed. "You? Training with me? I have never seen you close a fist to hit anyone."

"Well, I prefer using my magic, but when you live long enough, you learn a thing or two. I promise it'll be time well spent."

"No, thank you. I can train alone."

"Not for combat, you can't."

"I'll just punch the dummy, and I don't need to train for combat every day."

She laughed. "Says the girl who so desperately wanted to learn how to fight."

"Well, I did learn. I'm not Keisha, but I'm getting better."

She walked to the farthest wall and examined the swords. "You know what makes a good fighter? Sparring with different opponents. Everyone has a different fighting style. If you spar with different people, you'll be better prepared."

Micah said the same thing, but somehow coming from Ceris, it wasn't a welcomed statement.

I frowned at her. "Why are you doing this?"

She arched a blond eyebrow at me. "This what?"

"Being nice, helping."

"It is who I am."

"Ugh, what a lie," I muttered.

"Nadine, you may not want to hear this, but I was Cheryl. I am Cheryl. All her worries, all her pep talks, all her smiles and hugs and nice words, they were mine and they were true."

"I don't believe you. I'm sorry, but I don't believe you. After all you did to Victor and me, you think I'll believe you're actually a good person? Goddess ... whatever."

"What do you want from me? Do you want me to say I'm sorry? Well, I'm not sorry. I don't regret anything I did. If we went back in time and was presented with the same facts, I would do everything the same way again."

"Even kill innocent people? Like Victor's parents, his grandfather, his friend, his girlfriend, and even that girl from whom you made the Black Thorn?"

She pressed her lips tight for a moment. "I did what I had to do."

"No. You did what you thought would bring Victor to you, even if it meant being as evil as Imha."

Her blue eyes flared. "Don't compare me to Imha! I'm not like her, and I'll never be. I know I did horrible things, but I would do them again if it meant we would get us to where we are now. Haven't you heard of sacrificing a few so that many can live? That was the situation."

"But his parents? When he was a little kid?"

"Those weren't his real parents. Like the Fates would say, they just served a purposed. Besides, I had to uproot him, otherwise he wouldn't let you get close. He wouldn't transfer to New York, and he wouldn't need you."

"I still don't understand why you simply didn't walk up to him when he was older and explain everything to him."

"Besides the fact that gods aren't supposed to interfere in humans' lives? He would have freaked out, or thought I was a freak."

I crossed my arms and stared at her. "You interfered in mine."

"The only thing I did was give you the Destiny Gift. And, if you actually think about it, it was a gift from the Fates, not me. Being Cheryl didn't interfere with anything you did. I was just there when you needed to talk. I encouraged you, and I never told to do something you didn't want to."

I thought about it for a moment. It was hard to admit, but it was true. She never obligated me to do anything. Like the Fates pointed out to me once, Ceris had told me about the job at Langone, but I was the one who applied for it. She never told me I *had* to. She was there when I was heartbroken about Victor, and she suggested I go after him. More than once, she had been there for me.

I hated this ambiguous feeling in my chest. I wanted to despise her until the day I died.

Then she spoke words I never thought I would hear. "My only regret over everything I've done was not to have taken you more seriously after everything. I should have listened to you at Cathedral Rock. I should have taken you and Mitrus from there and kept you both safe. I should have acted like a friend."

I stared at her, completely in shock. No, she couldn't do this to me right now. She couldn't use Cheryl, couldn't pretend she cared, or say things to melt my resolve.

First, I hated her, I really did. I wished she would burn at a stake for eternity like the bad witch I thought she was.

Then, my hate subsided and I learned to live around her, to deal with her, even to fight beside her. I could do that. I could pretend she was an ally, but nothing more than that. However, having her come to me and tell me she regretted not being a friend to me was too much.

Feeling emotionally exhausted, I took off my gloves, threw them on the floor, and walked to the door.

"Where are you going?"

"Anywhere else." I stopped at the door and looked at her. "I can't deal with you right now."

FOUR AGONIZING DAYS WENT BY.

Ceris and Izaera were gone, trying to locate the other gods and goddesses and, I hoped, to convince them to join our team. Morgan didn't stop with his rituals. Victor spent most of his time in a conference room with Zelen, meditating, of all things. Keisha had woken up and was feeling slightly better. According to Victor, she would make it through but she would feel her shoulder for a few weeks. She —and I—was just relieved she was out of risk. Micah was up and better. He spent all of his free time catching up with his friends. Deven, Chael, and Eklan seemed enthusiastic to have Micah, or Mitrus, back, putting Micah's doubts of their loyalty to rest.

On the fifth day, Ceris and Izaera came back. They hadn't located any gods or goddesses, but they did some exploring.

"Time is ticking and finding the scepters is now our priority," Ceris said, standing in front of the table in the conference room. "We have visited every place of power we could think of." She extended her arm in front of her. A large rolled paper, much like a scroll, appeared in her hand. "Cathedral Rock, the pyramids, Chichen Itza, Stonehenge. Nothing."

She unrolled the paper in the center of the table of the conference room, revealing a map on yellowed paper with torn edges. We all leaned over to get a better look. The map looked a lot like the one I had seen when Imha had me, but this one didn't have any magical symbols hovering over it.

"We can't think of many other places," Izaera said. "The remaining ones seem improbable locations."

"Or," Ceris continued, "there are other places of power we don't know about."

Victor shook his head. "That's not possible."

"Why not?" Ceris asked. "Until thirty years ago, which is a short amount of time considering how long we've been on this Earth, we thought killing gods was impossible."

"You have a point," Zelen spoke. "But do you have any leads as to where those places of power could be?"

Ceris sighed. "No."

Izaera tapped her index finger on the map. "Our idea is to find a well-equipped library, borrow lots of history books, and research locations where important events happened."

"I like that idea," Morgan said.

Micah leaned back in his chair, clearly bored with the map. "I thought finding the scepters was time sensitive," Micah said.

"It is," Ceris responded.

"Then how do you suggest we research hundreds of books?" he asked.

Ceris glared at him, not afraid of showing how she hated when he interrupted her. "Every one of us will have to help. We'll have to sleep less, train less, meditate less, and research more. All of us."

Micah kicked his heels up onto the table. "That sounds boring."

"It may be," Ceris said through gritted teeth. "But it's the only idea we have."

"And if we find something, it'll be worth it," Izaera added.

Ceris rolled up the map. "Then, it's decided. Izaera and I will search for libraries tomorrow, and we will start our research the next day."

<hr>

I STEPPED OUT OF THE CONFERENCE ROOM AND TURNED TOWARD my bedroom.

"Nadine," Micah called. I slowed down and let him catch up with me. "You were quiet in there."

I shrugged, not sure how to answer. It wasn't as if I made a habit of speaking up.

"How are your days with your buddies?" I asked, hearing the jealousy and irritation in my words.

He smiled. "Do you miss me, darling?"

Shaking my head, I hurried my steps down the corridor.

"I know why you're walking fast, darling," Micah said, sounding annoyed. "Point taken. Can you please wait?"

Huffing, I slowed down. "You don't need to walk with me."

"I know, but I've barely seen you the last five days, and I have two things to talk to you about."

I raised my eyebrows at him. "Oh?"

"About what Dane said." He pressed his lips into a thin line and his jaw worked. "And you still didn't promise me you won't try ... doing again what you tried to do at the beach."

I shook my head. "I can't promise you that. I really can't. I won't be tortured again, and I won't let anyone else suffer or be killed because of me." I couldn't really talk about it without remembering my family. It hurt too much.

He grabbed my shoulders, forcing me to stop, and turned me to him. "I'm not sure if you believe me or not, but I told you I'll never let that happen again. I meant it."

I looked into his eyes. This was one of those rare moments when he was too serious. Well, perhaps it wasn't that rare anymore.

"I believe you, but in case you fail, I'll do it."

He leaned closer, holding my stare. "I won't fail," he said, his voice low. I held my breath, aware that his lips were a couple of inches from mine.

Knowing it was better not to argue, I nodded. I glanced down the corridor—we were three doors from my bedroom. I retreated, causing him to let me go.

"Thanks for bringing me here."

He reached one hand to me, but I retreated one more step. "Wait. I need to explain about what Dane said."

"You don't need to explain anything."

"But I want to."

I closed my eyes for a second, gathering strength to resist him and his charms. "Micah, I don't want to hear it. Seriously."

Hurt flashed on his features, but it was so quick, I may have imagined it there.

He nodded and before he could say anything else or stop me again, I rushed to my bedroom. I pushed my door closed, and then jumped into my bed, hugging Pinky as if the stuffed animal could save me from the madness I lived in.

26

"No!" I cried as the fire surrounded me, engulfing my family with its flame.

A tiny hand shot out from the fire. "Nad, help," Nicole croaked.

I took the little hand in mine, and it became dust.

"No!" I sat up, waking.

Breathing hard, I looked around. I was in my room in the underground bunker in northern Greenland. It was okay. I inhaled slowly. It was okay. Everything would be okay. I would fix everything.

I laid back on my pillow, but couldn't close my eyes without seeing Nicole's terrified face and her bloody body on my lap.

I kicked the covers away, dropped Pinky over my pillow, put on sweatpants over my shorts and a cardigan over my tee, and left my room. I tiptoed in my heavy socks down the hallway, afraid of waking up anyone else. Nobody had to suffer through the night with me.

A nice soda, or maybe even black coffee, sounded good

even if it was three in the morning. Besides, I knew I wouldn't go back to sleep tonight; I might as well eat an early breakfast and start training.

A clink noise, like a pin dropping on a hard floor, brought me to a halt.

"Hello?" I whispered. Nobody answered. I wouldn't call out with my normal volume; I'd wake up everyone, so I continued down the hallway, sure I would find whoever was also having trouble sleeping.

I turned a corner and something grabbed me, yanking me back. Panic shot through my veins. A hand over my mouth stifled my scream as I bumped my back into a hard surface.

"Shhh. Stay quiet," Micah whispered in my ear.

I nodded and he removed the hand from my mouth, placing it around my waist, keeping me close to him. Not that I was complaining, but it felt somewhat silly.

"What is it?" I asked in an equally low tone.

"I think someone is here."

I tilted my head to the side and glanced at him. "Of course there's someone here. There are eleven people in this shelter."

"No, I mean someone else."

"Oh."

Wait. Who did he think was here? Before I could ask, the clink noise vibrated through the walls again, louder this time, but still too faint to wake up anyone who was sleeping.

Micah tugged me with his arm around my waist, and we retreated to the closest door and into an empty bedroom. We leaned against the wall, leaving a tiny crack of the door open.

I could hear my heartbeat as the seconds passed. We peeked through the door as footsteps shuffled along the floor.

Demons. A bunch of demons.

Fear and repulsion burst through my system, and I shrunk into Micah's arms.

Micah lowered his forehead to my shoulder. "By the Everlast."

"I don't understand."

"Neither do I."

Hauling me with him, Micah scooted farther into the room.

"All right," I muttered, trying to keep my fear in check. "Let's think about the logical action here. We have to find a way of waking the others and getting out."

"I don't really see how we're gonna make it past the demons."

Disentangling myself from Micah, I peeked through the crack in the door. "Let's pray they take a wrong turn and go in the direction of the tech room instead of the other bedrooms."

Micah stood behind me again, spying out the door with me.

I held my breath as the demons approached the end of the hallway where they would have to turn left or right. I counted the monsters. I stopped at thirteen, but I didn't think there were many more. Not on this level at least.

The demons turned left, to the tech room.

I sighed in relief.

"Okay." Micah turned me around to face him. "Chances are we won't be able to wake the others and get out without being noticed, so go to the gym and grab as many swords as you can while I wake up everyone."

"But ... you'll be too close to the demons."

"We don't have any other option."

I watched the door. "Do you think there are more demons around?"

"I do." He pressed his lips in a tight line. "Are you ready?"

"Yes," I lied. It didn't matter if I was ready or not. We had to do it now, or we were all demon dinner.

We looked out the door. It was clear.

Taking a deep breath, I stepped out, but Micah held my hand. "Be careful."

I squeezed his hand. "You too."

He winked before letting go, and as silently as possible he rushed toward where the demons had gone. I watched him for a few seconds hoping he was quick.

I turned the other way, imitating Micah's hurried tiptoes. In my mind, I prayed not to bump into any demons, at least not until I had grabbed a few swords from the gym.

Oh God, there were demons in the compound!

I inhaled deeply again. No time for freak out mode now. I pushed those thoughts and feelings aside and focused on action.

I got to the gym without seeing anyone or anything. I picked a belt and fastened it around my waist before filling it with daggers from the wall. Then I reached for the swords. Some had scabbards, and I simply slung them across my shoulders. I didn't know how many weapons I had gotten when a noise came from outside the door.

My heart stopped.

Oh God.

Fighting a full-on panic, I hid behind two big weight lifting machines to the left side of the room, somewhat close to the door. I held my breath and waited, hoping luck was on my side.

Seconds later, Chael, Eklan, and Deven entered the gym.

Relief coursed through me. Micah must have woken them first and sent them here to help me. I started to stand to call them.

"Just lock the door?" Chael asked.

"No," Deven said. "Unlocking the door wouldn't be too hard. Let's destroy the weapons."

Destroy the weapons? What were they talking about?

"I like this idea," Chael said. "Destroy the weapons so they can't use them."

Oh. I crouched again, ignoring the rage building in me demanding I jumped out of my hiding place and kicked their butts. However, they were three deities and I was a tiny human. They would kick *my* butt. I prayed for Micah to wake everyone and come back soon.

"Hey," Eklan called. "Some swords are missing."

"How?" Chael asked.

Then silence reigned and I held my breath afraid they would hear my heart beating out of my chest.

Metal scrapped as they picked swords from the wall and pulled them from their scabbards.

Careful not to make a sound, I dropped three of the four swords I had in my hand, gripping the remaining one tight.

As soon as my pinky closed around the hilt, Chael and Eklan jumped to my sides, flanking me.

"Gotcha," Chael said, a naughty shine in his eyes.

I stood, willing my expression to mask my feelings.

Deven pointed his sword at me. "Let go of your weapons. All of them."

Slowly I squatted, pretending to drop my sword on the floor. Taking a deep breath, I grabbed another one with my left hand, whirled back—just as Deven's sword fell where I was—and swung both swords, grazing their tips against Chael's and Eklan's legs.

Both of them staggered back hissing.

The three Death Lords lunged at me. I sidestepped behind another piece of gym equipment, jumped over a bench, and ran to the door.

Someone threw their sword at me, and I saw it just in time, turning my body to the side. The sword grazed my arm. I flinched but didn't stop. Panting, I reached the door and ran out and into Victor.

Sensing what was going on, he closed the door behind me and locked it. He took one of the swords from me, grabbed my hand, and we ran.

"Where are the others?" I asked, out of breath.

"Waking the rest."

"Micah sent you after me?"

Victor nodded and pulled me to a stop before a corner. He glanced around it and cursed.

"Demons," he mouthed. "They are searching the rooms."

I glanced back to the end of the hallway where the locked door wouldn't hold the three Death Lords for long.

The exit of the building, the stairwell that led outside, was on the other side of the same hallway, but everyone else was still in the back beyond the demons.

Victor looked again. "I see Micah at the other end of the hall."

"We have to fight our way to them then."

Victor nodded. "On three," he said. "One, t—"

"Three," I said, running around him and into the hallway with a bunch of demons.

Cursing, Victor rushed behind me.

For a moment, the demons seemed surprised, and past them, Micah seemed furious, with his black eyes fuming.

Before the demons could react, I grabbed a dagger from my waist and threw it to the back, in an arc above the monsters. As I expected, Micah jumped up and grabbed the dagger in the air. Then I threw another, and he caught it the same way.

A demon swiped its claws at me. I parried it, drawing gooey blood from its thick skin. When it raised the other claw, I spun to the side and pulled my sword up, leaving a long slash on its chest. I kicked the creature out of my way as another demon came at me.

One good thing about fighting in a narrow hallway was Victor and I didn't have to worry about more than one or two demons at a time. I could do this. I could fight one at a time.

However, on the other side, Ceris and Izaera didn't have much space to use their magic. Pink bolts flew around, then green bolts, then pink bolts, but never the two colors at the same time. Even so, the sea of demons diminished.

I used my sword to parry an incoming claw. Another big hand full of talons came at me, and I ducked under it, taking advantage of my position to pierce the creature from below.

Beside me, Victor wasn't doing badly either. Actually, he was faster and more elegant than I was, and that inspired me to try harder.

After we battled a couple of demons each, I could see more of Micah. He was still behind six or seven monsters. He had a dagger in each hand, and his movements fast and precise, his eyes holding a predatory shine.

Besides the lethal stance, he looked badass. It was beautiful to watch. I could stare at him like this for hours. I could stare at him for hours—and days.

Until a hand clutched my throat and pulled me backward.

A scream ripped from me and, by instinct I thrashed against the hold. Someone else grabbed my arms and twisted the one with the sword until I yelped and lost my grip.

"No!" Victor yelled.

Beside me, Eklan pierced half of his sword's blade into Victor's back.

I screamed. With a loud groan, Victor arched his back and fell on all fours.

Oh, God.

"Levi!" Ceris shouted. A pink bolt zipped above his head, exploding on Eklan's chest and making the Death Lord stagger back.

She fought the remaining demons with new energy.

Chael held up a sword and looked past my shoulder to Deven.

"Finish him," Deven said.

Chael nodded. He turned to Victor and lifted his weapon above his head.

I kicked him, and he staggered over Victor, losing the grip on his sword and falling to the ground.

"Bitch," Deven said. He tightened the grip around my throat. I jerked, but he passed a heavy arm around me, keeping me still. Limping, Eklan approached us. He took a dagger and placed the tip to my chest, just as Chael stood up, aiming his sword at Victor.

"Say goodbye to this world," Chael said.

"You too," Eklan spat to me.

I closed my eyes.

The tip of the dagger pierced my skin and then cut to the side as Eklan fell, a dagger in his throat.

My heart hammered in my chest, and I gaped at Eklan's collapsed body.

I stripped my gaze from the body and glanced to the side. From above the demon he was fighting, Micah had thrown one of his daggers. He disposed of the demon and turned to Deven.

Grunting, Deven let go of me and faced Micah. Weak and gasping for air, I dropped to my knees.

I looked up, remembering Chael had been about to kill Victor. Thank the Everlast that Ceris had gotten to him in time, and now she held Chael to the wall, squeezing his throat with magic.

Meanwhile, Morgan and Izaera rushed to Victor and me. Zelen stayed behind with Keisha, helping her walk through the mess.

"How are you?" Izaera asked.

"I'm fine," I assured her. "Victor ... help Victor."

She turned to him. He had fallen to the floor, blood oozing from the wound on his back.

Someone knocked into me, and I glanced up.

Micah recovered from a punch, rubbing his chin, and then he charged Deven again.

"How is it? To have your own kind betray you?" Deven provoked him. "Oh, wait. You know how it is. You betrayed your own kind."

Micah groaned. "You don't know what you're talking about."

Deven flung his sword and, groaning, Micah deflected it with his dagger. The impact caused him to drop it, leaving him weaponless.

"Don't I? I did the same thing you did. Eklan and Chael too. We joined Imha. We work for her." Deven circled Micah, taunting him with his movements and words. "We were always watching over the other Death Lords. When we overheard Dane telling the others about an important meeting, we passed the information to Imha. She didn't think it was important at the time but asked us to spy on them. Then, at the meeting you revealed you're Lord Mitrus! I couldn't believe it, but I knew we had to come with you and contact Imha later."

Micah's stance changed as he gaped at Deven. "Then she's here?"

"She's on her way."

"Fuck," Micah muttered.

When Deven swung his sword at him again, Micah ducked, stepping around his opponent.

Using the wall as support, I stood up and held my sword by the blade. "Deven!" I called.

He turned to me reflexively, and I threw the sword to Micah. He closed his hand over the hilt and buried it in Deven's back, much like Chael had done to Victor. However, Micah wasn't taking any chances. He pulled the sword out and plunged it in again.

Deven fell, his head a few inches from my feet, before his body erupted in black smoke.

His eyes on mine, Micah took a deep breath. He had a couple of bruises and superficial cuts but no visible or grave wounds.

"Are you okay?" he asked.

I nodded, glancing to the side. I was okay, but Victor didn't seem to be. Beside him, Ceris ripped the end of her dress as she fought back tears. Morgan and Izaera held Victor's shoulders up, and Ceris wrapped the ripped cloth around him, using it as an improvised bandage.

Sweating and too pale, Victor didn't utter one sound, didn't move one muscle.

With his arm around Keisha, Zelen approached us. "They know where we are. We need to leave before more arrive."

"Can someone help me carry him?" Ceris asked.

Micah knelt beside Victor. "I can carry him." He passed an arm under Victor's shoulders and another under his knees and pulled him up.

"Come on," Izaera said, beckoning us to the exit.

I started following as everyone was exiting but then paused. I shouldn't but I couldn't help it. I ran to my bedroom, jumping over the bodies, slipping on gooey blood, and breathing through my mouth—the place reeked. The door was open, but apparently they hadn't done more than look inside. Thankfully, I found Pinky on my bed. I tucked it under my arm and rushed out before they left without me.

I ran up the stairs and met them outside, shivering in the cold.

"Where were you?" Micah asked, his eyes accusative.

I shrugged, but he glanced at the stuffed bunny in my arms and the knot between his brows smoothed.

Shrieks echoed through the frigid air. The sky was dark, but the white snow reflected enough that it was easy to see the black cloud of Akuma coming toward us. A similar wave of Ornek and Arak appeared on the horizon.

"Get us out of here," Morgan said, as the winged demons began their descent, flying too fast toward us.

Ceris extended her arm, and her scepter appeared in her hand. She closed her eyes, and the pink orb of her scepter shone brighter and brighter. I squinted against the light, looking through it. A ray shot out of it, crossing the dark sky in half a second, illuminating it with a baby pink glow until it hit the wave of bats and spread out like lightning. The bats shrieked.

"What the hell?" Micah snapped. "Get us out of here."

Ceris pulled her scepter back. A silver line danced inside the orb. I took a step closer to it, but the scepter disappeared from her hand.

Morgan grabbed my hand as Ceris closed her eyes and transported us out of there.

—————

27

Ceris took us directly to the shack on the Croatian island.

Micah carried Victor inside and placed him on one of the beds while I grabbed the first aid kit from the bathroom cabinet. Ceris stood beside the bed, looking like she would break down at any moment, and I was thankful the others stayed in the living room. This place was too small for all of us.

Micah turned Victor on his side, and I knelt beside the bed. I peeked under the cloth she had tied around him. It wasn't pretty. The sword had pierced him on the left side, half an inch from his heart.

"I'm not sure if there's anything I can do," I said, watching Ceris.

"I know," she said, sounding too calm. "But I need you to try something. Anything."

I nodded, believing it was best not to argue with her. As I cleaned the wound, Victor shook.

"Is he convulsing?" Ceris asked, leaning over the bed, her eyes wide in terror.

"I don't think so." I nudged Micah. "Hold him, please."

Micah held his shoulders, and I stitched the cut the best I could with him trembling. Done. It was clean and closed. That was all I could do.

Micah positioned Victor on his back, and the tremors increased.

I had seen him trembling this way before, when I first saw him in the parking lot of Langone, and when he came to see me a few weeks ago.

I rested my hands on his cheeks, and he gasped. A warm jolt prickled my palms as my energy seeped into him. With each second, the tremors lessened, until the transfer of energy was done and the trembling gone.

Removing my hands, I stood. A wave of dizziness assaulted me, and I staggered back. Micah rushed to my side and held my elbow.

"Are you okay?"

"Yes. He just took more than usual."

Ceris looked at me, unshed tears glistening in her eyes. "Thank you."

I nodded.

I thought about telling her I didn't know what was going to happen, if my healing had saved him, if it had bought him time, if the wound was too deep, if it had ripped something of importance, but she seemed so sorrowful, I decided to give her time to recover.

Micah followed me out of the bedroom and closed the door behind us.

Watching me with hooded eyes, he crossed his arms. "I don't understand. I thought they were on our side. I-I can't believe I fell for it."

"Shhh." I stepped into him, uncrossed his arms, and

placed them around my waist. I didn't care if he didn't really like me; I didn't care about the push and pull of our relationship. "Just let me hold you," I whispered, hooking my arms around his neck.

His hands splayed on my back, pulling me tighter against him. I buried my face in his neck, savoring his familiar sandalwood scent and the feeling of safety. I kissed his warm skin on his neck, and he shivered.

Tilting his head to mine, Micah rested his chin on my cheek. "You can hold me any time you want, darling." His voice was sincere.

I pulled back, expecting to see the smug grin on his face, but it wasn't there. His face was solemn, his eyes intent on mine. My gaze flickered to his full lips. He leaned into me, and I held my breath, certain he was going to kiss me again.

Then, he pulled back, clearing his throat.

"I've gotta ..." He pointed to the living room. "Yeah."

And he marched away.

Since Ceris wouldn't leave Victor's bedside, Izaera went on a few shopping trips for us alone. First, she brought the most urgent: medical supplies, including blood bags, IVs, gauze, antiseptic, morphine, ibuprofen, and a bunch of other things. Then she went out for food. The next trip was for clothes and shoes for all of us, and the last trip was for camping gear, since the shack only had two bedrooms—at first, she wanted to bring tents, but it was too cold outside. She ended up bringing several sleeping bags so we could camp in the living room. Micah insisted Izaera, Keisha, and I take the second bedroom, though one of us would to have to sleep on the floor.

Later, while Keisha helped Morgan in the kitchen with dinner, we all took turns in the only shower in the cottage. After my quick turn, I went to my bedroom, turned off the lights, laid down in my bed, and hugged Pinky.

I tried keeping thoughts of Micah out of my mind, but it was too damn hard. I didn't want to wonder why he almost kissed me and then backed out. I also chided myself for not having more self-control and for allowing these moments to happen. I should have pulled back when I noticed his eyes boring into mine, seeing through me, into my soul. A soul that belonged to him anyway.

Grunting, I rolled in bed and willed sleep to come and carry me away from here because I didn't want to deal with any of this.

However, sleep didn't come easily. When Keisha called me out later for dinner, I pretended to be sleeping. Later that night a nightmare visited me, and I did my best to stay in bed, awake but quiet so as not to wake Keisha and Izaera.

The next two days were completely boring. The cottage was too small for all of us, and there was nothing to do on the island, especially since it hadn't stopped snowing outside.

Keisha and I stretched and did some exercises a couple of times per day, mostly to pass the time, but she was rusty after being in a bed for a few days.

Ceris didn't leave Victor's bedroom, even after he woke up on the second day. He seemed conscious and fighting his wound, though he still needed lots of rest. And lots of my healing, which made me wonder if he was truly recovering at all.

On the third day, Ceris emerged, carrying Victor with her,

putting my doubts to rest. "He wants to walk a little," she explained. Half an hour later, they were back in his bedroom.

"We can't wait for them forever," Morgan said. We were huddled around the dinner table, eating Izaera's chicken noodle soup, which was delicious. "I mean, we could at least talk about finding the scepters, hash out a plan or two."

Micah nodded. "I understand, but there isn't much we can do without them. Even if we hash out a plan, Ceris will want to revise everything, every little detail, and we'll waste the same amount of time."

"It's not like we have anything to do now," Keisha muttered.

"I know what we could do," Zelen said. "We could improvise a sled and enjoy this shitty island."

Everyone chuckled. I only smiled.

After that the conversation drifted, I went to wash the dishes, and Keisha was by my side drying them.

"So," she said. "What's the problem?"

"What you mean?" I asked.

"You haven't spoken much these past few days. Like, at all."

I shrugged. "There isn't much to talk about. There's nothing happening."

She offered me a knowing look. "Ah."

Micah cut between us, placing a dirty plate in the sink. He took his time, his body looming too close, and his eyes on mine.

When he stepped back, warmth invaded my cheeks, and Keisha snorted. "Yeah, nothing happening."

I shook my head and focused on my important task. To wash dirty dishes.

———

THAT EVENING I PUT ON A THICK COAT OVER MY CLOTHES AND headed outside.

I didn't know why, but I wanted to walk around the snow-covered island, even though it didn't hold good memories. I had been here for three days and had managed to avoid it, but after so long inside the cottage with everyone around, all I wanted was a moment of peace and quiet.

I wandered to a rocky parcel, my snow boots crunching the snow, watching the waves as they crashed on the white sand at the farthest corner of the tiny island—where Micah had left with the Fates a little over four months ago.

The cold wind blew around me, and I adjusted my beanie and the collar of my coat, pulling it tight against my neck.

Snow crunched under heavy footsteps, but I didn't turn since I was sure I knew who it was.

"Isn't it too cold to be out here?" Micah asked, coming to stand beside me. He zipped up his coat and blew on his gloveless hands.

I raised my eyebrows at him. "You tell me."

"Well, I know how you can get warm pretty fast, darling." He wiggled his eyebrows, and I chuckled. He was already back to himself. "You can't say you don't want it."

"Always full of yourself."

He put his hands in the pockets of his coat and nudged me with his elbow. "As if it wasn't true."

I shook my head, returning my eyes to the beach. I didn't understand him. One minute he was pushing, the other he was pulling. I was tired of that. I was tired of everything.

He followed my gaze. "Why are you on this side of the island?" he asked. I shrugged. A long moment of silence passed before he spoke again. "I stood right there"—he pointed to the beach before us—"when the Fates took me away from here."

Oh, he remembered that too. Maybe he also remembered how that had hurt me—more than I was willing to admit.

"You know I did that for your own good, right?"

"No, I don't know," I muttered.

"I was … am not a good influence. I wanted to stay away so you would be free to make your own choices."

I scoffed. "My own choices? First, Ceris commanded me like a puppet, then the Fates owned me, and now my soul is yours. Who has any choice here?"

He sighed. "You have no idea how I wish you never got involved in this."

Ouch. I knew he didn't mean it like that, but it hurt anyway. "I'm sorry if my presence bothers you. Believe me, it wasn't my choice."

I turned around and marched away.

"Nadine …" He cursed and caught up with me, stepping in my way. "That's not what I meant. We are at war. We have barely begun to fight and look at us. Levi is hurt, and we don't know how or if he's going to be okay. Keisha and Morgan have had some rough patches too. My Death Lords betrayed me. Imha and Omi discovered our first hideout. The—"

"I was captured, and my family killed," I interrupted him, adding to his list, but my voice broke and I flinched at my words.

He clasped my shoulders. "You have no idea how sick I felt knowing they had you, knowing they had your family." His hands slid down my arms, and he cupped my elbows, pulling me closer. "You don't know how many times Ceris had to hold me back so I wouldn't march into Imha's place myself."

I stepped back and he let go of me. "You can't do that."

"Do what?"

"This." I gestured to him. "I can't take this. Your mixed signals. One minute you kiss me, the other you run away from me. One minute you say something sweet, the other you yell at me." I shook my head. "And it doesn't matter. You can't—"

"Why doesn't it matter?"

I pressed my lips together, fighting back the tears burning in my eyes. "Because you're a god. You'll live forever and won't settle for a mortal. Who cares if you're sending me mixed signals? We both know you're only playing. Oh, and let's not forget the Soul Oath. You and I know that my living days are getting closer and closer to their expiration date."

The muscles in his jaw tensed. "Nadine, I—"

"It's okay," I said. "I'm okay with it. It was my choice, and I would do it again." I sounded like Ceris ... crap. "Just please, stop it. Don't lead me on, don't stare at me, and don't help me out with anything. You're just gonna leave me anyway."

"No—"

"I should go in," I said, cutting him off. "I should help with dinner."

Without looking at Micah, I walked around him, back to the cottage.

After dinner and after Keisha and I had straightened the kitchen, I wanted a nice shower and some sleep. I entered the room I shared with Izaera and Keisha, and halted. Izaera and Ceris stood in the middle of the room, talking in hushed tones.

They noticed my presence and shushed.

"Sorry," I muttered, stepping out.

I was a little curious as to why they would be whispering, but I guessed being goddesses and living for thousands and thousands of years, they had lots in common. They trusted each other and were probably just talking, or discussing the next plans.

A tiny thread of jealousy swirled in my stomach. I remembered days with Cheryl and how easy it was to be with her, to talk with her. Just like Cheryl, uh, Ceris was now talking to Izaera.

I shook my head. Nonsense. Ceris meant nothing to me other than someone I had to put up with for the greater good. A powerful goddess who ...

A goddess with a pretty scepter, topped by a pink orb—an orb I had seen something inside of before we left the compound. How could I have forgotten this?

I had seen the same thing inside Izaera's scepter when we were in the forest.

Oh my God.

I rushed to the living room and almost threw myself at Morgan. He was mediating with Zelen in the center of the room.

"Morgan, I need to see some of your books," I blurted, disturbing his concentration. They looked up at me, their expressions a little annoyed. "It's important."

Morgan pointed to a large duffel bag beside the couch. "That's all I was able to save before we fled the bunker."

"Thanks," I muttered.

They exchanged an irritated glance then went back to their meditation.

Not wanting to disturb them further, I grabbed the duffel's straps and dragged it away. God, this damn thing weighed a ton.

"Let me help you," Micah said, taking the straps from me and lifting the bag as if it was filled with cotton balls. I glanced around. Where had he come from? "Where do you want it?"

"The kitchen table," I said, opening the kitchen door for him.

Keisha prepared coffee on the other side of the room. She arched her eyebrows at me, and I shook my head, not in the mood to explain anything.

Micah dropped the bag between two chairs.

"Thanks," I said, taking a seat.

He sat beside me. "What are we looking for?"

I stared at him. He held my gaze, serious but not closed, not annoyed, not pushing me away, and not drawing me in. Just serious and here. With me.

My heart squeezed.

"I'm not sure," I whispered, taking one of the books from the bag. "I want to see symbols, but I think there are too many of them."

Micah grabbed one book from the bag. "Symbols it is."

LATER THAT DAY, WHEN I WAS READY TO DISTURB CERIS AND call a meeting, she did before I could.

The sleeping bags were rolled up and thrown in a corner, Morgan and Keisha made coffee and sandwiches for everyone, and Ceris helped Victor to an armchair. I sat in another armchair, and Morgan took a stool by my side. Micah chose to stand by the wall to my left, and Keisha, Izaera, and Zelen squeezed on the couch.

We were ready. More than ready.

And I couldn't wait to tell them what I had found.

"We need to plan a couple of things," Ceris said, seated on the arm of Victor's chair. "If we are discovered here, where we will go next, who will we try to contact next, and the most important, what is our next step in finding the scepters?"

"I kn—"

"Ceris and I think," Victor started, not even noticing he had interrupted me, "that after this injury, my human body is much weaker than before. We believe it won't hold on for much longer."

"So we need to find the scepters now," Morgan said, his voice quavering.

Victor nodded. "We do, but I'm not strong enough to go out yet. We can't expect this to be simple. I need a few more days to rest and heal before we do anything, but that doesn't mean we can't start planning."

"I kn—"

"That's why I asked for this meeting," Ceris said. "Because once Levi feels better, we need to be on top of this matter."

"We *need* to get our hands on our scepters," Victor added.

"I kno—"

The door burst open, interrupting me. The Fates walked in.

Beside me, Morgan almost had a meltdown and knelt on the floor, his head low. Keisha lowered her head as if in a bow, and even Zelen showed them more respect than I did.

"Hello, child," the one who entered first said with eyes on

me. She halted behind the couch, while the other two remained a couple of steps back. "You don't look happy to see us."

"I never know what to expect from you," I confessed.

She offered me a lifeless smile. "Have we ever deceived you?" Well, when she put it like that. I shook my head. "Good."

Ceris stood. "Nay, can we help you with anything?"

"No, child. We are here to help you." Nay extended her hand, showing us a small crystal vial with a bright turquoise liquid.

Ceris's eyes bugged. "Is that what I think it is?"

Nay nodded.

Beside me, Morgan had another meltdown.

"Water from the Lake of Life," Victor said.

Nay nodded. "As you suspect, your human body won't hold for much longer. If we let it be, you would heal a little on your own and with Nadine's touch, but that would take quite some time. However, you'll need this right now."

"What do you mean?" Ceris asked, eyes narrowed.

Nay looked at me. "Tell them, child."

With the room's attention on me, I took a deep breath and held my head high. "I think I know where the scepters are."

28

———

Everyone spoke, or actually yelled, at me at the same time.

Everyone except Micah. He stared at me from his place along the wall with a deep frown.

When we were researching Morgan's books, he noticed I was on to something, but he didn't ask about it, and I didn't tell him either.

"Silence," Nay said in a normal tone, but energy coursed through the air and everyone quieted down. She gave the vial to Victor. "Drink it. You'll feel stronger in a couple of hours. Be aware this won't cure you. It'll only give your human body the stamina you need to keep going for a few more days."

With everyone watching, Victor uncorked the vial and drank it in one gulp. He wrinkled his nose. "By the Everlast, this tastes horrible."

Ceris grabbed his mug of coffee from the table and handed to him. I almost rolled my eyes at how caring she was with him. However, that was probably jealousy for not having —and knowing I would never have—what they did.

"Now, Nadine, tell them," Nay said.

I cleared my throat. "Just before we left the shelter, Ceris used her scepter and I saw something inside the orb. Yesterday, I remembered I saw something inside Izaera's orb when we were in the forest. I researched through Morgan's books and found out what I saw was Ceris's and Izaera's symbols."

"And?" Ceris asked, her voice harsh.

"When I was ..." I closed my eyes and swallowed the lump in my throat. It was always hard to speak about it. "When I was with Imha, she had a large world map covering an entire wall. I saw symbols on that map, and now I know what they meant." I glanced to Ceris. "I'll need a map."

She extended her hand and a scroll appeared on her open palm. I pushed the food and drinks to the side of the table, and she unrolled it over the cleared area.

The symbols sprouted to life. Several tiny bright marks danced along the map too fast to get a good look on them.

"What's happening?" Victor asked.

"Do you see the symbols?" Morgan asked.

Ceris shook her head. "I don't see anything. I mean, I know they are there, I can feel their magic, but I don't see them."

I pursed my lips. "It wasn't like this."

"What do you mean?" Izaera asked.

"Just ..." I stared at the map. Nothing happened. I took a deep breath and focused on a central point on the map, willing the magic to happen. Dizziness rushed through me, my vision darkened.

"Nadine," Micah called me.

I blinked and the darkness faded. Micah knelt beside me, watching me with concerned eyes. More mixed signals. Who needed that?

When I turned my sight back to the map, the symbols were slower than before. I focused on them.

Stop.

They did.

I gasped in amazement.

Holy shit, I had made the symbols stop!

"What do you see?" Keisha asked.

There were too many symbols, everywhere. Izaera's symbol shone over the destroyed forest, Ceris's flashed at Saint-Pierre-aux-Nonnains Basilica in France, and Micah's and Victor's glowed in the same place. I rested the tip of my index finger on the spot on the map. "Here."

Everyone spied over the map.

"A mountain in Mexico?" Morgan asked, squinting at me as if doubting me.

"Not just a mountain. A volcano," Victor said.

"The Popocatepetl volcano," Micah said.

"Their scepters are in a volcano?" Keisha asked, disbelief laced within her voice.

"An active volcano," Izaera added.

"Are you sure this is the place?" Ceris asked.

What did she mean? "Hmm, no, but with all I saw and felt, this has to be it." They looked at the map, as if answers or a detailed plan would pop out at them. "And I believe Victor's scepter is around the crater, you know, free and close to the sky, and Micah's scepter is deep down, near the lava bed because ... underworld and underground." I closed my mouth as heat spread through my cheeks.

"It makes sense," Micah said.

My head whipped to him. It did? I was afraid I was delirious.

He held my gaze, but Victor's hand on mine ripped my attention from him.

"Thank you," Victor said with a smile. He looked at the others. "The water of the Lake of Life has a quick effect. I already feel better. We should get ready to leave within a few hours."

Everyone stood and walked around the tiny living room, talking at the same time, disorienting me.

Wait. Where were the Fates? I glanced around. They were gone.

***

I CHECKED MYSELF ONE MORE TIME. ARMOR TIGHT, BOOTS strapped, hair pulled up and away from my face, daggers inside my boots, another dagger in the scabbard attached to the right side of my belt, and a sword on my left. I felt like carrying more weapons, but what difference would that make if I had only two hands to wield them?

With nothing more to do, I decided to use the bedroom's rare peace and stretch out a little.

While we got ready, Ceris and Izaera decided to go to the volcano and check the surrounding area, see if there were any demons around, if there were humans there, or if they could sense the scepters. They promised not to try anything without all of us.

"Why the arsenal, darling?"

I whirled around at the sound of Micah's voice. He leaned against the doorframe, looking too good to be true with his cocky grin and wearing his armor. God, how I loved seeing him like this. Beige wasn't really his color, but the way the thermal and the vest adorned his shoulders, arms and chest, and the way his pants hugged his legs, the color didn't matter. He looked much hotter in a warrior outfit than in his biker-rocker clothes.

I raised my arms over my head and stretched. "I want to be prepared."

"Hopefully, it'll be a quick trip."

"We don't know that."

"*Hopefully*, we'll get in, grab the damn things, and get out. Ten minutes tops."

"Hopefully," I repeated, extending my arms and bending at the waist to the side.

He took two steps into the room. "You don't sound hopeful."

I showed him a sorrowful smile. "Nothing has been quick or easy on this journey. I doubt this part, the important part, will be either."

"I'll be there to protect you, darling." He winked. "You don't need to worry."

I rolled my eyes. Hadn't I asked him to stop with his charm games? "I thought you had figured out by now that I can take care of myself."

He leaned closer. "I know, but that doesn't mean I can't protect you if I want to."

I stared at him. What was his deal? Why was he telling me this? Didn't he have more important things to do—like plan with Victor what to do once they got their scepters?

Panic rushed through me. They would get their scepters. They would become full gods with full powers, like Ceris and Izaera. They would be immortal once again. They wouldn't need me anymore.

I swallowed the lump in my throat. "Promise me you

won't let Ceris kick me out of here once you are ... Mitrus again."

He gaped at me. "What?"

"I won't be needed anymore. You won't need my healing. Since Ceris hates me, she might ditch me, and well, I won't be able to do anything about that. But I want to stay. I know I'm not a deity. I know I have no powers, but I want to stay. I want to help. Promise me I can stay."

He took my hands in his. "First, she doesn't hate you. Second, I won't let her ditch you because *I* want you here."

My heart skipped a beat, and then rushed the next ten. Oh, the mixed signals again. I couldn't take that. Not now.

Averting my eyes, I pulled my hands away. "We should finish getting ready."

However, he didn't let me and held on to my hands more firmly. "Nadine, there's something I need to tell you." Not trusting my voice, I just stared. He inhaled. "I—"

"There you are," Morgan said, appearing in the doorway. "Lady Ceris and Lady Izaera are here. We are ready to go."

Saved by the bell. I took a step back from Micah. "Good. Let's go."

I started after Morgan. Micah's fingertips caressed my elbow. "Nadine ..."

I shivered from his touch, briefly ensnared by the way he said my name.

"Come on," Morgan called, going back to the living room. "They are waiting."

I paused but didn't look back. "We should go," I whispered.

I rushed out the door before Micah could say something else that might make me cry. Like telling me our kiss had been a mistake. Or worse—that he wanted more.

29

CERIS AND IZAERA TOOK US TO AN OPENING ON THE VOLCANO'S side, supposedly halfway to the top.

Hugging myself against the cold air, I glanced around. The damn volcano was huge. Like gigantic. The view of the surrounding area, though mostly white because of the snow, was breathtaking. I closed my eyes for a minute and tried to imagine how it would be with the sun shining high. Sadly, I had never seen the sun outside of my visions, but I hoped I would see it someday. We were getting closer and closer to that. I would see it even if for only a second before the Soul Oath claimed my soul.

"This is the only entrance we discovered," Ceris said, pointing to the opening. It looked like a normal cave from where we were.

"We didn't explore it, though," Izaera said.

"Once we sensed the scepters and checked the area for demons, we went back to get you," Ceris explained.

"How about we talk about this inside? It's cold here, you

know," Micah said, his teeth chattering. "Don't want to waste time."

"Good idea," Zelen said, taking the first step toward the entrance.

"We can sense old magic in this place," Ceris said, following the forest protector. "Be careful and don't touch anything. When we find the scepters, let Levi and Mitrus get to them first. Understood?"

Everyone mumbled a half-assed, "Yes," turned on the flashlights, and she took us inside.

Once I crossed the entrance, I felt the power in this place. It hummed along the walls and brushed against me, against us, not good, not evil. If I could feel it this strong, I wondered what it felt like to Ceris, Izaera, Zelen, Victor, and Micah.

We walked along a narrow corridor with no openings in sight.

"We have only one way to go," Ceris said, at the head of the line. Victor was second, Morgan third, Zelen next, and then Keisha and me followed by Micah.

We walked a linear course for over ten minutes toward the middle of the volcano; the only sound was our boots on the stones.

"I see an opening," Ceris shouted after a while.

I sighed in relief.

We crossed the archway into a large, round room. The walls were smooth, like someone had sanded the stones. The ceiling was like a dome, high and curved with the symbol of The Everlasting Circle carved in its peak, and there was some kind of altar in the center, three feet high, with holes around its perimeter.

The power was even greater here, dancing and hopping

around the room like a charged bunny. If I read too much into it, I would say it was waiting for something.

Ceris rushed to another opening across the room. She peeked into it. "Another corridor, but it's short and ends in a stairwell. One staircase going up, another going down."

Victor reached her first. "Separate, then?"

"I don't think we should separate," Zelen said.

"I don't like the energy here and would appreciate if we could speed things along," Izaera said.

Micah nodded. "If we go to one first, then the other, we'll be wasting time."

"All right, let's separate the group then," Ceris said, stepping to the side.

Izaera stepped to the other side. "If you're going up with Levi, I'm going down with Mitrus. If anything happens, each group has a full goddess."

"Good thinking," Ceris agreed. "All right. So"—she looked at us—"Zelen and Keisha are coming with us." They stepped closer to Ceris. "And the rest of you go down with Izaera and Mitrus."

Micah glanced at me, offering me a satisfied smile. With a smile of my own, I shook my head.

Izaera turned around to us. "The plan is to go down or up, find the scepter, and come back to this room as fast as we can so we can get the hell out of here. Everyone fine with that?"

We all nodded.

"Good luck," Ceris said.

She stepped into the stairwell. Victor, Keisha, and Zelen followed her.

"Here we go," Izaera said, taking the lead. Morgan went after her, then Micah and me.

The stairwell was almost as narrow as the corridor, fitting

only two people side by side. It was uneven and high enough that Micah brushed the top of his head on the stones every few steps.

After eight flights of twenty steps—I counted—Morgan spoke up. "Whoever designed this needs to go back to architecture school." We chuckled. "Hmm, if it was you, Lord Mitrus, please forget what I said."

Micah laughed, and it sounded close to me. It brought goose bumps to my arms. "It wasn't me."

"I think the Everlast energy carved this place," Izaera said.

How was that possible?

We stayed quiet, and I wondered if these steps would ever end. I had counted them to one hundred four times and then given up because I didn't really want to know how many there were or I would hate it more than I already did, and there was nothing I could do about it.

"Iz," Micah said from the back, startling me. Iz?

"Yes?" Izaera said from the front.

"I'm sorry," he said, and by his steady, solemn tone, I knew he meant it. Which made me more curious. Micah was sorry? About what?

"I know," she said. "Apology accepted."

Morgan glanced back with a what-the-hell-are-they-talking-about look, and I shrugged.

"Iz used to have a pretty garden inside the Clarity Castle," Micah explained. "She kept a sample of the rarest plants on Earth there, the ones in extinction, and the newest ones so she could study them. On the day prior to my death, we argued about humans and their belief in us. During the argument, she brought up Levi and his ideas and how great he was and that we should follow him blindly and such. I lost my temper and burnt the entire garden."

"Oh." I wasn't sure if there was anything else to say.

"Mitrus's temper has always been a problem." Izaera glanced back. "Perhaps it isn't anymore."

"I'm still not sure about that." Micah sighed. "Iz, I promise I'll help you build it again. And I'll even help you care for it."

Izaera snorted. "That's something I'll only believe when I see it."

I chuckled.

"What?" he asked, nudging his finger against my back.

"I can't imagine you caring for flowers and plants."

"Well, you'll see it."

I came to a halt, and he bumped into me. I would have tripped if he hadn't put his arm around my waist and held me with my back pressed to him.

I tilted my head to the side and looked up. His eyes were intent on mine, much like his tone had been, but there was something else there, something that made my decisions more difficult to carry out.

Why did he say that? Why did he look at me like this? He knew, better than anyone, that when the world reached that point, when they were in the Clarity Castle once again caring for flowers and whatnot, I would be long gone.

Besides that, I kept in mind the same thing I told myself after finding out what Victor really was. Micah was a god, and he would live forever. Even if I didn't have my death day on a calendar, he would never waste time with a mortal. Yes, he was all flirty and knew exactly how to spin me around his finger. I didn't doubt that in his long life he had had affairs with humans, but that was all. Affairs. I wasn't an affair kind of girl.

Holy shit, what was I thinking?

A wave of rage coursed through me. I brushed his arm

away from me and rushed down to catch up with Morgan and Izaera.

A new tension filled the crammed air of the narrow stairwell as we continued our descent. I blamed Micah for it.

Morgan asked, "Any idea how deep we are?"

"We've been going for forty minutes," Izaera answered. "I would say two miles or so."

"That's a lot," Morgan mumbled.

"Which means we should be almost there," the goddess said.

Silence returned.

I hoped it didn't take much longer because each time I realized we were deep inside the earth with no windows and no central air system, I felt panic building inside me. I had no idea how we were still breathing in here, but I hoped it didn't change any time soon.

"We're here," Izaera said several minutes later.

"Here where?" Morgan asked, watching over Izaera's head.

"I don't know," she answered. "I just see a doorway ahead."

I shifted to the side and looked past Morgan. The glow from the flashlight showed the faint contours of an opening about thirty yards down.

Eager to reach it, we raced down the remaining steps and crossed the doorway. Red-hot heat washed over me, and I gasped. The air was excessively stuffy here, and I felt dizzy.

"Oh God," I whispered, glancing around.

We were in an underground chamber, not too tall, but wide and deep. Singed rocks lined the walls, the ceiling, and the ground. They lined everything except the lava river flowing forty feet from us. It surged up from the wall on the left and disappeared once again behind the wall on the right. Never before had I thought I would see real hot lava.

"Wow," Morgan whispered, big eyes on the lava. "For some reason, I don't really like being here."

"Me neither," I said.

Izaera closed her eyes. "Can you sense it? It's stronger here."

Micah narrowed his eyes. "Yes, I can."

I glanced around once more. There was no other opening, no other door. It had to be here. But where? Other than rocks and lava, there was nothing.

Morgan paced in front of the doorway. "What do we do now?"

"I don't know," Micah said.

I took a few steps toward the lava. The heat increased exponentially with each step, and I wondered if I could be burned without touching it. Besides being deadly, it was a beautiful thing. Thick, orange magma, looking like creamy fire, flowing away like a wave.

A hand clasped around my wrist. "Careful," Micah said, holding me back. "Don't get too close."

I glanced over my shoulder and found his worried eyes on me. Was he afraid I was still trying to kill myself and would jump in? "I don't plan to," I told him, halting. He let go of my arm but came to stand by my side. "Where could it be?"

"I don't know," he said. "But I bet my powers you'll be the one to find it."

I looked at him. "How come?"

"You're the one who finds everything. Without you, we wouldn't have done anything. We wouldn't have gotten to Cathedral Rock, we wouldn't have found out who we are, and we wouldn't be here."

I shook my head. "I'm sure Ceris would have found a way to help."

"To help Victor, but not me." Once more, his expression was solemn and his voice sincere.

I hated when he was serious. It was hard to be mad at him, to keep my distance from him.

"I can't pinpoint the source of the power," Izaera said, cutting through our trance. I lowered my eyes from his, noticing she was standing on my other side. "How are we supposed to find it?"

Micah nudged me with his shoulder, and I almost rolled my eyes. Almost.

Instead I decided to believe in his belief in me. I closed my eyes, imagining the scepter I had seen during my visions, and focused on it.

A current of energy replaced the stuffy air. I felt tendrils of power dancing around me. They twirled around us, and then shot around the room, zigzagging without any apparent pattern.

The tendrils formed a long line and disappeared through the ground, right behind us, taking its tangible energy with it. What the hell? I concentrated on it, calling it out. But it was gone.

I opened my eyes.

"Anything?" Micah asked in a low voice.

"I don't think so," I said, frustrated for disappointing him.

I whirled around toward the entryway and Morgan, and I saw it. The silver symbol on the ground, right where the energy had gone through.

I pointed to a large, broken rock a few steps from us. "There."

Micah gave me a sidelong glance. "Are you sure?"

Hadn't he just said he believed in me? "I can see your symbol over that damn rock, okay? It's there."

"Good enough for me." Izaera approached the rock. "You don't know what Mitrus should do, do you?"

I shook my head.

"It's okay," Micah said, going to the rock. "We'll figure it out."

Curious, Morgan and I got close to the rock too.

Micah placed his hand over the stone, and a black light shone from the broken slit. With wide eyes, Micah jerked his hand away and the light was gone.

"Oh," Izaera muttered.

Without hesitating, Micah rested his palms, one on each side of the long slit. The shine came back, stronger this time. The slit grew wider and Micah smiled. He reached inside it and, after a few seconds of struggle, pulled his arm out.

He held the crystal scepter in his hand.

30

MICAH SCRAMBLED TO HIS FEET, A BIG SMILE ON HIS FACE. HIS gaze met mine, pride and realization shone on his handsome features, and I smiled.

The scepter was more beautiful than I remembered. A long, round staff, topped by an orb shining with a black light, all made of crystal. It probably weighed a ton, but Micah held it as if it didn't weigh more than a rose.

He tightened his grip around the scepter. "Nothing is happening."

Hmm. Something nagged in my mind. The scepter was round and somewhat thin ... the first room. The altar and the holes on it.

"You have to take it to that first room we came through," I said. "I think you and Victor have to take the scepters there."

"Are you sure?" Izaera asked.

I put my hands on my hips. "Why does everyone keep asking me that? No, I'm not sure. I'm never sure."

"And yet, you haven't been wrong once," Micah said. "Let's go."

"Wait a second," Izaera said. She closed her eyes, and I thought she was entering a deep sleep. A few moments later, her eyes fluttered open. "All right. I told Ceris where we found the scepter. They will try that and meet us in the altar room as soon as they have Levi's."

Morgan frowned. "Can we go now?"

We didn't answer, but we moved to the stairs. At first we skipped the steps, rushing up, but after ten minutes of happy climbing our legs were tired.

"The others have it better," Izaera said, leaning against the wall to catch her breath. "They got tired first, but now they will breeze to the entrance."

I leaned beside her.

"Then we better keep moving," Micah urged, gently pulling me off the wall.

We continued to climb the steps, but not at the same pace as before.

When we predicted there couldn't be much more painful climbing ahead of us, the sound of a loose rock bouncing down the steps brought us to a halt. A few seconds later, the rock came into view, a tiny little thing, rolling down the steps and created such an echo.

Izaera put the tip of her boot over it, and the place became dead silent.

"That's odd," I whispered. "Why would there be a loose r—?"

The growls of demons rushing down the steps vibrated through the walls, making me shut my mouth.

Micah thrust his scepter into my hand and rushed forward to stand beside Izaera, his sword drawn.

I stood there, gawking at the marvel in my hand, and amazed, not only by its beauty, but because it didn't weigh one tenth of what I thought it would—and because Micah had trusted it to me.

The clash of metal, the bright green flashes, and the growl and grunts told more of the fight than my eyes showed me. Morgan held his flashlight higher, but still it didn't illuminate much.

An anxiety to help, to fight, built in me, like an itch I couldn't scratch.

Morgan scooted closer to me. "I can hold it, if you want to fight."

I started to turn to him, to hand the scepter to him, but stopped. "There's no space," I said, looking at the shapes that were Micah and Izaera. "All I can do is stand behind them and cheer. Not good enough."

In a matter of seconds, we moved up again crossing over the bodies of fallen demons.

"By the Everlast," Izaera groaned, throwing a green bolt into the darkness. I was sure it had hit a demon, but I couldn't see it from here. "Why are there shields everywhere? Like in the shelter, I can barely cast a decent bolt here."

"Better safe than sorry," Micah said, parrying a claw with his blade and drawing blood.

"It's nice when I don't want enemies casting anything at me, but not when *I* want to cast something!"

Micah chuckled, but it became a grunt as one of the demons swiped at his arm.

With an enraged shout, he slashed the demon's throat and stomped over its body, already lunging at another one.

"Come on," he shouted. "We need to get up there."

Only the Fates knew how many demons were in our way. I hoped not many because if the demons were here, it meant Omi and Imha knew where we were, and the longer it took us to do whatever we had to do, the more time they had to arrive.

I was about to ask one of them to trade places with me so they could rest, when they stopped fighting.

Izaera took a long, calming breath. "It seems clear now."

"Until the next wave comes," Micah said, panting.

"Let's hope there aren't many around," I said, coming up the stairs to stand before him. "Not yet, at least."

I handed him the scepter, and he clasped his fingers over mine.

I didn't object. I didn't have it in me to object. Not now. Instead, I stared at him. Really stared at him. Even with the sweat, the tired mien, and the few bruises, he was too gorgeous for anyone's sake. His black eyes met mine, and I wished I could read whatever secret message was in them because I would bet my soul, if it was still mine, there was a hidden message in there.

I wiggled my hand free from his and, as I turned to the stairs, the thick trail of blood on his upper arm caught my eye.

I brushed my fingers beside it. He groaned.

"Sorry," I whispered, the heat of embarrassment taking over my cheeks. Why did I touch him?

"It's all right."

"Is it bad?" I wanted to reach over and get a good look at it, but I was afraid of touching him again.

"I don't think so." He showed me his cocky smile. "I'll live."

He better because I had lost too much already, and I couldn't lose him too. I gasped with that realization.

"Let's move," Izaera called from several steps ahead. "Are you coming?"

Clearing my throat, I stepped back and rushed up.

I slowed down when I caught up with Morgan and Izaera, but I could feel Micah close behind me.

As I lifted my foot to reach the next step, a monstrous groan reached my ears. The ground shook. The walls shook. The ceiling shook.

"The volcano!" Morgan yelled. "It's awakening."

Bright orange glowed from far down the stairwell.

"Run!" Izaera shouted.

Oh, God.

On instinct, I placed my foot down to run, but with the tremors, it slipped. I was falling back, arms flailing at my sides, trying to grab anything, but there were only stones, rocks, and no edge to really grip. Then strong arms snaked around my waist, and I was pulled up, my chest flush with Micah's.

His wide eyes were on mine, and I could feel his heart beating almost as fast as mine.

"By the Everlast, I thought you were gonna fall headfirst," he whispered.

We looked back at the bright orange. It was getting brighter. And hotter.

"Shit," I whispered, disentangling myself from him.

He grabbed my hand and practically hauled me up. I had no idea where he got so much energy and stamina, but I wasn't complaining right now.

We reached the altar room, and I leaned against the wall, taking in the less stuffy air in big gulps.

"Nadine," Micah whispered.

I opened my mouth to send him to hell and tell him to leave me alone while I was trying to resurrect my lungs, but I lost my voice when I lifted my head.

Oh, God.

My legs wanted to give away, but I forced them to lock and hold on.

I straightened my back, stood beside Micah, Izaera, and Morgan, and pulled my sword from my waist, facing the eight demons in the altar room.

The monsters lunged at us.

Izaera quickly stunned three with her green bolts. Micah engaged two, fighting them as if he was a dancer on recital night. Two came at me, and I hopped over the altar, where I had an advantage.

Morgan ... I glanced around. Where was Morgan?

One of the demons swiped at my leg, and I fell on the ground. Pain burst from my knees, jarring my legs. I gritted my teeth, willing the scream to stay inside.

It came at me with its big claws again. I jumped up, and when its arm was pulled back I knelt again and slashed its throat. The gooey blood spilled on me, and I wrinkled my nose in disgust.

The other demon didn't waste time and jumped up on the altar. I was about to parry its attack, prepared to duck low and pierce it from the side, but it wasn't necessary as the tip of a blade appeared from its chest, immobilizing it.

The blade was gone, and the demon fell at my feet, revealing Micah behind it.

He had his smug grin on. "You're welcome, darling."

I marched around the demon and stopped a foot from him, pointing my finger at his chest. "I don't need you to save me all the time."

He looked like I had slapped him. "What? So I'm supposed to let you fall into the lava, or let you fight demons alone while I watch? Why not help you?"

"I don't need your help!"

"Why is it so hard for you to accept my help?"

I pressed my lips together, but the words slipped anyway. "I am not a damsel in distress! I'm not helpless!"

He leaned over me. "I know that. Believe me, I even think it's quite hot actually. But you can't blame me for wanting to protect you. I—"

"Protect me?" I scoffed. "Did you forget our deal? How will you protect me from that?"

"What is she talking about?" Izaera asked, coming up to the altar with us. Micah and I stepped back, turning away from each other. "Neither of you will answer? Mitrus, what deal did you make with her?"

"It doesn't matter," I said before he could answer her. "It's *my* deal and it won't affect anyone or anything else, so you don't need to worry about it."

Tilting her head, Izaera squinted at me, as if trying to read my soul. "And because you said that, I'm now worried. What is it?"

I wouldn't tell her, no matter how many times she asked or what she did. I just hoped Micah didn't tell her either.

Morgan appeared from the shadows along a wall. "Tell us, Nad."

"It doesn't matter," I repeated in a low tone. There were just the demons' bodies and us in the room now. I turned to Micah. "Here." I pointed to one of the holes on the edge of the altar. "Place your scepter here."

Matter forgotten, he inserted the end of his scepter in the hole and let go. It fit perfectly, making the scepter stand tall.

"I don't understand," he said.

"We probably have to wait for Victor," I said.

Micah puffed in frustration. He clenched and unclenched

his fists, probably trying to hide from me that he was trembling.

Shaking my head, I reached to him and cupped his cheeks. "When will you learn to ask for it?"

A cold jolt prickled my palms and energy seeped into him.

Closing his eyes, he inhaled deeply. "I was hoping we could end this soon and I wouldn't have to bother you," he whispered.

"I don't like seeing you hurt," I said.

The energy stopped flowing, and Micah opened his eyes, staring into mine. I pulled my hands away, but he took them in his. "Careful, darling. I'll think you care."

Fighting a smile, I retreated and jumped off the altar.

Morgan kept glancing at the doors, his eyes wide, his hands shaking, and Izaera communicated with Ceris often.

"They are on their way down," she informed us. I wasn't keeping track of time, and honestly, the minutes felt like hours.

Micah paced from one edge of the altar to the other, visibly impatient. "Tell them to hurry, before more demons arrive."

"Too late for that," a new voice said.

My blood froze, and I nearly dropped my sword. Everyone froze.

I didn't need to turn around to find out to whom that voice belonged, but I did anyway. Omi stood by the main entrance with a crap load of demons.

31

———

Like the raging sea, demons and more demons came out from the doorway, flanking Omi.

"What? No welcome? And I thought you would be glad to see me." He turned his big smile to me. "Especially you, Nadine."

Rage burned in my veins, and I lunged at him. Micah jumped off the altar, grabbed my arm, and held me back.

"I'm gonna kill you!" I shouted.

Omi laughed. "Ah, how I love when humans speak nonsense." His smile slipped away from his face as his eyes shifted to Micah. "So it's true. Mitrus. Long time no see, brother."

"Do not call me brother," Micah said through gritted teeth. "You and that bitch plotted against me, you played me against Levi. And Imha and you are the reason the world is in this mess."

Omi arched one eyebrow. "Mess? Imha and I don't think so. The world is the way we want it to be."

"You two are hopeless."

"No, brother, we are not. We are strong together. Imha and I make a good team. A good couple." The corners of his mouth twitched up. "Oh, wait. Is that why you are so wound up? Because she prefers me? But, brother, everyone knew that."

I couldn't help but glance at Micah. He shook his head, disgust on his face. "If I could go back in time, I would erase any association I had with her."

"The lies people tell themselves," Omi said, smiling at me. "He's a master liar, Nadine. Don't buy anything he tells you. He'll woo you with his confident smile and his sweet words, but he'll betray you. He'll betray everyone. He always does."

Micah turned his eyes to me. "That's not true," he whispered.

"Another lie," Omi said.

"Shut up!" Micah yelled, advancing a step.

"See? He doesn't want you to hear the truth."

"You ..." Micah leapt at him, and this time I held him back.

Omi laughed. "Aren't you two cute together?" His face hardened. "It's a shame you both will be dead soon." He raised his arm to the ceiling and yelled, as a wave of demons rushed to us.

Izaera cast a green shield in front of us, buying us time. Micah clasped my arm and pulled me around the altar, picking up his scepter on the way, where we would have an advantage.

The shield broke, and Izaera brought vines from the cracks between the rocks. The vines ensnared the demons, slowing and bothering them, buying us more time. If only Victor and Ceris would hurry ...

A couple of demons got free, and they charged us. Back-to-back, Micah and I fought them. Parry, dodge, duck, slash, stab. It was almost automatic and easy now, if it weren't for the fact that I was exhausted from coming up the stairs and the previous two fights.

We had killed a dozen or more when Omi must have decided it was taking too long and advanced. Izaera was ready and engaged him. I sighed in relief—it was only fair, since she was the only one with magical powers that matched his.

Meanwhile, we were busy with demons. I lost count after I killed my sixteenth. How many were there? And more kept entering the room. Each time a new wave surged I tensed, thinking Imha would be among them. Why wasn't she here?

And where was Morgan?

A claw came at me and I ducked, feeling the whoosh of air above my head. Once I straightened my back, I kicked the demon in its stomach, sending it back. Another pair of arms appeared by my side, talons ready to cut. I lifted my sword and parried its attack. The first one lunged at me, but I stepped back and used that opening to pierce my sword through the middle of its back. Buzzing with adrenaline, I stepped over the body and jumped, flying to the second monster. It readied its claws, but I struck them with my blade, sending them to the side while cutting him, then spun to the other side. While it recovered its balance, I slashed its throat.

They fell back revealing Morgan behind them.

I half-smiled. "You had me worried."

With hooded eyes, Morgan pulled the Crimson Dagger from behind his back. "You don't have to worry about me," he said, his tone cold. "My Lord is here now."

I glanced at the dagger in his hand. "Oh, Morgan, no."

Snarling, he pounced at me. I jumped back, trying to avoid him and bumped into Micah.

"Hey," he said between grunts and groans. He was still fighting two demons.

I remained close to him. "Morgan, I don't want to hurt you. Please, stay away."

Morgan swiped the dagger at me, and I blocked it with my sword, pushing him back.

"You're a good girl, Nadine," Morgan said, devoid of any emotion. "I'm sorry it has come to this."

"I'm sorry too," I whispered, tears building behind my eyes. No, this couldn't be true. Morgan couldn't have turned to Omi. He couldn't have betrayed us. "It was you who told Omi where we would be?"

He came at me again. I ducked under his arm, and careful not to hurt him too much, kicked him in the hip, causing him to stagger back.

"Yes. The forest and here."

"And NYC?"

"No. I wasn't committed to Lord Omi then. I only joined them after you survived Lord Omi and Lady Imha's tortures." He flashed me an evil smile and I cringed. This wasn't the Morgan I knew, and it broke my heart. "New York was the demons. They sensed a stronger aura in the city. That's why the population of bats grew within the city and why they attacked people outside the hospital, because they could sense you there. When Lord Levi showed up to see you, the demons sensed his stronger aura with yours and that's all Lord Omi needed to know the girl Brock had imprisoned was in the city."

Morgan took a step forward and thrust the Crimson

Dagger at me. I waited until the last second to duck under it, then pushed him aside with my shoulder.

I retreated a few steps and turned back to face him. "But ... how did Omi know about me? About me being a girl? I thought Brock was dead."

"He is dead, but Lord Omi had already been summoned and he appeared there right after we left. Brock had a few of your things in the school, mainly a bag with clothes and girly accessories you bought during our trip. Unmistakably feminine," he said, swirling the dagger in his hand. "Anyway, I didn't tell Lord Omi about the meeting with the Death Lords because I was hurt and stayed out of that, though I was able to disenchant Keisha's armor before you left."

I gasped. "You did that? How?"

He had an evil grin on. "I would have disenchanted all of your armor if Lord Levi hadn't interrupted me. Good thing I was quick to tell him a lie, and he believed me. I almost made him take me to the Death Lords' meeting, even hurt. But that went well with Deven, Eklan, and Chael there."

I gasped. "Holy shit, you helped them when they were in the shelter."

"Yes. But we had to maintain appearances in case Lord Mitrus and Lord Levi weren't killed that night. I continued to pretend to be on your side and left with you."

"I can't believe this," I whispered, feeling his betrayal weighing on my chest.

Micah stabbed a demon, pulled his sword out of its body, and whirled around to us, a mask of rage over his face. "Me neither."

He raised his sword, ready to strike Morgan, but I got in his way. "No!" I held his arm. "No. He's still in there. He has to be."

Watching Morgan and the dagger, Micah shook his head. "Once a human is touched by the power of our allegiance objects, there is no coming back. The Morgan you knew is gone."

I refused to believe that. However, I remembered Morgan saying something similar about Brock. Still, this was Morgan, not Brock. Morgan was a better man. He could get out of this, couldn't he?

Morgan charged us again. I spun around and deflected his blow.

Micah was about to strike him again—and this time I wasn't sure if I could stop him—when a demon showed up behind him and clawed his back. Groaning, he whirled and engaged his attacker, leaving Morgan to me.

Oh, God.

"Surrender, Nadine," Morgan said. "Surrender and they might let you live."

I almost laughed. Almost. If only he knew about the Soul Oath, he wouldn't be offering me such a deal.

But I didn't laugh. Instead new tears surged up. "Please, Morgan. Focus. You're not like this. You dedicated your entire life to The Everlasting Circle."

"Exactly!" He smiled. "Lady Imha and Lord Omi are the essence of the new Everlasting Circle. And I'm helping them."

He thrust that dagger at me, and I jumped to the side. "Stop!"

"Only when you surrender. Or when you're dead." He jumped forward, raising his weapon. I parried it, calculating in my head how I could disarm him without actually hurting him, and that meant hard kicks or punches.

He, on the other hand, didn't have such qualms.

When I ducked from the dagger, Morgan kneed my chest. My torso flew up, the air rushing out of me, and I staggered back, dizzy. I blinked in time to see his fist coming at me. My head whipped to the side, and pain exploded on my chin, spreading through my jaw and down my neck. I tripped on a stone and fell on my side, my vision darkening.

"Nadine!" Micah yelled.

Dear God, that hurt!

I blinked several times. Morgan stood above me, his feet straddling my legs. "One last chance. Surrender!"

I would have spat in his face if I wouldn't have made a fool of myself and drooled. Instead I held his gaze. "Never." I drew my knees toward my chest, and then kicked his shins. Cursing, he clambered back.

Taking advantage of the moment, I propped myself up on my elbows and reached for my sword.

"Bitch!" Morgan cried. He jumped at me and raised his dagger as the mountain roared and shook.

The dagger pierced my side, just above the hip bone. I yelled. Micah yelled. Everyone was yelling. And shaking. And fading.

My vision blackened, and my cheek grazed the stone under me.

"I'll kill you," Micah spat.

"No, Lord Mitrus, I'll have the honor of killing you and delivering your scepter to Lord Omi."

No, no, no. I pushed against the darkness in my mind, concentrated on the spots of light dancing in my vision, and willed them to grow and spread. A long breath in, a long breath out. Again.

My mind and vision clearing, I sat up and blinked at the scene.

With three demons holding his arms and neck, Micah thrashed like a caged lion while Morgan advanced to him, an evil smile on his lips and the Crimson Dagger in his hand.

Oh, God. Ignoring the sharp pain in my side, I closed my hand around the hilt of my sword and pushed to my feet as Morgan pulled his arm back, ready to pierce Micah's heart. Without really thinking about it, I flew to Morgan.

He saw me coming, though, and sidestepped. I was prepared. I whirled past his opening, ducking when he swatted his arm at me, and hit the back of his head with the hilt of my sword.

Unconscious, he fell face-first.

Not wasting time, I picked up Micah's sword from the ground, and turned to him and the demons holding him. One of them let go of Micah to come at me. Seeing his arm free, I didn't think twice. I threw his sword at him. He caught it as I dodged a claw swipe. Then I focused on my fight. The demon advanced, swatting his heavy arm at me. I slashed its arm, then jumped to the side and kicked him. Another demon came from behind and swiped its claws on my shoulder. I cried, whirling to it and cutting its arm off. It roared and jumped at me. Knowing they weren't bright creatures, I stepped back and out of the way, letting the two monsters bump headfirst. I almost laughed, but instead I slashed one's throat and stabbed the other's heart.

When I turned to Micah, he was pulling his sword from a fourth demon. God, they were multiplying!

He spun on his feet and stared at me.

"Thank the Everlast, you're all right," he whispered, running to me. He threw his arms around me, holding me tight. Surprised, it took me a brief moment to return the gesture. I buried my face in his chest, relieved he was all right too. He splayed his hands on my back, and I winced as he hit the spot where Morgan had stabbed me. "You're hurt," he said, sounding as if he had forgotten.

"I barely feel it now."

"It's because of the adrenaline." He twisted my shoulder to get a better look at it. "It's not too bad. It doesn't seem deep." He ripped the end of his shirt and tied it around my waist, making sure it secured the wound. "There. That should do the trick for now."

He smiled at me. I smiled back.

From the corner of my eyes, I saw movement behind him. I pushed him to the side and raised my sword. With his dagger trained to where Micah's heart had been a second ago, Morgan ran into my blade.

As if it had burned me, I dropped my sword and my hands flew to my mouth.

Morgan fell back, my sword buried in his chest. "You will burn in the fires of the underworld," Morgan wheezed.

A sob lodged in my throat, and I fell to my knees. Micah's heavy hand squeezed my shoulder.

Morgan gasped, blinked, and then went still.

Oh, God, I killed Morgan. I had killed Morgan. Me. Killing a person. And not just any person. Morgan.

Killing demons in self-defense was one thing. Killing humans—and a friend—was another.

A wave of nausea rolled in my stomach, and I pressed a hand to my mouth.

Footsteps and voices echoed inside my head, sounding distant.

With bruises and some ripped clothing, Ceris, Victor, Keisha, and Zelen stepped out of the back doorway and froze.

On the other side of the room, Omi seemed to have a

renewed energy as he was finally able to hit a bolt to Izaera's chest and send her flying to the farthest wall.

Immediately, Ceris cast a shield in front of them. Omi sent a red bolt toward them at the same time.

The bolt exploded on contact, breaking the shield.

"Go!" Ceris pushed Victor and the others to the side and stepped toward Omi.

"Ah, the brave, loving Ceris," Omi said. "Good to see you again, sister."

Without acknowledging him, Ceris threw a pink bolt at him. Their fight commenced.

Victor, Keisha, and Zelen stopped short between Morgan's body and Micah and me.

Holding his shiny scepter, Victor knelt before me. "What happened?"

I shook my head, unsure I could think of what happened, much less speak about it.

Micah's hand left my shoulder. "Keisha, stay with her. Levi, come with me."

Keisha appeared before me. "Are you okay?"

I shook my head and tears sprung to my eyes. Oh, God, I killed Morgan. I would never get over it. Nausea swirled in my belly again, and I clamped my mouth, breathing deeply through my nose.

Morgan didn't think the dagger had any more power, but it did. The dagger had intoxicated him, robbed him of his thoughts and life. *Omi* had robbed him of his thoughts and life. Because of Omi and his object of allegiance, Morgan had turned into a crazed man. I had killed him, yes, but he was too far gone to be saved. At least, that was what I wanted to believe, since now there was no choice. Besides if the real, old Morgan could have seen what the new Morgan had been up to, he would have wanted to die. That was how dedicated he was to the creed.

All right. Where was determined warrior Nadine? I needed her right now. Not the weak, stand back, hide wherever she can Nadine. I needed the one who could store all the bad stuff into an airtight container and lose that container in the back of her mind, while focusing on revenge, on retribution.

I could do this.

I shoved the container with my sentiments to the back of my mind where it would get lost, at least until we got past this situation. I took a deep breath and stood.

"What do I have to do?" Victor asked.

I pointed to the hole on the opposite side of the altar from Micah. "Place your scepter here."

He narrowed his eyes. "And?"

I opened my mouth to answer, but a different word came out. "Demons!" I yelled.

More demons emerged in the cave from the entrance. They rushed past the spot where Ceris and Izaera both fought against Omi—who seemed to be holding well on his own against two goddesses—and came toward us.

With their scepters in hand, Micah and Victor stepped down from the altar and came to stand beside Zelen, Keisha, and me.

We fought. I barely saw a thing. My mind was numb; all I knew was that I had to dodge, parry, duck, stab, slash, and repeat.

Keisha saved my neck more than once when I seemed too focused on one demon and didn't notice another approaching. I should have said thank you, but I was too caught up, too wound up, too not myself.

However, I did notice when the numbers of coming demons reduced.

"Victor, Micah," I yelled through the clanks of metal and the growls and grunts. "Go do your thing. We'll cover for you."

After they killed their current opponents, they jumped onto the altar. I nudged Keisha to help watch the sides, while Zelen took the back.

"Just place the scepters in the holes, right?" Victor asked.

I dodged a claw. "Yes, but I don't know which one, other than they should be opposites."

"But there are ten holes," Victor said.

I kicked the demon back as Micah answered for me. "Then we try all of them."

I ran my sword through the demon's chest and turned to the altar. Victor and Micah grabbed their scepters from two holes and placed them in the next ones. Nothing happened. They took their scepters from those holes and—

Across the room, Omi threw Ceris to the side and deflected Izaera's bolt with a shield, all the while, watching the guys at the altar.

A red bolt formed in his palm.

"Watch out!" I pointed to Omi.

Micah and Victor whirled around and jumped to the side, avoiding the bolt by inches. I stepped on the altar intent on crossing it and helping Ceris and Izaera against Omi, but energy surged up around my legs and stopped me in the center.

"What is this?" I asked, incapable of moving. The energy surrounded every inch of me.

Omi was ready to send another bolt, his eyes on me this

time, but Ceris knocked him back with one of her bolts, and then Izaera was on him too.

Victor turned to me. "I don't know."

"Can't you move?" Micah asked.

"No!"

"I don't understand," Victor muttered.

Since I couldn't move my head, I scanned the area with my eyes and I understood. "There." I tried pointing my fingers or jabbing my chin to my right, but nothing happened.

Thank goodness, Victor and Micah understood and looked the way I was looking. The hole on my right was shining.

"Is the one opposite to it shining too?"

"Yes," Micah answered.

"Then place the scepters there," I said.

"But what about you?" Victor asked.

I swallowed. "I-I think I'm supposed to be here."

Micah was in front of me in a flash. "What? What does this mean? Did you know this? Why didn't you tell me? Why—?"

"I don't know!" I cut him off. "I don't know any of it. Just ... just do it, okay? Please." He put a hand on my cheek, looking unhappy about it. "Micah, Ceris and Izaera won't be able to hold Omi much longer, more demons are bursting in, and only the Fates know when Imha is arriving. Please, do this so we can leave."

His eyes shone with indecision. Finally, he nodded, pulling his hand away, and went to my left, where he placed his scepter. Then Victor placed his scepter in the hole to the right. Energy burst through me and I gasped.

A bright white shine came from the altar, forcing me to close my eyes.

A ruckus sounded around me. The clanking of swords, the whoosh and oomphs of blows being dealt and received, the growls and the groans, the yells, and the rapid shuffle of feet on the rocks. I was aware of it all until the energy began pounding inside me, like a thousand jackhammers. The energy dragged me down to my knees, and then it slipped out from me.

I blinked my eyes open. My hands pressed against the stones on the altar, and lines of white energy ran down my arms and zigzagged to the scepters.

Eyes bugged, Micah reached for me. A shock coursed through us when his fingers brushed my shoulder. I yelped and he jerked away.

He cursed. "What is it doing? Is it hurting?"

"I-I don't know," I croaked.

Filling with the energy that had been in me, the scepters shone brighter and brighter.

My head felt heavy, my vision dimmed, and my muscles felt like jelly. The energy was leaving me completely. For a moment, I wondered if it had taken everything, even my own energy. I wondered if this was my purpose, if my aura was powerful to make Micah and Victor full gods again.

The last two lines left my arms and zoomed to the scepters, and I fell to my side gasping for air.

Once more bright light shone, blinding me for a moment, but this time they came from the scepters.

Micah knelt beside me, but I shook my head. "Go. Get your scepter. Now."

With a pained expression, he stepped back and stood

before his scepter. Victor and Micah shared a nod, and at the same time, they closed their hands around their scepters.

"No!" Omi yelled.

The lines of energy appeared on Micah's and Victor's hands, running up their arms and shoulders and chest, taking every inch of them until they were encased in white light and shone brighter than anything I had seen or encountered before. I closed my eyes again until the shine receded.

When I opened my eyes, the glow was gone and they were there, one on my left, one on my right, standing tall and proud, with their scepters. No bruises, no signs of weariness, and looking amazing in their own skins.

"Did it work?" I asked, pushing up on my elbows.

Micah beamed at me. "It did."

For some reason, I expected them to become the older men I had seen in my visions, but they still wore the same handsome bodies and faces from when I had first met them.

"My, oh my," Imha's voice echoed through the room. "It seems I'm late to the party."

32

———

Imha had brought chaos with her because everything and everyone suddenly went crazy.

Omi broke through Ceris and Izaera, and reached Imha. Side by side, Victor and Micah lunged toward Imha and Omi. More demons burst through the door, and Keisha and Zelen went to them.

I needed to help. If I didn't, they would be two short. Even though two of them had just recovered their powers, we were still embarrassingly outnumbered.

I sat up and my head spun. Oh God, what had happened to me?

Keisha showed up before me, striking a demon that had dove to me and I hadn't even noticed. My brain was mush. So were my muscles.

She fended off a couple more, while I scooted back. If I couldn't help, I had better hide because I would only attract unwanted attention and distract Keisha's focus. Feeling weak, exhausted, small, and alone, I reached the edge of the altar. I prepared to jump off and stopped. Morgan's body was right there, at my feet. A sob raked my body, and I pressed a hand to my mouth to keep it in. Oh my God. Morgan was dead. My family was dead. The world was destroyed. How many more would die before this mess was over?

Keisha roared and the sound made me turn around. She brandished her sword, dropping one demon after another with her sure strokes, her blade ripping through their grayish bodies like she was ripping through paper. Zelen and his staff weren't too bad either. He moved fast for a guy who appeared so old.

Farther away, Ceris and Izaera took turns assisting Keisha and Zelen, trying to thin the wave of demons running to them, and throwing bolts at Imha and Omi trying to catch them off guard. The beauty of it all was to watch Victor and Micah working together to beat Imha and Omi.

They looked like ninjas, moving fast, exchanging blows, spinning around each other, throwing bolt after bolt, a fierce look on their faces and a lethal glint in their eyes.

If I didn't know better, I would believe they had worked together forever.

"Isn't it fun?" Imha asked, flinging a huge purple ball at Micah. He slipped to the side and let it pass. "All of us back together. Playing, fighting, killing." She threw a purple bolt at them. Victor cast a shield and when it broke, it exploded in purple smoke.

That was new.

Coughing, the guys clambered back, and Omi threw several red bolts at them. The bolts hit them on the chest and shoulders, sending them flying several feet. They landed on their backs.

Imha charged them, producing two Black Thorns on her palms.

Oh, God.

I jumped from the altar, not sure what I was doing, but knowing I had to do something. I took a step and kicked something.

The Crimson Dagger.

Morgan had kept that damn thing all this time. I wondered if he also kept ...

I crouched down and searched his pockets. I found the vial in one of his belt pockets. There was only one drop inside. He probably used it to disenchant Keisha's armor. Ugh, only the Fates knew what else he had used it on, what else he had done against us.

Rushing, I opened the vial and let the drop fall over the blade. Without hesitation, I shot up and ran—or better, limped—around the altar toward Imha.

"Hey, bitch," I called her.

Surprised, she paused, giving me enough time to aim. I threw a dagger at her, missing on purpose, distracting her of my real objective as I threw the Crimson Dagger.

She tilted her head back and cackled. "By the Everlast, Nadine, what a lou—" She looked down at the Crimson Dagger in her chest.

I snickered. "Lousy aim?"

One second later she disappeared into thin air, taking along Omi and the demons.

Everyone else stilled, looking at me.

"What was that?" Ceris asked, carefully approaching me.

The adrenaline was wearing out. I leaned on the altar for support. "Morgan still had the vial with the fountain water. I put the last drop on the dagger and threw it at her, wishing her and all her associates to appear in a deep cave in the South Pole."

"Clever," Micah said, standing up. The wounds on his shoulders and chest were already healing. "I like that."

Heat crept up my cheeks.

Keisha put an arm over my shoulder and kissed my cheek. "You're my hero!"

Ceris stood before me, her eyes on mine. "You truly are a hero."

"Whatever you are, you're amazing." Zelen patted my back.

I winced.

"What is it?" Victor asked.

Micah pushed through them and reached to me. "Her wound."

The cloth he had tied around me was gone, and my shirt and the side of my pants were soaked in blood.

Exhaustion and pain flooded me, and I slid to the floor. Micah passed his arms under my knees and shoulders, and pulled me to him.

A huge groan shook the mountain.

"It's going to explode," Izaera said. "Any second now."

"We need to be outside to transport to another place," Ceris said.

"Let's go, then," Victor said.

Holding me tight, Micah ran back to the entrance with the others. I rested my cheek on his chest and closed my eyes, welcoming the sleepiness.

I could feel heat and more tremors, but I wasn't sure if it was the volcano or me.

"Stay with me, darling," Micah whispered. "Please, stay with me."

I tried to stay with him, I really did, but I had no strength or will left.

When the darkness closed around me, I couldn't fight it.

33

———

The front door opened, and Ceris stepped out onto the porch.

She sat in the rocking chair beside mine. "Here," she said, handing me a new mug with steamy coffee. "It's black."

I dropped the empty mug over the railing and took the new mug from her. "Thanks." I sipped the hot liquid, kind of pleased when it burned my throat.

"How are you?" she asked.

Everyone asked me that every two minutes.

Apparently, I had lost consciousness when we were halfway through the first tunnel, right before the volcano erupted. They got outside with a second to spare and took us back to the island. Victor tended my wound. It was deeper than Micah first assumed, and I had lost a lot of blood. Victor performed a small surgery, transfused blood, and all that jazz. I stayed in bed, in and out of consciousness for four days. Keisha told me Micah barely left my side. Meanwhile, Ceris, Victor, and Izaera were out most of the time, looking for a new place for us. Since Morgan had been working with Omi, we didn't know if the island had been compromised or not, and we didn't want to risk it.

When I woke up, I cried nonstop for a couple of hours, feeling extremely guilty for having killed Morgan. They all assured me there was nothing we could have done to save him. I had saved Micah's life. Oh, I had saved all their lives, which was another thing they kept saying every two minutes.

Ceris explained to me what she believed happened at the altar. I had the ability to heal Victor and Micah, and this same healing power was the key ingredient to "heal" them from human to god form. My healing was the power required for the altar to do its thing. Which sounded crazy, but we seemed surrounded by crazy.

I was freaking tired of it all.

I had escaped to the porch early in the morning, when I knew everyone was still sleeping. This was the third day that I sat here, surrounded by snow, with a mug of coffee and Pinky, under a heavy blanket, and stayed quiet, my mind blank, my soul calm. My moment of peace. Peace I didn't deserve.

Today though I wanted my peace and quiet. I wanted to stay alone and keep my mind blank, so I wouldn't remember what day it was. In vain, though. Each time I closed my eyes, images of Raisa and Olivia dragging me to a bar to celebrate invaded my mind. It made me more frustrated because I didn't deserve to feel a happy warmth remembering those times.

Ceris sighed. "Nadine, you can't live your entire life with this guilt. It's not right."

Ha, if only she knew. Now that Victor and Micah were full gods, my days in this world were halfway over. Now all we needed to find more allies, strategize a war, fight, and win.

"I know there was nothing we could have done for him," I

said. "I know that. I believe that. But that doesn't change the fact that I killed him."

She placed a hand on my arm. "I don't think there is anything we can say to you that will lessen that feeling." She paused. "The first time I killed a human I cried for days, then I disappeared for almost a year. I neglected my duties. Families everywhere began fighting, relationships crumbled, and wars began because of discord. Obviously, every deity in the world was franticly trying to find me. In the end, I realized I had to move on. Though that human had deserved it, I couldn't stop living and neglecting my subjects and my own family because of my guilt. They deserved better. I pulled myself together and worked through it."

"So I should pull myself together." I hated when people lectured me.

"You should, but I understand if you don't want to do it yet. Just don't take too long. We have tons of things to do, and we'll need your help."

I scoffed. "Now that the guys are gods again, you don't need anything else from me."

She squeezed my arm, and I stared at her. "That's not true. More than once you proved you are part of this family. We need you. We truly do." Tears brimmed in my eyes. This family? Had she really said that? She offered me a sweet smile. "And Mitrus would go cuckoo if you left."

Would he? I hadn't really spoken to him since we came back. We had exchanged a few words. How are you? Are you hungry? Do you need help? But we hadn't been alone and talked—really talked.

"Speaking of him," she whispered, standing up.

As if on cue, the front door opened and Micah appeared behind it. "Hey," he said, with a half smile.

"I'm gonna make more coffee." She winked at me, and I shook my head, fighting a smile. How had we gotten here? Why wasn't I wanting to jump at her throat anymore?

She left and Micah leaned on the porch's railing, a couple of feet in front of me.

"How are you?"

I groaned. "If one more person asks me that, I'm gonna punch him."

Bending over, he smiled. "Promise?" I punched his shoulder. "Ouch. Darling, I was teasing."

"I wasn't."

He stared intently into my eyes. "I'm glad you're okay."

I nodded, turning my eyes to my coffee. "And you? How's life as a god?"

"The same shit it always was."

I lifted my eyes to his. "Why is that?"

"It's lonely," he said, surprising me. "Right now it's different because we need to help each other, but once we win this war, it'll be lonely again. Levi, Ceris, Izaera, and the others are my family. We fight a lot, but each of us has his or her own life. Some, like Levi and Ceris, Sol and Lua, and sometimes Omi and Imha, have a life together, which probably makes eternity more bearable."

"Wait ... are you telling me you don't like being a god?"

One corner of his lips turned up. "I never said that, darling. I love the power, the rush, the adrenaline, but when things are calm, which is most of the time, it can be lonely and boring, which is Imha's explanation for her sick actions."

I sipped from my mug, unsure where he was going with this topic or what I should say.

I whirled my finger around a strand of my hair. Micah smiled. "What?"

He pointed to my hand. "You haven't done that in so long."

Ugh, I hadn't noticed. But he had. "Have you always been this observant?"

"I notice everything about you, darling. For instance, I know you haven't sung in a long time, which is a shame."

Wow, he was right. With everything going on, I hadn't noticed that. But he had. I wondered if he knew more about me these days than I did. Now that he had mentioned it, my heart squeezed. I missed singing. But what good would it do? Singing wasn't a weapon I could use in the war.

"So." Clearing his throat, he pushed away from the railing and extended his hand to me. "Come with me. There's something I want to show you."

I watched his hand for a moment, unsure. Then I watched him. His expression. His eyes. The way they conveyed how he was really hoping for me to accept it.

I took his hand, expecting him to guide me inside the cottage, or out to the beach.

Instead he took us somewhere else.

We stood in the middle of a desert. There was sand and sand and more sand, an occasional cactus or two, a few rocks, a couple of dried trees, and more sand. Oh, yes, *more* sand.

"What the hell?" I asked, letting go of his hand.

"Through here," he said, approaching the short, dead-looking trees. He stood in front of two of them, and then he beckoned me to follow him. "Come on, darling. You want this, I promise."

Letting out a frustrated sigh, I strutted to him.

With one of his smug smiles, Micah touched the center of the trunk of each tree and a black veil formed among them.

"A portal?" I asked and he nodded. "To where?"

"You'll see."

He offered to take my hand again, and this time I didn't hesitate. Curiosity was a hard thing to push back.

Together we stepped into the portal and into—I gasped—the underworld.

My mouth hung open as I glanced around. It was dark all right, but even so, there were spots of lights here and there, and it looked like a huge cave. We stood on a high ledge on a wall made of rocks, looking down at what seemed to be a park, with dark green grass, some trails and paths, even flowers and bushes, but what caught my attention was the lake. It was large and deep black, and several people—dead people—surrounded it.

"What is this place?" I asked, looking over the ledge.

"The Lake of Life."

"B-but I saw it before, in a vision with Ceris. It was in a cave."

"There are many caves around the lake." He pointed to a stone wall on the far left. A small opening swallowed the water. "The dead come to the lake every once in a while to check on the loved ones they left behind."

I whirled around to face him and almost tripped. "Wh-what are you saying?"

With a hand on my back, he steered me back to the edge and pointed to where a couple, three kids, and a baby walked down a path, going to the lake.

My knees buckled, and I crouched down. Tears blurred my vision, but I quickly wiped them away because I wanted to see them. I needed to see them.

My father, my mother, Nicole, Tommy, Teddie, and Troy sauntered down the path. They had smiles on their faces. The kids played with each other, pushing and teasing. And Troy—oh, God—baby Troy was with them, looking healthy.

Micah knelt beside me. "Happy twentieth birthday."

I whipped my head so fast to look at him, my neck hurt. "What? How did you know?"

He shrugged. "I just know. Do you like my gift?"

I didn't deserve any gifts, but at this moment, he was giving me more than I could ever ask.

Tears brimmed in my eyes. "I love it."

"From what I've learned, they come here once a week to check on you."

"They can see me?"

"Yes, through the reflection in the lake."

"And now? Will they look at the lake and see I am here?"

He sighed. "Humans aren't supposed to have contact with the dead. It disrupts their peace. I was hoping you would agree to leave before they reach the lake."

"But ..." I tried estimating the time it would take them to get there. "That's only five, maybe six minutes."

He rested his hand on my back again. "I know, darling, but think about it this way: at least you got to see them. You know they are all right. You know they are together. Isn't that enough for now?"

Tommy poked Teddie and then raced around Mom and Dad. Nicole seemed annoyed, but when Teddie poked her too, she smiled and chased after them. All the while, my father grinned at them, and my mother made baby faces at Troy.

A small smile took over my lips. "Yes. For now."

Micah sat down beside me, and I rested my head on his

shoulder. Being here, watching my family with him, it was like paradise.

We observed my family for a minute more before he broke the silence.

"Nadine. About what Omi said, about me betraying everyone, I—"

"You don't need to explain it."

"I want to explain. To you." He took my hand in his. "I was never a saint. Far from it, actually, but I wasn't entirely evil. I argued with and contradicted everyone in my life, but I never betrayed them. At least, not all of them." Like he betrayed Victor—a mistake I knew he regretted. "But ... I've changed now. I don't know how to explain it. I guess being human for over twenty years and actually living like them, under-standing them, changed me."

I knew it had changed him. I remembered the vision I had seen, of those men attacking his family and him at the open market, and the men killing his parents. I remembered his pain, his ache. I knew he would never forget that.

I squeezed his hand. "I believe you."

Letting out a long breath, he kissed my temple before rising, gently tugging my elbow. I let him guide me upward.

I tried to etch the image of my family in my mind. During the tough times ahead of us, I had to hang on to one good thing. And my family was the *best* thing. Followed closely by Micah, who, among all this mess, was stealing my heart. I glanced at him. He already had stolen my heart with his rough face, his bad boy act, his caring side, his sweet touches, his hot kisses, and everything in between. My heart was his, even if he would never accept it.

I sighed. Even if he wanted to accept it, I knew there was no future for us. In a couple of months, I would die and he would forget I had ever existed. But for now, I wanted to enjoy these perfect moments.

With that in mind, I turned to Micah, stood on my tiptoes, and kissed him. A quick peck on his soft lips. "Thanks," I whispered, pulling back.

Shock flashed on his face, before being replaced by that cocky smile of his. "Anything for you, darling."

He entwined his fingers with mine, and we walked back through the portal.

Hello there!

Thank you for reading *Soul Oath*!

Reviews are very important for authors. If you liked my book, please consider leaving a review on amazon and/or on goodreads, please!

And you can read the first chapter of *Cup of Life* on the next page!

CUP OF LIFE

CHAPTER ONE

THIRTY OR FORTY YEARS AGO, I WOULDN'T HAVE STARED AT THE girl in front of me for more than five seconds before charming her into going to bed with me.

But this girl ... this girl was different.

"I think that's everything," Nadine said, stepping out of the cottage as Rok flew from the roof.

It was early January. The lights around the cottage reflected off the three feet of snow and illuminated Nadine's long brown hair, tinting some strands bronze. Her hair, her dark green eyes, and her red lips contrasted with her fair skin; the only thought on my mind was that I had never seen a more beautiful girl in my entire life. And I had been alive for quite some time.

Nadine approached me, and as it was every time she looked at me, I fought the urge to reach to her, to pull her against me, to kiss her, to—

"It is everything, isn't it?" She glanced at the bag slung across my shoulder and the box in my arms. She held her sister's stuffed bunny in one hand and a duffel bag in another.

We had been moving to our new location all day, making several trips to and from, and now we were the last ones here.

"I think so," I replied, quickly glancing to Rok hovering above our heads. "Ready?"

She walked down the porch steps, into the snow, and turned to the cottage. Her eyes scanned it, as if she wanted to take every little detail with her.

She slung the duffel bag over her shoulder and flipped the collar of her jacket up. "It's odd. I feel like I should feel bad for leaving this place after fleeing so many others, after losing so many people." She sighed. "But I don't, and I totally should, especially after seeing the new place Ceris got us."

I nodded, knowing too well that the new place brought her depressing memories.

No matter. It was a new place, a new path on our journey, a new beginning. We were on the right track.

I offered my arm to her. "Let's go, darling."

With a half-smile that made my heart skip a beat, Nadine sauntered to me and hooked her arm with mine.

I scooted closer to her, closer than necessary because I could and because I wanted to, and then I transported us out of there.

NEW FREAKING YORK FUCKING CITY. THAT WAS WHERE CERIS found a couple of intact buildings and apartments, one of the few Omi and the demons hadn't completely destroyed when they invaded the city over a month ago. She had found many bodies in them though. Levi, Izaera, and I helped her clean the large third floor, four bedroom apartment she had chosen before she brought the others to the city.

"They will never look for us here," Ceris said, using her powers to scrub the walls clean of blood.

She was probably right, but I knew Nadine wouldn't be okay with it.

When we brought the others, Nadine didn't disguise her disgust, but made no other objections. She understood why Ceris had chosen this place, and she agreed with the goddess's reasons. Still, it wasn't easy for her.

"Are you all right?" I asked as we walked among the debris, rumble, and flipped cars that lined the area around the apartment.

Ceris, Levi, Izaera, and I had united our powers to build a strong ward around the place with a radius of three blocks. Then we cleaned paths that led to the building while moving bodies, cars, and broken glass out of the way.

"I'm fine," she answered, pointing the flashlight to our improvised trail. She wrinkled her nose at the smell of the decay and avoided looking around too much.

We arrived at the building, crossed through the front doors, walked up three flights of stairs—the elevator was destroyed—and opened the door to the apartment.

It wasn't bad. A large living room with a fireplace, two sofas and four armchairs, a coffee table, lamps, and other decorative stuff, though most we had to throw away. Vases, pictures, paintings, rugs, pillows—all broken or tainted by blood—were now in the trash. Then there was a dining room for ten and a fully equipped kitchen. There was an office and half-bath in the front. Next to them was a corridor that led to four bedrooms, one being a suite, and two separate bathrooms.

We had to replace most beds, comforters, and pillows, since those had also been destroyed during the invasion. We had to find generators and fuel for the electricity, and we had gone to a grocery store in Australia—so not to leave a trace around here—for food and drinks.

We took all the furniture from the front office and transformed it into a gym. It was half the size of the gym we had in northern Greenland, but it was a place to burn some energy and stay sharp.

Ceris and Levi had chosen the suite. Apparently, they were mending things between them. Zelen and I were sharing one of the bedrooms, while Izaera shared another one with Keisha. Nadine had picked the spare room all for herself. Lucky girl.

I dropped the box in the living room as Nadine walked to the door of her bedroom and stared at the inside.

"What is it, darling?" I followed her gaze. The furniture we had found was simple. A brown wooden queen bed and matching nightstand, thin mattress, and a dark blue comforter. Nothing else. No curtains, no rugs, no decorations, no drawer, no dresser—the same as the other bedrooms.

"It's so lifeless," she muttered. "If the bed was made of metal, I would think we were in a prison."

A prison. That was what this was for her. This situation, this place, this war, the Soul Oath. Her prison.

I leaned closer to her and kissed the top of her head, not sure what to say. She turned to me, with suspicion in her pretty eyes, as if she doubted my intentions. I guess she had no reason not to suspect my intentions. She once said she was tired of my mixed signals. I was too, but I couldn't help myself. I tried with all my might to stay away from her, to not touch her, not hug her, not kiss her. So far, I was failing.

"Come on, darling. You love it when I kiss you." Teasing came naturally to me, and she actually reacted the way she always should react with me: her brows knotted and she dismissed me. I should have stopped there. I should have walked away and left her be. Instead I nudged her arm with my elbow. "What?"

"Nothing," she said, her tone indicating it wasn't really nothing. She sighed and stepped into her bedroom. "I guess I better ..." She gestured around the room, and I had no idea what she meant.

Nevertheless, I went along with it. "Sure. Yeah."

She closed the door in my face.

ABOUT THE AUTHOR

While USA Today Bestselling Author Juliana Haygert dreams of being Wonder Woman, Buffy, or a blood elf shadow priest, she settles for the less exciting—but equally gratifying—life as a wife, a mother, and an author. Thousands of miles away from her former home in Brazil, she now resides in North Carolina and spends her days writing about kick-ass heroines and the heroes who drive them crazy.

Subscribe to her mailing list to receive emails of announcement, events, and other fun stuff related to her writing and her books: www.bit.ly/JuHNL

For more information:
www.julianahaygert.com

ALSO BY JULIANA HAYGERT:

Free

Into the Darkest Fire

Tested

Secret Santa

The Everlast Series

Destiny Gift (Book 1)

Soul Oath (Book 2)

Cup of Life (Book 3)

The Everlasting Circle (Book 4)

Willow Harbor Series

Hunter's Revenge (Book 3)

Siren's Song (Book 5)

The Breaking Series

Breaking Free (Book 1)

Breaking Away (Book 2)

Breaking Through (Book 3)

Standalones

Playing Pretend

Captured Love

Dazzle Me